DYING
to Live Here

Edited by Twyla Beth Lambert

Cover Design by ambient design

Print ISBN 978-1-957529-47-9

Ebook ISBN 978-1-957529-48-6

Library of Congress Control Number 2026931415

For my mother
Thanks for every "kiss of encouragement"

ONE

"My neighbor is dead," Laura said.

It was a strange way to begin a phone conversation, even for my flighty best friend. Trained by my Southern mama to always be polite, even to crazy people—plentiful in my home state of Florida—I replied, "I'm sorry to hear it."

"You shouldn't be."

"What are you talking about?" I turned down the volume on my TV, thinking perhaps I'd misheard. Laura's exemplary manners wouldn't normally condone gloating over death. "Why are you telling me this?"

"It means there's a house available in my neighborhood," she said.

Comprehension finally dawned. Laura had been urging me to move closer to her ever since my divorce. She lived a short walk from the beach in a community called Harbor Shores. The neighborhood was located east of Florida's Coastal Highway A1A (a most desirable spot), but the homes were priced within the means of young families. An available home there was a rare find. My humble townhouse, crowded with my treasures from the estate sales I frequented, didn't have a yard for my dog. Getting to walk him on the beach every day and living closer to my best friend would be a dream come true.

"If the owner is dead, who's selling it?" I asked.

"His daughter. She works for some big bank in Charlotte, and she has no intention of coming back to Florida." She sounded out of breath, and I pictured her on the stair-stepper she kept in a spare bedroom, knowing that she devoted a large portion of her day to exercise. Laura's life as a wealthy, suburban housewife was very different from my workaday existence. She belonged to the Costa Verde Women's Club, volunteered for charity committees, served on her neighborhood HOA board of directors, and had lunch at The Club with her other friends. She'd always been the more outgoing of our unlikely pairing from the first day we met at Florida State University fourteen years ago, when I'd shown up at our dorm with my poster of Albert Einstein and found she had already selected the best side, decorated it in pink, and invited our new suitemates over for a tour.

"How do you know so much about the dead guy's daughter?" I asked.

"Folks around here like to gossip," she replied. "I heard about it from a neighbor during our morning power walk."

Despite our dissimilar natures, Laura had been there for me when I lost my little sister and the bottom dropped out from under my world during our freshman year, and the experience bonded us for life. I would do anything for her, but tonight all I wanted was to chill out on the sofa with Hopper, my sweet-tempered bulldog, and watch *Antiques Roadshow*. A real estate opportunity provided by untimely death did not entice me at that moment.

A disturbing question popped to mind. "He didn't die *in* the house, did he?"

She paused before responding. "I'd prefer not to answer that question."

I felt my stomach clench. "Laura!"

"A home health aide visited every day," Laura clarified. "She found him."

"Still." I shook my head, trying to rid it of the image.

Laura huffed, "Emma, come on. He won't haunt the place."

"I hadn't even thought of that, but now I am." How depressing, dying alone with only the visiting nurse to find you. I surveyed the living room of my townhouse with its mismatched furniture I'd been so pleased to find. It was a single person's home, and I realized grimly that I was a future candidate for such an end. Hopper, the only male I'd ever invited into the house, curled up on top of my feet and burped loudly.

"You're missing the point, Emma," Laura continued, still huffing along on the exercise machine. "This is your chance to buy a home in Harbor Shores. We can walk on the beach every morning. Think of how much Hopper will like that!" She paused before adding, "Once you're in, you can back me up by volunteering to serve on the homeowners' association board of directors."

Ah-ha. I knew she had an angle in there somewhere. "Volunteering is your thing, not mine. I don't want to snitch on my neighbors."

"You won't have to. The management company does that. Anyway, I'm the president," Laura pointed out. "I set the tone, and it's a very cool, laid-back board of directors."

"There is no such thing."

"Excuse me? *I'm* on it! Are you saying I'm not cool?"

"I'd prefer not to answer *that* question. Anyway, maybe it's too much trouble to move."

"You said you wanted a bigger yard for Hopper, and I want you to live closer to me. Is that so bad?"

I sighed. Laura gave me guilt trips so often I had frequent flyer miles, but she was right about needing more space for the dog. "We're getting ahead of ourselves, anyway. How much do they want?"

"My neighbor, Sophie, is a real estate agent. She told me they're going to open it up to bidders on Monday. You have to act now, or someone will snap it up."

I sat up straighter. Hopper opened one eye to make sure I wasn't going anywhere without him—like the kitchen. "I don't know if I want it yet. Who knows? It might be infested with termites."

"You can make an offer that's contingent on inspection. You need to see this place right away."

"When is the open house?"

"There won't be an open house. I told you, people are lining up with bids. Someone else will snap it up. Sophie told me that a couple who currently rent in the neighborhood are planning to make an offer above market value."

"You expect me to make an offer on a house I haven't seen?"

"That's what I'm trying to tell you, I can get you in *tonight*. You can look inside and make the first offer sight unseen. But, you *will* have seen."

"Tonight?" I twisted in my seat to look at the clock, and, in the process, disturbed my furry foot warmer. He snorted, then scratched at the lap blanket until it fell onto the seat cushion. He proceeded to tug and nudge it into an acceptable shape before turning around in circles and settling down on top of it. "It's after nine o'clock. How do you plan to do that?"

I heard an electronic beep as she slowed down her machine. Her voice became clearer. "A couple of years ago, when he was in the hospital, his daughter gave me a key so I could water the plants. I still have the key."

"I'm not sure that's legal," I said.

"I think it's a gray area."

"I think it's breaking and entering."

"Right. We should do it at night."

"Should we synchronize our watches?"

My sarcasm whizzed past her undetected. "Good idea. Meet me at my house at ten o'clock. Wear black."

"You are certifiable. Do you know that?"

"Of course. That's why we're friends."

"Just like Thelma and Louise," I said, but she'd already hung up.

As I took Hopper on his last walk of the night, I debated what to do. Laura could be very persuasive. Back when we were college roommates, she talked me into all kinds of crazy things, but we always had fun. Once, we dumped red dye in Westcott Fountain at Florida State. It was supposed to honor the school colors of garnet and gold, but the result was gory. The dye stained our skin, so we were literally caught red-handed. Still, Laura's adventures were always fun, and I'd never learned how to say no to her. So, after I'd taken care of Hopper, I changed out of my favorite pair of comfy pants and dressed entirely in black. What could go wrong?

Feeling like an idiot in my ninja wear, I showed up at Laura's house at ten o'clock. She answered the door sporting an animal-print shirt she usually reserved for Jaguars football games.

I cocked my head. "Why are you wearing *that*?"

Smoothing the front of her shirt, she replied confidently, "Camouflage."

I sighed. "Let's get this over with before we get arrested."

The late August humidity lingered. A trickle of sweat traced its way down my back. The night air rang with the high-pitched hum of katydids and crickets. I slapped at a whining noise near my ear. Laura led me through darkness punctuated with the feeble orange glow of streetlights.

"It's one of the closest to the beach," she whispered as she pointed to our destination.

In the dim light, the vacant house had an ominous aura. The dark windows gaped like empty eyes. My heart began to race. I stopped walking.

"I'm having second thoughts about this, Laura."

She ignored me, leading the way past the overgrown lawn through a tunnel of hedges flanking the front door. The jungle-like shrubbery blocked any moonlight and hindered Laura's initial efforts to insert the key. The keychain jangled as she fumbled with the key. I swiveled my head, checking for nosy neighbors. Swiping upward on the screen of the phone clutched tightly in my hand, I activated the flashlight.

"Turn that off," she hissed. "Someone will call the police."

I wiped my sweaty palm on my pants and turned off the light. "Come on, Laura," I wheedled. "Let's forget about this."

A click and a squeak of the door hinges answered me. Laura crossed the threshold and fumbled for a moment, searching for a light switch. Suddenly, she tumbled forward into the darkness and squealed.

Quickly, I reactivated the light and aimed it at the foyer. Laura lay sprawled atop a dark lump on the floor. I quickly realized it wasn't a lump. It was a body—the body of a woman. Long strands of red hair splayed out in the puddle of blood beneath her.

Suddenly spotlighted, Laura scrambled to her feet, squealing, "Ohmygod—ohmygod—ohmygod." A large splotch of blood stained the front of her shirt. She peered down and started to breathe so rapidly I thought she might hyperventilate.

My head spun. A coppery smell wafted out through the doorway. I focused on my phone, trying not to faint. "I'll call 911."

"Wait." Laura grabbed my arm. "Think about what this looks like."

My finger stopped before sending the call. "Are you suggesting we turn around, lock the door, and pretend we never saw anything?"

"I don't know. Just let me think." She ran both hands through her blond hair, transferring a streak of red to one of her curls.

"Who is that? Do you know?"

"Yes, I know her."

At that moment, headlights illuminated the driveway. A police cruiser pulled to the curb. Laura's eyes met mine, wide with panic. The car doors opened, and a cop got out, brandishing a flashlight. He swept it across the front of the house. The beam stopped when it spotlighted us. He took in the sight of Laura covered in blood and went on high alert.

"Sheriff's Department," he shouted. A second officer emerged from behind him. "Let me see your hands. What's that in your hand?"

"Just my phone. I'll put it away," I said, reaching toward my pocket.

"Freeze! Keep your hands where I can see them."

"Officer, we were just checking on the house," I babbled. "My friend has a key. We walked in and found that. She tripped."

I turned to Laura, but she remained silent, frozen in the beam of his flashlight like a deer—a deer wearing an animal print and a large bloodstain.

Struck by the coincidence of a policeman showing up so quickly, I asked, "Why are you here?"

"We received a report of an intruder in a vacant house. You're both under arrest."

HOURS LATER, Laura's husband, Jack, drove us home from the police station. A huffy silence hung in the car like a bad smell. I pushed the hair out of my eyes and realized the smell was real—the musty odor of the holding cell clung to my clothes and hair.

Laura turned and beamed at me, oblivious to the tension inside the vehicle. "Now we're truly sisters—jail sisters." They'd taken her bloody shirt for evidence and given her the top from a set of khaki prison duds.

I squinted at her. Exhaustion overwhelmed me, draining away my usual sarcasm. From my spot in the back seat, I caught sight of my reflection in the rearview mirror. A nimbus of tangled, dark-brown hair framed my pallid face, and my gray eyes were bloodshot with fatigue. I longed for a shower and clean clothes.

Jack spoke for the first time since leaving the police station, his voice startlingly loud. "What were you thinking? Why go look at a house in the dark?"

"It seemed urgent," Laura said. "Someone else might buy the house before Emma."

He grunted. "I imagine the price will go down now that it's the scene of a murder."

She reached over and squeezed his arm. "You know how to spot a silver lining."

He grunted and lapsed back into silence.

I stared out the window, worst-case scenarios filling my head. How fortunate the murderer had been so kind as to leave the body right inside the doorway. I had not entered the property, nor had I touched anything. I was simply in the wrong place at the worst possible time. My best friend's situation seemed less certain.

Jack dropped me off at the curb in front of my townhouse. As I shuffled up the walkway to my home, I sighed with relief. Laura's neighborhood no longer felt so desirable.

THE NEXT AFTERNOON, my doorbell rang. Through the peephole, I saw Laura standing outside, and, after a moment's pause, I opened the door.

"I brought a peace offering," Laura said, holding up a bottle of wine.

I squinted at the label. "Isn't that the brand that's 'buy one, get one free' at Publix this week?"

Abashed, Laura hid the bottle behind her back. "Can I come in? Please?"

I gave a long-suffering sigh but stepped aside and led the way to the kitchen table where we had shared many secrets and best-friend talks. It was only because of our long history that I was willing to let her back in. This was the worst mess she'd gotten me into, ever. I dug in the drawer for a corkscrew and retrieved two glasses before joining her at the table.

I filled mine to the rim. "I can't believe you got me arrested."

"Not really," she said, reaching for a glass. "No charges were filed. We literally stumbled across the body."

"You did," I corrected.

Her eyes widened. "That reminds me. Do you have any club soda? I really loved that shirt."

I shot her a level look and took a swig of wine before speaking. "What did Jack say when you got home?"

After her first sip, she wrinkled her nose. "Oh, he chewed me out for a full hour. Said he couldn't believe I got myself arrested on his poker night."

"You think he was upset about the poker?"

"I guess not." She chewed her lower lip, considering. "Well, maybe a little."

"Did you get a phone call from that detective today?" I had gotten a call of my own, and I wanted to compare notes.

"Yes." She swirled her wine and watched it spin. "He warned me the investigation would be ongoing, and that even though they couldn't hold us, we're still suspects and shouldn't go anywhere."

"He told me that. Tried to scare me. Even though, technically, I wasn't inside the house, I'm still a 'person of interest.' He also said if I had any additional information I wanted to share, I should call him."

Her eyebrows shot up. "Additional information? After all that grilling last night, he still thought you were holding back?"

"I got the feeling he was trying to get me to give him more information about you. A divide and conquer routine. I told him I still didn't even know who the dead woman was."

She took another sip before replying, "Her name was Rose Martin."

I examined her face, which was suddenly grim. "I thought the house was supposed to be vacant. Do you have an idea what she might have been doing there?"

"Snooping, probably. She was a professional busybody. We called her Nosy Rosie. Constantly interfering in everybody's business. She was the president of the HOA for a long time. Before I challenged her for the position, that is. She hated me."

"Why?" Laura had many friends. This was the first I had heard of an enemy.

"I unseated her as president. She assumed she'd be president of the board forever, but I decided to challenge her for the seat. The neighborhood held an election, and she lost. Rather than take it graciously and continue to serve as a volunteer, she quit. Left the board in a huff. She never forgave me." Laura hesitated, glancing out the window into my tiny backyard. Bumblebees investigated a hanging basket filled with bright yellow moss roses, the only flowers able to withstand the late summer heat. She seemed to gather herself before speaking again. "You're mad at me right now, and that's understandable, but I need your help."

I took her hand. "You know I'll always help you. What do you need?"

Her green eyes were pleading. "Everyone is going to think I did it. Because she hated me, and I hated her back. We had some very heated, very public arguments. That's motive, right? But you know I didn't do it. So, I thought you could help me figure out who really did it."

"Sure, we can do that." I patted her hand. "Just let me go get Scooby, and we'll hop in the Mystery Machine."

"I'm serious, Emma. My neighbors are already staring at me when I go outside. But you're a neutral party. I can introduce you to them, tell them you're thinking about moving into the neighborhood. One of them might be the murderer. You can get a read on who it is because you're so intuitive." She gave me an imploring look.

"Not that intuitive. I let you talk me into breaking into a house and ended up in jail."

"I promise to make that up to you, Emma."

I pursed my lips and examined her skeptically.

"Please. You've got to help me."

I sighed, remembering all the times she'd helped me in the past. I owed her. On top of that, my innate pragmatism told me we'd never be able to move past this until the real killer was caught. The previous night had been one of the worst of my life, and I was eager to put it behind me forever. "What's your plan?"

She smiled at me triumphantly. "I want to introduce you to my neighbors at the block party on Friday night. That's where we'll find Rose's enemies."

"Won't they think it's weird, me showing up at one of their parties? I've never met your neighbors."

"Why is that weird? I've never met your neighbors, either. Have *you* even met your neighbors?" Laura, an extrovert, had never accepted my introverted ways.

I crossed my arms defensively. "I've met the ones with dogs."

She cocked her head. "Do you know their names?"

Counting on my fingers, I replied, "Coco, Rocky, Milo, Daisy—"

"Not the dogs' names!" Laura sighed heavily, directing a puff of air upward and dislodging a curl that had fallen over one eye. "This is why you need to move closer to me. You never go out of your way to meet anyone."

Not wanting to repeat a conversation Laura and I'd had many times before, I deflected. "Why do you assume the people in your community are Rose's enemies?"

With a careless shrug, she said, "When Rose retired, she turned her energy to remaking the neighborhood in her image, and a lot of people resented it. Come with me on Friday. I can introduce you and tell them you're thinking of buying a house."

"Seems tacky to have a party right after one of their neighbors was murdered."

She smirked. "What better opportunity to gossip?"

two

ON FRIDAY NIGHT, I pulled into one of the parking spaces near the community clubhouse, turned off the ignition, and sat in my car, thinking. There was still time to leave. An enormous privet hedge blocked the view of the entrance, and no one had seen me arrive. As I stared out the windshield, a knock on the passenger window made me jump. I turned and found Laura waving and smiling maniacally. Perhaps an insanity plea was the way to go.

As I stepped out of the car, the humidity smothered me right before Laura did. "I can't thank you enough for doing this." She squeezed me tightly. "I know how much you hate small talk."

"No big deal," I mumbled into the cloud of her curly blond hair.

"It'll be great having you by my side. Jack never wants to attend these neighborhood parties. He's such a fuddy-duddy." Laura linked her arm through mine and led me through the double doors of the clubhouse into a large, open room filled with groups of people making polite conversation. The back wall was lined with windows overlooking a patio surrounded by lush, tropical foliage and a lap pool glowing blue with underwater lighting. A high ceiling soared above, crisscrossed with wood beams. An imposing Spanish-style wrought iron chandelier loomed overhead, providing tastefully dim lighting, while music played from hidden speakers. On one side of the room stood a table laden with food. On the other, a full bar beckoned, complete with bartender.

Laura pulled me toward the bar. "Come on. Let's get you a drink. Our neighborhood likes to party. These people even bring booze to the annual Easter Egg Hunt."

While we waited for our drinks, I evaluated the crowd. Some had gray hair and wore brightly colored resort wear. Others appeared to be middle-aged, casually dressed in T-shirts and shorts. Nearby, a couple of young mothers wrangled small children, trying to tempt them with offers of chicken nuggets and cookies. Conveniently positioned near the bar stood the women without children. Each held a glass of chardonnay. In their matching uniform of coiffed blond hair, Lilly Pulitzer sundresses, and Tory Burch sandals, they brought to mind *The Stepford Wives*.

After we visited the bartender, Laura led me toward the Sundress Squad and proceeded to interrupt their conversation. "Hey, ladies! This is my friend Emma. She's thinking about buying a house in Harbor Shores." The women all smiled politely. Some raised their glasses in a toasting gesture.

I nodded and smiled. "I think I met you last winter at Laura's thirtieth."

Laura made an exasperated noise. "Let's forget about that party. I know I have. Will you excuse me for a moment?" Laura promptly abandoned me, leaving me struggling to remember their names and hoping they'd reintroduce themselves.

"I'm Miranda," the tallest blonde obliged. "I think I missed that party." Her hair added an extra two inches to her already considerable height. As the apparent leader of the couture cadre, she motioned toward her companions, who bobbed their heads on cue. "Perhaps you remember Ellen and Sophie."

"Don't you live nearby, Emma?" Ellen asked. The shortest of the trio, she wore her hair in a bun reminiscent of Tinker Bell.

I nodded. "I own a townhouse near South Beach shopping center."

"West of A1A?" Miranda's tone curdled the words, making the question sound more like *near the dump?*

I resisted her attempt at intimidation. "Yes, but it's on the Intra-coastal."

Sophie visibly perked up at my words. "I'm a real estate agent, available to help you if you're selling." She produced a business card, seemingly from midair.

I took the card to be polite. Beneath her name and company logo it read, *Happiness resides at the beach*. I raised an eyebrow—my default expression. Laura always accused me of being a cynic (while warning me I'd get wrinkles above that eyebrow if I didn't lighten up). "I'm not sure happiness has an address."

"I can't say that this neighborhood is always a happy place." Miranda gestured at her surroundings with one ring-laden hand. "Things have been rather eventful around here lately."

Recognizing an opportunity to probe for information, I spoke up. "Such a tragedy. Was she a friend of yours?"

"Oh, dear, no. I doubt she had any friends around here. She was not an easy person to get along with." Miranda took a sip from her glass of white wine.

"Really? What did she do?"

"She was constantly finding fault with her neighbors, reporting them for minor infractions of neighborhood rules. Once, my stepson left his car parked on the street in front of our house, and she called the towing company. She knew very well whose car it was. Such a meddlesome woman." She patted her poufy hair as if to calm it down.

"Miranda, you shouldn't speak ill of the dead," Ellen said in her girlish voice.

"Why not? She did nothing but speak ill when she was alive. Remember the Simpsons' dog?"

"Nobody could prove she ran over him on purpose," Ellen murmured.

Miranda flicked her hand dismissively. "He only had three legs! How fast could he be?"

"She did complain a lot about him pooping in her yard." Ellen shook her head. "Poor guy lived next door and probably couldn't walk any farther than her yard."

I coughed as the sip of cocktail I'd just attempted to swallow jumped down my windpipe instead. When I'd regained control, I asked, "Wasn't she on the HOA board? If she was so mean, how did she get elected?"

Miranda shrugged. "No one else wanted the job, I suppose. And, certainly, no one wanted to stand in her way."

A statuesque woman with dark, flowing hair plowed through the crowd like a masthead on a ship, complete with a proud, perky bosom. She held up a dish in her hands and said brightly, "I made vegan quinoa cookies!"

"Step aside for the stampede," Miranda muttered.

"Lovely," Ellen said. "Emma, this is Francesca Rinaldi. Emma is considering moving into the neighborhood."

Francesca shook my hand with a firm grip. "How wonderful. You will love it here." She had deeply tanned skin and a melodic accent.

"Have you lived here long?" I asked.

"I moved here from Italy ten years ago. Do you have children?"

"No, just a dog."

"That's nice," Francesca replied a little condescendingly. "What do you do for a living?"

"I'm a web developer. How about you?"

"I am a fitness instructor. I teach a class on Mondays, Wednesdays, Fridays, and Saturdays, at my house."

"Don't you mean in your driveway?" Miranda said with a sneer.

"Yes, we need space to do the exercises," Francesca replied, crossing her sculpted arms. "It is quite intensive. A boot camp."

Sophie covered her mouth and whispered in my ear, "My husband told me it looked more like a booty camp."

Miranda gave Francesca a scornful look. "Didn't the HOA tell you to stop the class because you couldn't run a business out of your house?"

"They tried. Rose Martin tried hardest of all. She rallied neighbors against me, to vote in the next meeting," Francesca said with a dark look on her saturnine features. "Rose claimed it was against the bylaws."

"Running a business in your front yard?" Miranda said.

"There is no rule in the HOA covenants that states I can't operate a home business," Francesca said emphatically. "Sophie, as a real estate agent, don't you have an office in your home?"

"That's different," Sophie said, sticking out her freckled chin.

Francesca threw her hands up in the air. "I don't see how. And don't you host a book club at your house, Ellen?"

"Yes, she does," Miranda interjected. "What's your point?"

"People complain because the women in my class park their cars on the street, but I imagine there are many cars in front of your house when you host your book club."

"I guess that's true," Ellen admitted.

"Not at all," Miranda objected. "A book club is totally different."

"Yes, it is different. This is my livelihood! They tried to take away my job." She thumped her hand against her sternum. "More than my job—my identity."

"Francesca, I would never complain about you having that class," Ellen said in a conciliatory tone of voice.

"I know you wouldn't, Ellen. I didn't mean to get so... *irritata*," Francesca said, taking a deep breath that lifted and lowered her *irritatas*. "I'm just making a point."

"Yes, I believe you made it," Miranda said. "At any rate, I imagine that complaints to the HOA management company will decline sharply now that Rose Martin is gone."

Ellen's eyes widened. "Miranda!"

Miranda shrugged and took another sip of her white wine.

Laura finally returned and pulled on my arm. "Sorry, ladies, I need to steal Emma. I want to introduce her to a few more people."

As she directed me away, I whispered angrily at her. "Why did you abandon me? Those women are vicious."

"Since we're looking for a murderer, it seemed the best place to start. Did you learn anything?"

"Everybody hated Rose Martin."

"We knew that."

"Miranda seems to carry an extra helping of hatred."

She clenched her fist and bumped me on the arm. "I knew it!"

"Laura, don't be ridiculous. We don't know anything yet."

Laura pulled me toward a cluster of folks engaged in a heated discussion. We joined them and listened.

"That Gus Redding has got to go. He's been coaching for three years, and for three years, they've missed out on the championship." The tall, muscular man removed a Seminoles hat from his bald head and dabbed his forehead with a napkin.

"He's rebuilding the offense," said another man with a deep Southern accent. "It all depends on the freshman class. He's a good recruiter, but it takes time to build a team after you lose a quarterback like Marcus." The Southern guy had a handsome, friendly face, a deep tan, and brown hair that curled over his collar.

A petite woman laid her hand on the bald man's arm in a calming gesture. "Three years isn't that long, Ed. Give him a break."

"Nobody could ever hope to live up to Bobby Bowden," I interjected. I regretted my boldness immediately when all eyes turned toward me.

"Truer words were never spoken," said the good-looking one. He held out his hand. "Sam Turner. Are you new to the neighborhood?"

With his gaze fixed on me, I noticed his brown eyes fringed with dark lashes. I shook his hand, which was rough and warm. "No, I'm here with my friend, Laura." I glanced around only to find that she'd abandoned me again. We were going to have a serious talk later.

He squeezed my hand before releasing it. "So, you're an FSU fan?"

"Ten years ago, it delivered me a best friend. I'm a fan for life."

"Oh, we just missed each other. I was in law school by then." He gestured to the couple he'd been debating. "Have you met Ed and Mindy yet?"

"No, I haven't." I extended my hand to the woman. "Pleased to meet you. I'm Emma."

Mindy smiled and took my hand but barely squeezed it. She was petite, and standing next to her hulking husband made her appear even tinier. She had shoulder-length brown hair and a gingham shirt that made me think of Mary Ann from the *Gilligan's Island* reruns I'd loved watching on TV Land after school. "Are you visiting Laura from out of town?" she asked.

"No, I live in town. Laura is trying to convince me that I need to move to this neighborhood, though."

"Well, Harbor Shores is a lovely place. I'd have to agree with her. In fact, the house next door is for sale." She pointed at the Mayhew home.

Ed gave her a sharp look. "I'm not sure that one's available at the moment."

Mindy covered her mouth with her hand. "I'm sorry. I shouldn't have mentioned it." She searched my face, obviously wondering if I'd heard the news.

"Yes, that's the one Laura was trying to talk me into. I don't think I'm interested anymore. Did you know the victim?"

Mindy nodded, but Ed cut her off before she could reply. "Yes, we all did. I don't know what she was doing in that house. I heard she was stabbed. Maybe she interrupted a robbery?"

"Was anything stolen?"

Mindy shrugged. "Phillip Mayhew was wealthy. His daughter had been preparing for an estate sale. He had a lot of expensive things. The operators of the estate sale had already done an inventory."

"We don't know anything about it," Ed said sternly. He shook the ice in his glass, which was empty. "I need another drink. Come on, Mindy."

"Nice meeting you, Emma." Mindy meekly followed her husband who'd already headed toward the bar with long, determined strides. Her little legs struggled to keep up with him.

Ed and Mindy's departure left me alone with Sam Turner. "So, FSU, huh? What did you major in?" He raised his beer to his lips.

I noted the absence of a ring on his left hand. "Computer Science. You?"

"Law."

"Oh? What kind of law do you practice?" I asked, keeping my tone casual.

"Criminal. How about you?"

"I'm not a criminal," I said quickly.

He laughed. "I mean, what do you do?"

Inwardly cursing my Freudian slip, I felt my face grow hot. "I'm a web developer. It's boring, actually. Are you the kind of lawyer that defends people or the kind that puts them in jail?"

"I'm a defender of the innocent. And, sometimes, the guilty." He shrugged. "But I try not to ask."

"Ignorance is bliss?"

"Something like that. I just do my job, try to put up the best defense I can mount." He lifted his strong chin. "Everybody has the right to a competent defense."

"I guess that's true."

"Enough about me," he said, waving his beer bottle. "Tell me about you. Are you originally from here?"

"Nope. I grew up near Clearwater. Got a job in Jacksonville right out of college. Been here ever since. You?"

"Nah, I'm from Cairo, Georgia." He pronounced it *kay-row*. "'Bout an hour north of Tallahassee."

"You didn't stray far from home," I said.

He nodded. "True. My dad had just passed when I was a senior in high school, and I wanted to be close in case Mom needed me."

Instantly charmed, I inclined my head and smiled. "That was considerate of you."

He tipped an imaginary hat to me and grinned. "Thank you, ma'am. I do try."

His gaze softened, encouraging me to continue.

"My sister, Sarah, passed away while I was a college freshman. She was younger than me, still in high school. She was very athletic, good at everything, particularly basketball. She collapsed during a game due to an undetected heart defect." I wondered why I was confiding in him so quickly, but he remained intent, so I went on, "It was devastating. So unexpected. I wanted to come home, but my parents convinced me not to." I broke away from his sympathetic gaze and searched the area for Laura. I spotted her across the room, talking to one of the young mothers. "Laura was my freshman roommate. At first, we didn't seem to have that much in common, but Laura was so supportive when Sarah died. She got me through it. I probably would have flunked out if it weren't for her. She got me out of bed and made sure I went to class. Even wrote a paper for me, but don't tell." I laid a finger across my lips.

He mirrored my gesture. "My lips are sealed."

Ed and Mindy returned. Ed had a fresh drink in his hand but the same grim expression on his face. With a twinge of regret that the one-on-one with Sam had been interrupted, I made an attempt to draw them back into the conversation. "So, Mindy. Tell me more about the estate sale. How did you hear about it?"

"I'm friends with Phil's daughter, Alice. She was in town last week to sort through all his things. She invited me over to see if I wanted anything. A few other neighbors too, I think. Alice has her own place up in Charlotte. She told me she didn't need any more furniture. Just sorting through the keepsakes, finding mementos, and getting rid of the rest." Mindy leaned forward and smiled brightly. "Do you like estate sales? I love them."

"Me, too," I said. "I like to look for quirky salt and pepper shakers."

Her obvious interest in the topic made Mindy's speech speed up. "Every Friday, I check out the estate sale listings. This is Florida, after all. There are estate sales all the time."

"Do you collect anything in particular?" I asked.

"Honestly, I enjoy peeking in other people's houses more than buying things. Costa Verde has some really beautiful homes."

I nodded. "You can tell a lot about the people who lived there by the things they collected."

Ed grumpily said, "Our house is full enough of geegaws as it is."

Mindy lightly smacked his arm. "Oh, hush."

"Did they list the estate sale at your former neighbor's house already? Before the body turned up, I mean," I clarified.

"Yes, come to think of it. Wonder if they'll take it down? Alice said she was in a hurry to get the house emptied and sold. Guess they'll have to postpone the sale now."

"I would think so." I made a mental note to check out the listing when I got home. It would have been smarter to attend the estate sale without resorting to breaking and entering. Leave it to Laura to pick the complicated route.

As if summoned by my thoughts, she reappeared by my side. "Emma, come over here and try this seven-layer dip. It is to die for." She waved at Sam, Ed, and Mindy, and pulled me away toward the food table. "Find out anything new?"

"How can I, when you keep yanking me away from people?"

"We need to circulate if we're going to interview everyone." She glanced around furtively. "I feel like people are looking at me like I'm guilty. They might talk to you more if I'm not right beside you. Did you find out anything yet?"

"Mindy told me the house had been inventoried for an estate sale. Maybe whoever killed Rose also stole something that could be tracked down?"

"That's an interesting idea." Laura handed me a small plate laden with multicolored goop: guacamole, cheese, beans, and who knows what else. Four other things, I supposed. I grabbed a tortilla chip and dipped it in the goop. It was indeed tasty.

A tall, thin woman wearing a shirt that advised us to *choose happiness* joined us at the buffet table. "Is that Kristin's seven-layer dip?"

"Hi, Carly," Laura said. "Have you met my friend Emma? She's thinking about moving to the neighborhood."

"Pleasure to meet you," Carly said. "We have such a fabulous community. You'd love living here. Say—were you the friend who was with Laura when she stumbled over Rosie?"

I'd been wondering when someone would put that together. "Yes, I am, unfortunately."

"What was it like? What did you see?" Carly had an avid expression on her thin face. She put a chip in her mouth without taking her eyes off me, as if seated in a movie theater, riveted by the show.

"Not much. It was dark. As soon as it happened, the police showed up and locked us in the back of their car."

"That's it? How about you, Laura?"

"When I unlocked the house—Alice gave me a key, you know—I couldn't find the light switch. I stepped forward while running my hands along the wall, and I couldn't see what was in front of me. I tripped over Rose's body. There was a lot of blood." Laura's voice faded off as she remembered. "The police said she'd been stabbed."

"Do you remember how she was positioned? Was it like she was running away from someone?" Carly the Curious asked.

Laura examined her memory, her expression distant. After thinking for a moment, she spoke. "I think she was facing up. But all the blood was spreading out from underneath her body."

"So, someone stabbed her in the back?" Carly chuckled. "That's appropriate."

Someone called Laura's name. She looked around to locate the source, who proved to be a short, round, gray-haired woman, vaguely resembling a Russian nesting doll. Laura waved enthusiastically. "That's Bina. Let me introduce you. Excuse us, Carly." Laura led me to the little round woman and bent to give her a hug. "I didn't see you over here. Have you been here for long?"

"Oh, you know me. I've been tucked over here in the corner, listening to all the gossip." Bina's blue eyes sparkled in her wrinkled face. "Lots to talk about."

"Yes, indeed," Laura said. She pulled two chairs to the corner where Bina sat. "I want you to meet my friend, Emma. I've been trying to convince her to move here."

"Now's not the best time to be promoting our quiet little seaside town. Not so quiet these days."

Laura leaned forward in her chair. "Bina, you've been here longer than anybody I know. What can you tell us about Rose?"

"Fetch me another drink, and I'll come up with something." She held up an empty glass.

Once Laura had brought her a glass of wine and a small plate of appetizers, Bina started. "I was here, back in the early days of the neighborhood. I remember how they made certain their house looked different from all the others. Put up an arbor on the front, painted everything a different color. She always wanted to stand out, but she wanted everyone else to blend in."

"Her husband?" I asked. "No one mentioned her husband."

"Their marriage ended long ago, no more than five years after they moved here. She got the house, and we haven't seen Paul around here since then. They never had children. I wonder what will happen with the house now?"

Laura nudged me with an elbow. "Guess that's another one for you to consider, Emma."

I rolled my eyes. "Great idea. Instead of reading the real estate listings, I should have been reading the obituaries."

"Sounds like Brooklyn," said Bina. "Rent-controlled apartments are hard to come by."

"Whatever works, I guess." I shrugged. "Do you remember where her husband went after they split up?"

"No idea. I think they were originally from up north. Possibly, he went back there."

"Or, possibly, she buried him in the backyard, but—" Laura raised an admonishing finger. "Not without submitting a request for a landscape alteration with the architectural committee."

Bina chuckled. "The divorce surprised everyone. They seemed like the perfect match. Both were unfriendly. Always complained about children playing in the neighborhood, blocking the streets with their games, leaving their toys out. And they didn't like dogs, either."

I winced. "I've heard all about that."

"I used to serve with her on the HOA board of directors," Bina continued, shaking her head. "She tried to pass rules about unsupervised children and pets. Lumped them together like that."

Laura's nose wrinkled with distaste. "That's crazy."

"That's Rosie," replied Bina. "There was some talk of her misusing HOA funds. She never thought she needed prior authorization for anything. Board meetings were battlefields when she was president." Bina reached over and patted Laura's knee. "Then you came along, and the War of the Roses really began. Everyone was tired of her ways, but no one was willing to stand up to her. I think maybe you didn't know better, little Laura. Didn't understand what you were getting yourself into. But when you defeated Rose for president, I worried she'd find a way to get back at you somehow."

"Oh, she tried. She left me the most hateful messages. It was serious enough to call it harassment, but Jack convinced me to leave it alone. He's not much for confrontation."

"I don't blame him. I've been keeping my head down myself ever since my term on the board ended." Bina patted Laura again. "I felt a little bad for abandoning you there."

"Don't you worry about that." Laura placed her hand over Bina's. "You did your time."

"Speaking of time," Bina said, looking at the gold watch on her age-spotted wrist, "I think it's my bedtime."

Laura helped her out of her seat. "Why don't we walk you home?"

"That would be lovely."

We flanked Bina as we exited the party, with the crowd parting for the tiny, rotund woman as if for royalty. I noticed a couple of people looking from Bina to Laura with concern. Laura kept a smile on her face and her hand on Bina's elbow. She shoved the double doors of the clubhouse open and took a deep breath. The humidity enveloped us like a damp towel.

Human sounds faded behind us as we made our way down the street under a moonless sky. Sparse streetlights emitted pale orange light, barely keeping the oppressive darkness at bay. The night air hummed with a symphony of croaking frogs and chirping insects in the nearby wooded area. An owl hooted loudly, and another responded with harsh, screeching notes. Finding a dead body had made me jumpy. Despite the humidity, I felt a chill. As I rubbed my hands up and down my arms, my skin felt like gooseflesh beneath my fingers.

Laura's voice penetrated my growing unease. "Bina, where's Hugh tonight?"

"Oh, his arthritis is acting up, so he stayed home, but I didn't let it hold me back. Thank you for walking me home. Can't be too careful after a murder occurs around the corner."

"I still can't believe it." Laura's curls glinted in the dim lights, bouncing in time with her steps. "Murder is something that happens in big cities, not here in Harbor Shores."

Bina clucked her tongue in displeasure. "Terrible. Just terrible. I don't understand how someone could creep into our little neighborhood without someone noticing."

"Unless it was someone who was already here. Might still be here."

Laura's words chilled me. I swiveled my head to see if anyone was behind us.

"Bina, why do you think Rose was killed?" Laura asked.

"She had enemies in the neighborhood, but it's hard to imagine anyone getting mad enough to kill. Strange, her getting killed so soon after Phil died. They were the first to buy homes in this neighborhood. The first two houses sold. Now they'll be the last. Assuming someone wants to buy them after this." Bina turned and peered up at me, her silver hair forming a halo in the streetlights. "You seem like a sweet girl, Emma. I think you'd make a good addition to the neighborhood."

I smiled down at the tiny, round woman. "We'll see. Everything is on hold for now. But I'm sure you'd be a wonderful neighbor, too."

We reached a single-story stucco house with a lamp glowing softly in the front window. Bina said, "Looks like Hugh waited up for me."

When we escorted her to her door, Bina hugged me as well as Laura. "Any friend of Laura's is a friend of mine."

As we turned back toward Laura's house, she said, "See? There are kind people living here."

"I didn't say otherwise." But the back of my neck tingled as if someone might be watching us. My pace quickened, and Laura's steps matched mine. Soon, we were practically running, our mutual sense of unease feeding each other's fear.

We reached her house, fighting to catch our breath, and resisting the urge to fling open the door and slam it behind us. Inside, it was dark, making it evident that Jack had already gone to bed. I placed my hand over my hammering heart and exchanged a glance with Laura. We began to laugh, though quietly, so as not to wake Jack.

Laura led me into the small study off the entry hall where Jack sometimes worked from home as a financial advisor. She placed her hand over her own heart. "That was silly."

"We're probably overreacting," I agreed, but my heart continued to race. "Maybe Rose's killer wasn't even a neighbor. Maybe it was like Mindy said: Rose interrupted a robber, and he's long gone."

"Mindy said that?"

"Yes, before Ed shushed her." I thought for a moment. "On second thought, maybe Ed said it. Why don't we look up that estate sale website she was talking about?"

She gestured to the desk chair. "You go ahead. Sounds like you know what you're doing."

I sat down and began typing. The familiar clicking of keys beneath my fingers soothed my jangled nerves. "Multiple companies run estate sales around here, but most of them use a common website to advertise. I'll check that one out first." I typed in the local zip code, and a string of sale listings popped up. I sorted the sales by distance, showing the closest first. "Bingo."

I found a picture of the house but no date. I clicked on the heading to check if the sale inventory was still there. It was. About sixty thumb-nail pictures filled the screen. I jerked my head back. "Damn. That is some ugly furniture."

Laura leaned to look over my shoulder. "Why would anyone steal *that*?"

She had a point. As I scrolled through the pictures, I quickly deter-mined that the previous owner had eclectic tastes. Cherry Queen Anne dining chairs were upholstered in jarring tropical prints. An antique settee sported a pillow in the shape of a frog. The brass coffee table had bird-like talons in place of feet. Lucite chairs flanked a Chesterfield sofa. "Some of it was probably expensive at the time it was purchased. I saw a settee just like that on Antiques Roadshow. Turned out, it was worth thousands. But combined with all that, it seems like a child put it together."

"The owner became reclusive after his wife died, two years back. They owned another house located in a wealthy part of Charlotte. I think this house inherited all the rejects whenever she redecorated."

"Have you noticed anything worth larceny?"

"No, but I'm not an antiques expert. Besides, why not just wait for the sale?"

I turned around and raised an eyebrow at her. "Yes, that's a good point. Why wouldn't someone just wait for a house to be open to the public rather than breaking in at night, dressed in black?"

Her forehead creased. "Maybe *someone* just didn't think of it. Why are you looking at furniture, anyway? Nobody breaks in and takes a settee. Look for smaller items like jewelry."

I scrolled down. "Hard to tell in these pictures. They have jewelry, but I have no idea how valuable it is." I pointed at a bracelet displayed on the screen. "Like that. Looks like one of those rubber bracelets that people wear to raise awareness for a cause. It's engraved." I leaned forward for a better look at the stylized letters. I thought they read, *T&CO*. "Does that say TACO?"

Laura squinted at the screen. "That's not an A. It's 'Tiffany and Co,' darling."

"You're kidding? Tiffany makes rubber wristbands?"

She rolled her eyes and pointed at the description, jabbing at the words for emphasis. "Black. Titanium."

"Too bad. Tacos are a cause I could definitely get behind."

Laura exhaled with a huff. "Can we focus, please?"

"Sure, sure. What are those other numbers for?"

Laura peered at the screen. "Hmm, 1837 and 1997. It must have been the year of an anniversary. One hundred fifty years."

"One hundred sixty," I corrected.

She waved away my pesky math skills. "Whatever. But I don't think this is useful. It would be better to see it in person."

"I'll sign up for updates and they'll send you a notification when the sale is rescheduled." I began typing.

Laura looked over my shoulder again. "Hey, that's my email."

"I don't want a bunch of junk mail."

"Oh, sure. Send it to me. I'm going to sign you up for Hair Club for Men tomorrow," she threatened.

"Should I tell them Jack referred me?" When she lightly smacked the back of my head, I said, "Fine. I'll use my email."

She nodded, satisfied. "When they have the sale, we can go and determine what's missing."

"That's a great plan. As long as no one buys anything before we arrive." I leaned back in the office chair and rubbed my eyes. "I think we need to call it a night and regroup tomorrow."

"I agree. This is going downhill, fast." Laura walked me to the door and kissed me on the cheek. "I'll call you tomorrow. We can go out for lunch."

I nodded. "How about tacos?"

three

Early the next morning, the ringing of my phone woke me from a deep sleep. I rolled over and checked the number on the screen. With a groan, I accepted the call.

"Laura, it's seven a.m. on a Saturday."

"Oh, good. You're awake," she said brightly.

"I am now. You're the only person I'd answer at this ungodly hour. Why are you calling so early?"

"I have an idea. Remember the fitness instructor from last night?"

"Yes."

"I texted her and told her we want to try out her class this morning."

"Laura! Ugh. Not only did you wake me up on Saturday morning, but now you expect me to show up at boot camp?"

"It's not boot camp. It's a beginner's class."

"I need something easier. Does anything come before beginner? Larva, maybe? Or is it pupa? I always get those mixed up."

"Don't ask me. You were the science major."

"Computer Science," I corrected.

"Whatever. Anyway, you need to get up and get moving. The class starts at eight. Wear something cute."

"Why does it matter if I look cute while some perky exercise instructor humiliates me?"

"Looking cute always helps. Let's meet at my place and walk over together."

I looked at the clock with dismay, realizing there was no way that I would be able to get back to sleep. "Fine. But you're buying me breakfast afterward."

"We'll probably be all sweaty."

"You said it was for beginners."

"I did, didn't I? Okay, we'll see. Gotta run." She ended the call. Living closer to Laura looked even less enticing.

Half an hour later, I pulled into Laura's driveway. She was waiting outside in a fuchsia Fabletics tank and leggings, looking just like Kate Hudson. She peered at me in dismay when I emerged wearing gray shorts and a black T-shirt with a picture of a dog and the message "I SHIH TZU NOT."

She put her hands on her hips. "Did you wear that just to spite me?"

Who, me? "No, I wore it because I like dogs."

"You don't even own a Shih Tzu."

"True, but I do enjoy swearing."

Laura sighed heavily.

"Anyway, if I'm going to be tortured, I want to be as comfortable as possible."

She swatted the air. "Whatever. Let's go." She led the way in a rapid stride. I would be winded before we arrived at the exercise class.

I stopped in my tracks when I saw the large group of svelte women stretching in Francesca's driveway, overflowing—in some cases, literally —into the adjacent community pool parking lot. "They don't look like beginners."

I knew it was too late to turn around when I saw Francesca waving enthusiastically. She wore a running bra with the Italian flag across her chest. It was waving, too.

"All right!" she said. She turned and addressed the group of fabletes. "Let's start our warm-up. Find a space at least five feet away from the person next to you. We're going to start out with high knees in place. I want you to lift your knees up past your hips and swing your arms as fast as you can. We're sprinting in place. Let's raise that heart rate, ladies."

This is going to be bad. I chose a spot on the back row. From there, I had a view of a squad of ponytails swinging in front of me. *At least no one could see me.*

"Let's circle up and face each other!"

Naturally.

"Make a big circle! Now, I want you all to lunge walk to the center. Say, 'Hello!' and then jump-squat backwards."

You have got to be kidding me.

All the perky ladies faced each other, lunged toward the center of the circle, and cheerily called out, "Hello!" Then, they lowered their bottoms almost to their heels in a squat and launched themselves upward, hands stretched high towards the sky.

Where is that murderer when I need one? Kill me, please.

"Now line up again as before. We're going to do some mountain climbers. Start in a simple plank position. Make a nice straight line from your head to toe. Imagine that you're climbing a mountain and bring each knee up to your chest, one at a time. Keep that back flat! Imagine there's a glass of water balanced on your back. If you need more of a challenge, pull your knee toward the opposite side instead of straight forward."

More of a challenge? No, thank you. That's a hard pass.

I lay prostrate on the ground. I glanced up and saw a mountain range of bottoms in the air. I noted that most of the women opted for the extra challenging technique.

I remained face down in my puddle of sweat. Everyone was facing forward, away from me. Recognizing an opportunity to escape, I aimed for the hedge surrounding the clubhouse and pool. I didn't want to draw attention to myself by standing, so I performed an awkward crab walk in a semi-crouch. When I reached the hedge, I checked again to see if anyone was watching, and then I lunged around it.

I ran directly into Sam Turner.

My perspiration-laden, ugly-shirt-wearing body smashed fully in contact with Sam's bare chest. At eye level, I saw water droplets sparkling on his smooth, tan skin. I jumped away from him and raised my hands to my burning cheeks. Despite my already flushed complex-ion, I felt the telltale warmth of an intense blush creeping up my neck. I smelled the chlorine wafting from the pool and from his skin. *I probably reek.* I wanted the ground to open up and swallow me. Boot camp was preferable. Anything was better than this.

"Sorry about that," he said. "Did I get you wet?" He removed the towel he wore draped around his shoulders and held it out to me.

I took a step back. "That's okay. I'm fine."

He struggled to suppress a mischievous grin, wiping his face with the towel. "Working out with Francesca this morning?"

"Laura convinced me to try it out."

Through the bushes, I heard Francesca call out, "Double time!"

"Seems too humid for all that hoppin' around. I prefer swimming laps." He began rubbing his hair with the towel while I tried not to stare at his biceps.

"That does sound better. Maybe I'll try that next time."

"I'm here every morning," he said, draping the towel back around his neck. "Run into me anytime." He bobbed his head and walked away, turning left at the hedge. I noted that he would pass the booty camp on his way home.

Probably going that way so he can see sweaty women in leggings. I looked down at my ensemble and wished I'd listened to Laura. Better yet, I wished I'd stayed in bed. I dragged my beaten, sodden, humiliated body back to Laura's house, retrieved my car, and drove home.

four

AT THE SOUND of my key in the door, Hopper began howling impatiently. He greeted me with joyful abandon, though I'd been gone less than an hour. I rubbed his ears, and he grunted with pleasure.

"You're my boy, aren't you?" I asked him in a singsong voice. "You're a good boy. We don't need any other boys around here, do we? No, sir, we don't." He licked my face, and I took it as a sign of agreement, though I probably just tasted salty.

Kicking off my sweaty shoes, I padded down the hallway to my bedroom with Hopper following, always at my side. I paused to scratch him behind the ears. "You're the only loyal male I know, Hopper."

I stripped off my smelly, unattractive clothes, tossed them in the hamper, and stepped into the shower. As I stood under the spray, with the warm water pouring over my head and face, a memory of the day I became a dog owner flashed into my mind.

I wasn't alone that day. My ex-husband, Ryan, accompanied me to the animal shelter. The problems in our relationship were already becoming obvious after only a few months of marriage. He worked long hours at an investment firm, and I was part of a team developing new software with a looming release date. The differences between us, which had been significant to begin with, were only widening. We thought adopting a dog would bring us closer together. In the end, our relationship lasted less than two years. *But could we say it was fourteen in dog years?*

That day at the shelter, Hopper caught my attention right away with those big, sad eyes. Unlike the other dogs, his demeanor was calm and attentive. He sat quietly near the entrance to the enclosure, never taking his gaze from me. His smooth fur was a mixture of browns and blacks, and his small ears lay snug against his broad, flat head. When he opened his mouth, he appeared to be grinning.

"Not that one," Ryan said. "Looks like he might be part pit bull."

"So? A neighbor owned one when I was growing up, and she was a sweet dog."

He jerked his head back and looked at me incredulously. "Sweet?"

"You train them, obviously. They have to know who's boss. Does that bother you?"

Never one to shirk off any perceived affront to his manhood, Ryan stuck his chin out. "Fine with me. Sure that's the one you want?"

I was sure he was the one—the dog, not Ryan. I nodded.

Ryan had been my college boyfriend. We met at a party. He was a business major, and I was a science nerd, but physical attraction overruled our personality differences. He was ambitious, and from the beginning, it was clear he was going places. I just didn't realize those places would include his coworker's bedroom. The minute he started working at that firm, insisting that the job demanded long hours and weekends, I should have recognized the signs. When he assured me that Thea, his associate with the long black hair and luminous blue eyes, was nothing more than a coworker, I believed him at first. However, when I found a long, raven strand of hair clinging to his undershirt on one of those late nights, I couldn't ignore my niggling worries. By tracking him on Find My iPhone, I saw he was lying when he said he was at the office. He was at Thea's. Our marriage ended after twenty months. Twenty months of wasted time.

Thinking about it was another waste of time. I got out of the shower and dressed in a fresh pair of shorts and a T-shirt. Deciding I needed to clear my head, I padded to the foyer to retrieve Hopper's leash from the hook beside the front door. "You're my good boy. You want to go for a walk?" He barked in affirmation. I reached down and scratched his rump. He circled with a full-body wriggle, tail curved up in the air.

After our stroll, I began to feel human again. A cup of coffee would complete my transformation. I was adding dark roast to my little four-cup coffeemaker when I heard the doorbell. *What now?* Too much had happened to me already that day, and it wasn't even ten o'clock. I opened the door and found Laura on my doorstep. She had taken the time to shower and change and appeared fresh and crisp in her white peg pants and pink floral top.

"You ditched me!" she said with her hands on her hips.

"It was an act of desperation," I said. "I'm sorry. Would you like some coffee?"

"I thought we were going out for breakfast." Laura bent to scratch Hopper behind the ears.

"That was before boot camp. I'm making coffee. Come on in." I led the way back to the kitchen. "Do you want eggs?"

"Nah, just coffee is fine." She opened the cabinet where I kept my mismatched collection of mugs and selected her favorite—a souvenir from a charity dance marathon in which Laura and I stayed on our feet for twenty hours. I'd wanted to give up, but she wouldn't let me. Laura never gave up on me, either.

I cracked two eggs in the pan and began pushing them around with a spatula. "What was the point of me embarrassing myself at that exercise class, anyway?"

Laura sat down at my little table and fiddled with my salt and pepper shakers shaped like black and white poodles. "You were supposed to be identifying suspects," she said.

"By looking at their backsides?" I turned from the stove to look at her incredulously. "Something like a police lineup, but in reverse."

"No. You were supposed to stay and chat with them after class."

"I couldn't breathe after that class, let alone talk. Did *you* stay and chat with them?"

"I tried, but they all rushed off." She sighed deeply. "I swear, people are avoiding me. I've been tainted by that murder. It's like I have a big red M stamped on my forehead."

"You're imagining things. Besides, you're the president of the

HOA. Nobody likes the HOA." I pointed my spatula at her. "You guys are always sending them letters telling them to cut their grass or weed their flowerbeds. They hated the last lady so much, someone killed her."

"I'm not imagining things. I found this in my mailbox when I got back this morning." She pulled out a folded sheet of paper and laid it on the table. I stepped away from the stove and peered over her shoulder to read it. Handwritten in block letters, the note read, "STOP ASKING QUESTIONS OR END UP LIKE ROSE."

A chill swept over me. "This was in your mailbox when you got back from Francesca's class?"

"That's right."

I stepped away again, wanting to distance myself from the menacing words. "That means we can eliminate anyone who was in the class this morning."

She bit her lip. "I haven't looked in my mailbox since yesterday. Someone could have placed it there any time since then."

I turned off the stove and sat beside her at the table. "You know, you probably should have taken this to the police right away. Maybe they could have gotten fingerprints from it or something."

She released a breath, an anguished expression on her face. "I didn't even consider that. Do you think it's too late?"

"Probably." I shrugged.

"What if we put it in a Ziploc bag?" she suggested.

It seemed unlikely, but I stood to retrieve one from the pantry. Anything to make Laura feel better. "Maybe we should forget about our investigation."

"The only way I'll get out from under this cloud of suspicion is if the real killer is found." She pushed around the salt and pepper shakers as she considered. "I wish I knew what Rose was doing in that house. I heard the police say that the sliding glass door was unlocked."

"You didn't mention that before." The coffee machine gurgled, signaling it was almost ready. Although I drank it black, my best friend was used to having things sweetened for her. I searched in the pantry for the stevia packets I kept on hand for her frequent visits.

Laura stared at the twin shakers in her hands as if trying to decide between them. Twin creases formed between her eyebrows. "Do you think she might have been meeting someone there?"

"Why there?" I placed the coffee carafe, a spoon, and a green packet on the table.

"Maybe they wanted somewhere clandestine."

"Are you suggesting she was having an affair with someone? All I've heard is how disliked she was." I returned to the stove to retrieve my plate and mug before sitting down across from Laura. "Can I have the salt and pepper, or are you too attached to them now?"

She pushed them across the table. The saltshaker fell over, and a small amount spilled out. She swept it up into her hand and tossed it over her shoulder.

"Why do you do that?"

"I've told you—it prevents bad luck."

"I could use something to turn my luck around." I sprinkled the salt on my food, where it belonged. "I ran into Sam Turner today while I was making my escape from Francesca's class. I looked like a total mess."

She gave me an arch look. "You're interested in Sam? You didn't mention it."

"We've been too busy playing Nancy Drew. Besides, I'm sure he's not interested in me. Not after today." I shoveled a large bite into my mouth.

"I told you to wear something cute."

I rolled my eyes at her. "What can you tell me about him?"

"Not much. He hasn't lived there for long. He bought the Clark's house when Dan was transferred to Utah. I know that he's a lawyer, and he lives there alone." She waggled her eyebrows at me.

"I was just curious. That's all. Forget it."

"Sure," she said, but I knew she wouldn't. She didn't. "You've been alone too long, Emma. Jack and I don't have a perfect relationship, but it's nice to have someone to come home to."

"I'm not alone. I have you. And Hopper." My pup perked up, seeking a handout.

Laura reached down and gave him a pat on the head instead. "Hopper is a good guard dog, and you'll always have me, but a man in your life would be nice. I worry about you." She reached for the ominous note. "I worry about me, too. I'm scared, Emma. I was already afraid of jail but this—" She held up the paper, and it shook in her hand.

I covered her hand with my own to stop the trembling. "We'll give this to the police, and that will take care of both problems. Did you show it to Jack yet?"

"He was on a call with a client when I left." She glanced at her watch. "Now that I mention it, he'll be wondering where I am. I swear, you break into one vacant house, and all trust goes out the window." She carried her mug to the sink, washed and dried it by hand, and returned it to its spot in the cabinet. Cleaning things always calmed her.

I walked her out to her car. When she got in, she turned the key, but the car only emitted a grinding noise and refused to turn on. She peered at me through the windshield in bewilderment, tried once more, and got back out of the car.

"What were you saying about bad luck?"

"Terrific. Can you give me a ride home?"

I went back inside to grab my keys and refilled Hopper's water bowl before driving Laura home. As we pulled up to her house, we spotted someone walking up to the front door. Laura got out and called to the visitor, "Can I help you?"

It was a young man with spiky red hair. In his arms, he held an extremely large three-ring binder. "Are you Laura Benton?" he asked.

"I am. Are you selling something?"

"No, ma'am. My name is David Garrity. Rose Martin was my aunt. I'm helping my mom clear out her house. We found this binder full of HOA stuff, and a neighbor suggested I should bring it to you." He held out the huge binder.

"Thanks." Laura smiled at him. "Do you need help sorting Rose's house? I'd be happy to lend a hand."

"That's awfully nice of you. I'll let my mom know." He gave a friendly wave and left.

Laura shrugged and opened the binder. Her eyes widened, and she gestured to me to hurry inside. I rolled up the window, lowered for eavesdropping, and complied.

She dropped it on the dining room table. "Emma, check this out. Rose collected information on everybody in the neighborhood. She has records in here of every house in Harbor Shores: the sale price of each house, how many people live there, how many kids and pets in each, types of vehicles... This is crazy."

"She really was Nosy Rosie. Unbelievable." I looked over Laura's shoulder as she turned the pages. Rose had collected every neighborhood newsletter for the past twenty years. She saved all the notes from each board meeting along with financial reports. There was a section dedicated to public records, including land surveys, county tax records, and public utility records from the electric company. "Did you have any idea she collected all this information?"

Laura shook her head slowly, stunned. "No. I had no clue."

"Do you think anyone else knew?"

She glanced up from the binder and met my eyes with her own. "I wonder." She glanced out the window and pursed her lips. "I think I'm just going to walk over and introduce myself to Rose's sister. Want to come?" She raised her eyebrows and widened her green eyes innocently.

I squinted suspiciously. "What are you planning?"

"Just a friendly visit," Laura said. "I'll grab some juice or lemonade from the fridge to share with her."

"You have juice?" I said incredulously, following her into the kitchen.

She opened the refrigerator and bent down to examine the contents. "You know, for mixers. Screwdriver, Tequila Sunrise, Gin and Juice."

"Got it. That makes more sense."

She removed a plastic bottle and placed it on the counter before turning to the large cabinet where she stored her hospitality serving items. Laura's father had been an Army Colonel, so her mother became skilled at hosting promotion parties, change of command receptions, and monthly coffees. Laura learned hospitality at her mother's knee, and her vast assemblage of serving items attested to the fact. After surveying her collection, Laura selected a large, elaborate, glass bottle with a swing-top stopper attached and carefully filled it with lemonade. Then, we set off down the road toward Rose's former home.

"I never knew Rose had a sister," Laura said as we walked. "It's difficult to imagine her even having a mother and father. I wouldn't be surprised if she grew from a spore."

"You probably shouldn't speculate like that as we approach her house," I said. "I doubt that her sister would appreciate it."

"You can't assume anything about the way her sister feels either," she replied. "Lots of siblings don't get along."

I tried to shake off the sadness that fell on me at the mention of sisters. We walked in silence for a couple of minutes, but I could practically hear the gears moving in Laura's head.

"Rose and her sister could have been like the Wicked Witch of the West and Glinda, the Good Witch."

"We'll know for certain if she's wearing a pink ball gown when we arrive," I speculated, grateful that Laura's comment had lightened the mood.

"Funny," Laura replied.

"Actually, that gives me a great idea for how we might make her feel welcome in Harbor Shores." I began singing in a squeaky voice and with a flourish, I presented her with an invisible giant lollipop.

Laura elbowed me. "Knock it off, Mayor Munchkin."

I continued the song in my best munchkin voice.

"Emma, quit it!" She jabbed me with a finger, then pointed to a house just ahead of us. "We're almost there. That one with the arbor on the front is Rose's place."

I looked in the direction Laura was pointing and saw a pink stucco single-story home. The house featured a courtyard with an iron gate. On one side was a two-car garage, discreetly angled, so the doors didn't face the street. The other wing of the house showcased a broad picture window. An attached metal arbor held brilliantly blooming roses that climbed the posts and spanned across the top of the entrance to the courtyard.

"Rose actually planted roses?" I said, astonished.

"Probably because all the thorns provided additional home security."

"Shh." I saw a woman emerging from the garage wearing work clothes and carrying a box. She had short brown hair with a few streaks of gray in it, and her face was smooth but free of makeup. "That must be her sister."

Laura put on her brightest pageant smile and waved. "Hi! You must be Rose's sister. I'm Laura Benton. I live around the corner. And this is my friend, Emma."

"Pleased to meet you," the woman said, placing the box down and removing her work gloves. She swiped a sleeve across her forehead, leaving a dirty streak. "I'm Gwen."

"Looks like hard work. We thought you could use a refreshment." Laura held out the lemonade. In her other hand, she held a stack of disposable clear plastic cups, a not-so-subtle suggestion for an invitation inside.

"Oh, lovely. Thank you so much. I'm afraid it's quite a mess inside," Gwen said. "Let's sit in the courtyard." The courtyard was formed by the U-shape of the house. We followed Gwen to a bistro table and chairs in the shade. "I've been going through stuff in the garage today. Rose sure accumulated a lot of things." She sat down heavily in her chair. "It's so thoughtful of you to bring cups. I already wrapped up all the glassware."

Laura passed out cups and filled them with lemonade. "I'm so sorry for your loss. Were you close?"

Gwen shrugged. "Maybe when we were children, but we'd grown apart since her marriage." She motioned towards the house. "I've never visited here before now."

Laura glanced at the door, obviously disappointed that we hadn't been invited inside. "Are you holding an estate sale?"

"No," Gwen said after taking a deep gulp of lemonade. "Too much trouble. I'm donating a lot of it, and my son, David, is taking some of it to set up housekeeping at his apartment. He graduated from high school this year, and he's starting at the University of Wisconsin this month on full scholarship."

"Oh, how fortunate," Laura said. "You must be proud. Do you live in Wisconsin, too?"

"Yes, in Eau Claire."

"Guess you have some pretty rough winters up there. Did you give any thought to keeping Rose's house and staying in Florida?"

Gwen waved away the suggestion. "Too hot for me down here. That was Rose's thing, but I'll never leave Wisconsin. I'm too attached to my home to change now."

"I understand." Laura nodded sympathetically.

Meanwhile, I was thinking, *why would anyone choose to live in Wisconsin?* We Floridians never understood why anyone would want to live anywhere else.

"Plus, I'd never live in an area that's prone to hurricanes," Gwen added.

Well, there's that.

A car door slammed. David entered through the courtyard gate, carrying a six-pack of mover's tape and a roll of bubble wrap. "More supplies." He spotted us sitting with his mother. "Oh. Hello, again."

"Thanks, David," Gwen said and gestured at us. "I guess you met Laura when you delivered Aunt Rose's binder."

"Yes, that's right."

"And this is Laura's friend, Emma," Gwen continued.

David nodded. "Yes, we met at the same time. Nice to see you." His voice and manners were extremely polite. He seemed more mature than his freckled face would suggest.

"I'm afraid we're keeping your mother from getting anything done," Laura said. "Is there any way we can help?"

"No, thanks. I appreciate it, but I have to go through everything first," Gwen said, then raised a finger. "Actually, it would help if you could tell me where the closest Goodwill or Salvation Army is located. I'd like to donate some of these things, and it's going to take me a few trips."

"There's a Goodwill on Valley Road," I said. "It's not far."

"Gwen, why don't you let us take the first load over there for you?" Laura suggested in a voice dripping with charm. "That way you don't have to stop what you're doing. Emma's got a big ol' SUV."

Gwen's mouth popped open. "Oh, I couldn't trouble you like that."

"No trouble at all. Emma and I can go grab the car and be back in a couple of minutes." She stood before Gwen could make any more objections.

As we walked away, I whispered, "Laura, you're being a little pushy."

"Nonsense. I'm just being neighborly."

We drove back to Rose's house in my Pathfinder. I parked at the curb and opened the rear hatch.

David came outside carrying a sealed box. "I'll load it up. We really appreciate it." He added three more cardboard boxes, about two feet long, with the word EGGS printed on them.

"Do you need any more boxes?" I asked. "My office just got a load of new computers, and they've been unpacking them all week."

"I'm sure we can use them," David said. "That will save me another trip to the store. Oh—Mom said to ask you to bring back the tax receipt from Goodwill if it wouldn't be too much trouble."

"No trouble at all. Is that the last box?" Laura asked.

David closed the cargo door. "Yep. Thanks again."

When we reached the exit to the neighborhood, Laura said, "Turn right."

"But the thrift store is on the left. Where are we going?"

"Your place," Laura said. "I want to go through these boxes in case there are any clues."

"But we told her we'd donate them."

"We will. After we look through them."

Slowly, I shook my head in wonder. "Boy, Nosy Rosie sure did meet her match when you moved to Harbor Shores, didn't she?"

"I was more than a match for her. I bested her."

"I wouldn't let anyone else hear you talking like that."

"I didn't say I killed her."

"Still... you should watch what you say, Laura."

A few minutes later, I pulled up to my house. "Do we have to carry all this in and unpack it? Can't we just open them, peek inside, and then go to Goodwill?"

"I guess so. But I don't want anyone to watch us. Is there enough room in your garage to pull the car in?"

I turned to her and arched an eyebrow. "You imply that my garage is messy."

She narrowed her eyes. "Yes, I know you well."

"As a matter of fact, I cleaned it recently." I pushed the button attached to my sun visor, and the garage door slowly opened.

Laura's mouth fell open as she took in the state of my garage. All the contents were pushed to one side, stacked precariously on top of other stuff. "That's what you call cleaning? I bet when you were a kid, you just shoved everything in the closet when your mom made you clean your room."

"Shows what you know," I said, sticking out my tongue. "My mom just shut the door."

"That explains a lot."

I made a three-point turn at the foot of my driveway and carefully backed into the narrow opening. I pressed the trunk release button, got out, and did a crab walk in the cramped space between my car and the mountain of stuff.

Laura stood behind the SUV and surveyed the boxes sealed with tape. "Got a knife?"

I rummaged through the contents of a wall cabinet and retrieved a box cutter. "Maybe I should do it. I'm not sure you're allowed to have a knife." I sliced the tape on the first box to reveal a stack of carefully folded clothing.

Laura wrinkled her nose. "Ugh. It smells like her awful perfume."

I sniffed. "What did she wear? Poison?"

"It sure as hell wasn't Joy," Laura replied, fanning the air with one hand. "Open the next one."

The second box contained mismatched dishes and glassware.

The third box held old books.

"This is going to take forever," I complained.

"Then you'd best get to it," Laura replied, holding a book upside down by its spine and flipping the pages.

We had searched three-fourths of the books before something fluttered out of a worn hardback copy of *Scruples*. I bent down to retrieve the fallen piece of paper. It was a picture of a newborn lying in a clear plastic bassinet, wrapped in a hospital blanket. The baby had a thatch of bright red hair.

I picked it up and handed it to Laura. "Think that's David?"

Laura held the photo closer to her face and peered at it. "The tag on the foot of the bed says, 'Baby Martin.'"

"Show me." I took the photo from her hand and examined it. "You're right. David's last name is Garrity. Why would Rose have a picture of a redheaded baby named Martin? I thought Bina said Rose and her husband, Paul, never had children."

"Could be another baby on her husband's side of the family. Red hair can pop up in any gene pool."

An awful thought occurred to me. "What if she had a child that died?"

Laura tucked her chin and grimaced. "That's an awful notion."

"True, but if she'd lost a child, that might explain why she was always yelling at kids to stay away from her house."

"I would think it would have the opposite effect. People who always wanted kids but can't have them often become attached to other people's children."

I returned my focus to the photo. "What should we do with this? It seems a shame not to give it back to Gwen, but if we do, how can we explain the way we found it?"

"I guess we could just say it fell out of the box."

I passed the photo back and forth between my hands. "Maybe."

"We should hold on to it, though, in case it's evidence."

"Evidence of what?" My gaze shifted from the infant's face to Laura's.

She crossed her arms and rested her chin on one fist. "I don't know. This could be Rose's secret. She hoarded other people's secrets. It makes sense that she would have had her own."

After we searched the rest of the books without any more discoveries, Laura said, "Let's take this stuff to Goodwill now. She'll be wondering where we are with her receipt."

After we visited Goodwill, we returned to Gwen's house with the receipt. The garage door was open, and Gwen stood inside, arms crossed, as she stared at stacks of boxes with dismay. When she spotted us, she swiped an arm across her sweaty forehead and waved.

I stepped out of my car and approached her with the donation record in my hand.

"One more thing to check off my list," she said, taking the paper. "Thanks."

"No problem," I replied. "I can bring you those empty boxes from my office tomorrow."

When she looked at me in confusion, I realized I had only told her son. "I work for a software development firm. We just got some new equipment, and I told David I could bring the empty boxes over."

She nodded. "Thank you. That would be helpful. Software development, you say?"

"That's right."

"Maybe you could advise me. Rose had an older model desktop computer, and I'm not sure what to do with it. I've heard there are recycling programs. What does your company do with their old equipment?"

"We do recycle it, after we've cleared all the data." I paused before adding, "I could take care of it for you. I might even be able to add it to our recycling collection. Some places charge you to recycle electronic equipment."

A look of relief lifted her features. "Would you? I hate to ask you for more help, but I am a little overwhelmed." She gestured to the overflowing garage behind her.

Laura had been standing behind me, listening to the exchange. "Is it inside? Emma can take it apart for you."

"David already did that." Gwen moved some boxes aside to reveal an old desktop computer and a boxy monitor.

"Oh." Laura, eyes mournful, obviously still hopeful for an invitation inside.

I used the key fob to unlock the hatch, Gwen hefted the main unit inside, and I loaded the monitor.

"Thank you again. It's nice to know my sister had such friendly neighbors."

Back in my car, Laura said, "'Friendly neighbors?' I hope you plan to snoop on that computer before you recycle it."

I turned to her and grinned. "Absolutely."

We returned to examining the binder splayed open on a table at Laura's place.

"What are you two up to now?" Jack entered the study in athletic wear and running shoes. His outfit was nicely coordinated, and I wondered if Laura picked out his clothes.

"Just some HOA business, dear," Laura said. "Going for a run?"

"I hope you aren't doing any more investigating. You've gotten into enough trouble as it is."

"Of course not," Laura lied. "Jack? The car wouldn't start after I drove it to Emma's house this morning. We left it there, and she gave me a ride home."

"Oh, great. Did you leave the dome light on again?"

"I don't think so."

"Did the engine turn over at all, or was it silent?"

"It made a grinding noise."

"Alternator. Great. That's gonna be expensive. I'll call Triple-A when I get back from my run."

"Thanks, honey."

He huffed in reply and left the room.

I turned my head to look at Laura. "What's up with him?"

"He's been a little testy ever since he had to retrieve me from jail."

I snorted. "Better leave you two alone, then."

"You don't need to rush off, Emma."

"It's Saturday. I have things to do around the house."

"I left my purse in your car." She walked back outside with me. A group of ladies wearing shorts and visors speed-walked by on the street. Laura waved. "Hi, Sharon! Andrea!"

The ladies nodded but didn't smile, briskly walking past.

Laura watched them with a bleak expression. "They all think I'm a murderer."

I waved her off. "Nah, they're probably just trying to keep their heart rate up. I think you're over-reacting."

She turned on me, enraged. "I am not!"

Hands up in surrender, I said, "Whoa! Honestly, Laura, all this investigating you have been drawing me into suggests that you think *they* might be murderers."

She squinted, confused. "Sharon and Andrea?"

"No, all of your neighbors."

Turning to watch the women walk away, she asked plaintively, "But who had a motive?"

"That's not your problem to solve."

Her face hardened. "But it is. I'm a suspect. When the police released us, they warned me that I could still be under investigation."

"They haven't followed up with me."

"You weren't covered in blood."

"Laura, why would you walk back into the scene of a crime you yourself had committed and throw yourself on top of the victim?"

She threw her hands in the air. "I don't know! To deflect suspicion? Maybe I killed her unintentionally, and then I led you back there to provide a witness to my innocence."

"I know you didn't do that."

"You do, but none of my neighbors do."

"You are entirely too concerned with what other people think of you. Too concerned with appearances. I considered living here because it's close to the beach, but now this place seems like a pretentious trap."

I'd gone too far. She crossed her arms and glared at me with her lips pressed tightly together. "If that's what you think of me, then you can just go back home to your little, old house and try to make the best of it. Why bother doing housework?"

I opened the car door and retrieved her designer handbag. "Take this. Why don't you and Louis Vuitton here get back inside before the neighbors start talking about you?"

She snatched the purse from my hands and stomped back inside, slamming the door behind her.

five

I DIDN'T HEAR from Laura for the remainder of the weekend. I worried I'd been too harsh with her. We'd had fights before, but they always blew over quickly. Laura stood by me through the roughest years of my life. I couldn't turn my back on her when she was in the middle of her own trials. My guilt grew as I replayed our argument, which now seemed petty. I'd been too hard on her, but I didn't know how to make it up to her.

When I checked my email on Monday morning, I found a notice from the estate sale website. It announced the sale at the murder house had been rescheduled for that coming Thursday. It didn't call it "the murder house," but that's how I'd begun to think of it. A preview of the sale was available on Wednesday afternoon.

I picked up my phone to call Laura, but she didn't answer. I presumed she was still angry and screening my calls, so I left a message. "Laura, I want to apologize for being such a jerk Saturday. Things have been so crazy lately. I got an email today that says the estate sale in your neighborhood is back on, and I figured we could go together and check it out. Give me a call, please."

Later that morning, my phone rang. Without preamble, Laura said, "So, when is the estate sale?"

"Thursday and Friday, with a preview on Wednesday afternoon. Want to come with me?"

"Of course."

"Are you still mad at me?"

"A bit."

"I'm sorry I said you were paranoid and pretentious."

"Actually, you didn't say it in those words, but now I know how you really feel."

"I don't think that. You're a decent person. I'm proud to be your friend."

She was silent for a moment. Then she said, "Thank you. You, too."

"Still friends?"

"Always."

"I've got a meeting on Wednesday, but I can swing by your place afterward. About five-thirty, okay?"

"Sure."

"And I promise not to dress like a bum."

"Whatever."

"See you then."

"'Bye."

I ended the call feeling I'd made some sort of progress.

WEDNESDAY EVENING, I left downtown early, trying to beat the traffic. One main highway led to the beach communities, and every evening it backed up with workers heading home. Despite my advanced planning, I got caught in the traffic as it crawled along. After I'd been stopped by every red light coming down A1A, I turned into Laura's neighborhood and pulled up to her house.

She opened her front door and immediately hugged me. "Let's never fight like that again."

I breathed a huge sigh of relief. "Deal."

She took a step back and surveyed my ensemble composed of a crisp, white Ann Taylor blouse with black trousers. "You'll do."

"Not that anyone dresses up for estate sales," I said. "I just wanted your approval."

Her expression softened. "I'm sorry. It's possible I was overreacting."

"No way. Forget it." I checked my watch and saw that the sale must have started. "Are you ready to go?"

She nodded and called back into the house, "Jack! I'm going out for a little while." I heard a grunt from the living room. She pulled the door closed and locked it behind her. "Dangerous neighborhood, you know."

Once again, we walked along the path back to the house where our recent trials originated. As we got closer, we passed cars parked along the street. It looked like the sale would be busy.

"Is this going to bother you?" I asked. "Going back into that house?"

"No, I'm fine," she said. But when we arrived at the front door and followed the instructions on the posted sign to "come right in," she looked down at the foyer floor and hesitated. No sign of the blood remained on the tiles. She stepped over the area with a larger-than-necessary stride, and we proceeded into the house.

Due to our unfortunate experience, I never got a good look at the house on my first visit. Honestly, I felt anxious about returning to the site of the crime myself. While then it had been dark and foreboding, in daylight, it was bright and airy. I smelled a scented candle burning somewhere, no doubt an attempt to make the home inviting to potential buyers.

A cathedral ceiling arched above the room, illuminated by a large, gleaming chandelier. As I stepped through the entryway into the living room, I saw a pair of wide French doors leading out to a patio. Through them, I caught a glimpse of a serene pond and a willow tree. Beyond the tiled entry, hardwood floors gleamed in the late afternoon sunlight.

"It is a beautiful house," I said.

"I told you."

The scene appeared peaceful, but when I inhaled, I caught a hint of bleach in the air. The scent reminded me of the blood-soaked floor that must have been thoroughly scrubbed in anticipation of the estate sale.

My stomach turned over. "But I don't think I could get past the whole murder-scene thing."

She gestured at the crowd. "Looks like it only increased the turnout."

Looking around, it seemed she was right. The crowd at the preview night was bigger than any estate sale I'd ever attended.

The ugly furniture was tagged and on display. All the contents of cabinets, closets, and drawers had been arranged on long tables and dotted with price tags.

In the living room, I thought I recognized the woman perusing the contents of a brass and glass étagère. "Mindy?"

The petite brunette looked up from the item she was holding and smiled. "Emma! I see you came to check out the estate sale."

"You bet." I noticed the knickknack in her hands was a ceramic mask with real feathers protruding from its forehead. "It's a remarkable collection."

Mindy grimaced, delicately placing the mask back onto the table. "It certainly is." She glanced around the room. "They really cleaned up the place."

"How can you tell?" Laura asked. "Had you been here recently?"

"I dropped in to visit Alice. Her father's health declined so much recently he hadn't been keeping the place up. He really needed a handy-man." Mindy replaced the mask on the shelf. "Well, enjoy exploring." She wandered off toward the kitchen.

I turned to Laura. "Where do you want to start?"

"The bedroom, of course," she said.

I raised my eyebrows but followed her back to the primary bedroom. Curiosity had replaced my earlier sense of foreboding about the house.

"Everything has been pulled out and moved around, Laura. I doubt we're going to find anything."

"I downloaded the 'before' pictures from the original sale listing so we can compare and see if anything's missing. Since this is only a preview, they haven't sold anything yet."

"That you know of."

"True."

We scanned the bedroom. The walls glowed with Pepto-Bismol-pink paint. Matching custom blinds obscured a set of sliding glass doors leading to a patio.

Laura jerked her head back as if repulsed by the hue. "They probably spent a fortune decorating this room, and it looks like a pink nightmare."

I nodded, stunned. "I feel like I'm inside a uterus. It's a womb-room."

Laura snorted. A pair of twin-sized beds were pushed together in the middle of the room. "Twin beds?"

"Just like a fifties' sitcom. Lucy and Desi, or Ozzie and Harriet." I examined the dresser. The surface overflowed with ladies' accessories and jewelry. "Wasn't he a widower?"

"I guess he didn't want to get rid of his wife's things." Laura checked her phone and compared the photo with the display in front of us. No noticeable differences stood out. "None of this is exceptionally valuable."

"They keep the high-end jewelry in a case up front where the workers sit and take payments for purchases," I explained. "Not that I ever buy any of that stuff."

"No. You buy tacky salt and pepper shakers."

"They're not tacky," I said defensively. "They're kitsch."

She moved on past the dresser and turned to investigate the walk-in closets. There were two: his and hers. The one on the left was considerably larger than the one on the right, presumably because it belonged to the lady of the house. The sale organizers had pulled out the most upscale ensembles, hung them on top and bottom connecting hangers, and displayed them facing outward. There was enough resort wear to fill a cruise ship. Some items still had the original tags attached. Lining one wall from top to bottom, a shoe rack displayed an extensive collection of footwear. Several small drawers, suitable for lingerie and accessories, flanked the shoe rack. Laura pulled one of the drawers open and found it empty. She continued down the row, opening each drawer and feeling around on the underside of the supporting structure.

"Everything is on display," I said.

Laura didn't stop her rifling. "They might have missed—"

"Can I help you?" A woman in a blue polo shirt with the words *Estate Sales by Barbara* stitched on her formidable chest appeared in the doorway of the closet.

"Just checking out the workmanship on these built-ins. What an amazing closet," Laura gushed.

The woman crossed her arms. "Please don't interfere with the displays. The sale will not begin until tomorrow at nine. Concealing items in advance of the sale will not be tolerated."

Laura jerked her head back and tucked her chin indignantly. "I would never—"

"Please exit the closet."

Laura stomped out of the closet and glared at the woman who had taken a seat in the corner to guard the room.

I slunk out of the room behind her. "That was fun. I'm going to get banned from Estate Sales by Barbara."

"Who needs them? Come on. Let's check this room next."

She proceeded into the study, an east-facing room with a large picture window. Sunlight gleamed off the polished surface of an enormous desk the size of a mattress. A matching hutch with drawers occupied the opposite wall. Floor-to-ceiling shelves loaded with books lined the other wall. The introverted bookworm inside me wriggled with delight. A room lined with bookshelves was my idea of a happy place, although most of the ones on display were about golf, history, or the military. I reminded myself I was on a mission, with "don't get caught" among my primary objectives.

"I'm sure they already cleared out the desk and all these drawers, too, Laura." I looked nervously over my shoulder. The fourth wall of the office consisted of French doors facing directly into the main area where the estate sale employees sat. Fortunately, they appeared to be busy managing the crowd out there.

"I'll be quick." She slid her hand along the underside of each bookshelf and pulled out drawers one by one. "You could speed things up by checking out that hutch."

With a glance over my shoulder, I opened the hutch doors. A waterfall of heavy, hard-backed books cascaded out and crashed loudly to the floor at my feet. Laura jumped.

The woman in the blue shirt appeared at the doorway. "I'm going to have to ask you to leave."

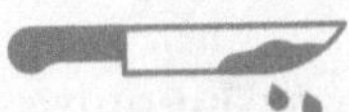

WE HURRIED OUTSIDE, hunched in humiliation. "Well, that was embarrassing," I said.

"If you hadn't been rooting around like a bull in a china shop, it wouldn't have happened," Laura replied.

"I was not. I opened one cabinet door. I didn't realize it was booby-trapped."

Laura did a facepalm. "I'm so disappointed that our search didn't turn up anything."

"It was a long shot," I replied.

"Maybe it would have gone better if we could have stayed longer." We'd reached her house, and she unlocked the front door. "However it happened, we got nothing out of that investigation."

She opened the door to find Jack standing in the foyer. He glanced up from sorting the mail. "Investigation? Don't tell me you are still nosing around in things that aren't any of your business."

"We were just out shopping, looking for bargains," Laura said.

Jack eyed her dubiously. He turned to me. "Emma, you need to keep her out of trouble."

"I'll do my best."

He snorted. "You'll be right there with her, more likely." He withdrew an envelope from the stack. "Laura, here's an HOA letter addressed to you."

She examined it. "That's strange. Whenever we get mail from the HOA or neighborhood management, it's addressed to both of us." She tore open the seal and scanned the letter. She put her hand over her mouth. "Oh my god."

"What?" I asked. "What is it?"

"I'm being removed from the board of directors."

"How can they do that?" Jack asked. "You were elected."

"The other board members asked me to voluntarily step down. They think my current troubles detract from the image of the HOA."

"The HOA already had a bad image. Nobody liked them to begin with."

At my words, Laura's lower lip quivered, and her eyes grew shiny with tears. Jack put a comforting arm around her shoulders.

I quickly backtracked. "Laura, I didn't say nobody likes *you*."

"But it's true," she sniffled.

"Laura, sweetie, I know you've been under a lot of stress, but I think you're becoming hysterical."

Jack's eyes widened, and he flashed me a look of alarm.

She scowled at me. "I thought you of all people would support me."

"I do support you, but I think you worry too much about what other people think. Anyway, how can they force you to do this? What happens if you don't step down?"

"They said they can have a vote at the next community meeting."

"When is that?"

"The end of this month."

"Maybe the police will have found the real murderer by then."

"I doubt it," she predicted glumly.

AFTER THE DISAPPOINTMENTS of the previous day, I expected Laura to withdraw for a while. So, when my doorbell rang the next afternoon, I was surprised to find her standing on my doorstep holding two brown paper bags labeled "Goodwill." She held them up and said, "I have a new plan."

I cocked my head and examined her face. "*You* went to Goodwill? You *bought* something from Goodwill?"

She blew out a huffed breath in frustration. "Yes, but I'd rather not stand out here and advertise. May I come in, please?"

I took one of the bags from her, and she followed me into the house.

"What's in this, anyway?" I lifted the bag and peeked in the top as I carried it to the kitchen table.

"Disguises," she answered.

I gave her a level look.

"I thought we could try to get back into the estate sale. I don't want them to recognize us since you got us kicked out yesterday."

"What do you mean, *I* got us kicked—wait, what did you just say?" I grabbed one of the bags. "*Disguises?*"

"You know, the kind of things that people who go to these estate sales would wear."

"I *am* one of the people who goes to estate sales, and I've never required a wardrobe change."

"You said it. I didn't," she replied snippily.

I reached into the bag and pulled out a crumpled flowered hat. "Are we disguising ourselves as grandmothers?"

"We need something to cover our hair." She pulled out a paisley headscarf, tied it on her head, and tucked her blond curls beneath it.

The bags also contained clunky footwear and shapeless dresses. I held one of them up, examining the brown calico print. "I am not doing this."

She crossed her arms and eyed me sternly.

Twenty minutes later, two babushkas walked into an estate sale.

As we entered the house, I glanced around furtively, sweat beading beneath my ugly outerwear, but the employees gave no signs of recognition. The house was crowded, and they were too busy ringing up sales to notice two strangely dressed women. The first display we examined was the jewelry case near the checkout desk.

Laura pulled out her cell phone and took a picture of the contents of the case. "I'll compare it to the before-sale inventory," she whispered. "Do you see anything out of the ordinary?"

"You mean besides us?"

She glared.

I held up my hands in surrender. "I told you, I don't know much about jewelry."

"Fine. Let's go look at the books."

"That's where we got in trouble yesterday."

"Then *you'll* just have to be more careful, won't you?" she replied huffily.

I made an exasperated sound but followed her.

"Open each book and flip through it to check for papers hidden inside," she instructed.

One by one, we lifted books from the large built-in bookshelves, opened them, and flipped the pages. I held each book upside down to see if anything fell out.

A short, balding man in glasses joined us in the study and reached for a book. Laura snatched it before he could remove it.

"Hey!" he protested.

"Just a minute." She performed the flip-and-shake maneuver before holding it out to him.

"You people are crazy." Abandoning the book, he turned heel and stalked out.

An uneasy feeling crept up inside me. "You shouldn't have done that. He's probably going to complain to one of the workers."

"I couldn't let him take it before I checked it."

"This is pointless, Laura. We're not going to find anything."

"Excuse me?" We looked up to find the same woman from yesterday looking at us censoriously.

Laura put down the book she was holding, bobbed her head, and said, "Mea culpa." We backed out.

When we were away from the penetrating gaze of the employee, I hissed, "You realize that's Latin, right? Were you pretending we didn't speak English? If so, you probably shouldn't have gone with a dead language."

"It was the first thing that came to mind. Anyway, she didn't throw us out this time, did she?"

"Maybe she's calling the police—or the loony bin."

"Don't be so dramatic. Let's go check the other bedrooms."

The upstairs was nearly empty. Most of the furnishings and the room contents had been moved downstairs for better display. Laura opened every closet door. On the top shelf of the last closet, shoved back in a shadowy corner, was a small cardboard box.

Laura stretched up on tiptoes, trying to retrieve the box. She turned to me. "Can you reach it?"

I could see why the sale organizers missed the box. Only about the size of a brick and a dull, neutral color, it blended in with the closet walls. I stretched as far as I could and managed to nudge the corner of the box with my finger. Little by little, I scooted the box closer to the edge until I was able to grasp it. I saw one word written on it: *ROSE*.

I slid the top off. The distinctive smell that wafted from inside the box triggered a distant memory of carbon copies. It contained a stack of yellow duplicate deposit slips. They were the old kind that banks used to use long before modern technology made it possible to deposit a check by snapping a photo of it with your phone. The paper was crumbling in places, and the ink had faded. The amount deposited was one thousand dollars. There were dozens of them.

Laura took the box from my hands. "What are they?"

"Bank deposit slips—all signed by Phillip Mayhew."

"He was the previous owner of this house."

"The guy who died in the house?"

Laura nodded. "They are all made out to the same account number. The fact that he wrote *Rose* on the box suggests that the money was for her, but there's no way to be sure without knowing her account number." She removed a stack and flipped it like a wad of bills. "If each of these represents one thousand dollars..."

"That would be over a hundred thousand dollars," I said, using my typically unappreciated math skills. "But there could have been more. Most banks stopped using these carbon-copy forms decades ago. The deposits might have continued after the last date using newer technology."

"Why was Phil paying Rose for so many years?"

"I don't know. Services rendered? Intimate companionship?"

Laura wrinkled her nose. "Thank you for that image. I was thinking more along the lines of blackmail. Hush money."

"Maybe Rose was sneaking into the house to retrieve this box. This could be evidence of whatever was going on between them," I suggested.

"That still doesn't tell us who killed her." Laura sighed. "We're back to square one." She tucked the box into a convenient pocket in her frumpy dress.

"That seems like a bad idea," I said. "You are such a bad influence on me."

She waved away my concern with a flip of her hand. "Always have been. It's my job. You were such a nerdy girl when we met at college. I like to think that I broadened your horizons."

"Broadened them to include breaking and entering, jail, and now committing a crime while trying to disguise my identity."

A look of pride crossed her face. "You must admit, I'm never boring."

Before leaving, we decided to make a final pass through the kitchen. I didn't expect to find anything there. The kitchen didn't seem to be a likely hiding place, so I was surprised when Laura stopped abruptly. "What?" I asked.

She pointed to the knife block on the counter. Like everything else in the house, it was of excellent quality with a recognizable name brand. It had six slots for various types of cooking knives.

One knife slot was empty.

We locked eyes, and Laura's eyebrows raised nearly to her hairline. "Could be the murder weapon," she hissed.

I looked around to find out if anyone had overheard, but no one was paying any attention to us. We were just a couple of little old ladies, and that meant we were practically invisible. I tugged Laura's arm and pulled her out the door.

We got into my car quickly to avoid being seen in our disguises by any neighbors passing by the house. As I drove, I pondered over what we'd learned at the estate sale. "One knife missing, and Rose was stabbed. You think the missing knife was the murder weapon?"

"Could be. That would tell us the person who killed Rose wasn't waiting there to kill her. They didn't bring their own murder weapon. They grabbed what was nearby. It was an impulsive act."

"So, you think whoever killed Rose was surprised when she showed up?"

"Not necessarily. But it wasn't premeditated. Whoever it was, they didn't come prepared to kill."

When we arrived back at my townhouse, I yanked the shapeless hat off my head. "We should toss these getups," I suggested, scratching my scalp. "That hat probably gave me lice."

"Don't worry. I wasn't planning on keeping my outfit, either." She surveyed her ensemble with distaste. "In fact, I think I'll change now and put it directly in the trash."

"Don't leave it in my trash. What if the cops show up with a search warrant, find the outfits, and connect us to the two frumpy ladies who robbed an estate sale today?"

"We didn't rob anyone. We picked up an old box of receipts. Nothing but trash." She turned the box over in her hands, examining it.

"What if it's evidence? We should have left it there."

"They would have thrown it out eventually. Besides, the police inspected that entire place. They must not have thought it was important."

"Maybe it's not. What good does it do us? We have no means of finding the purpose of those payments. Both parties involved are now dead."

Laura chewed on her lower lip as she pondered. "The only person I know who's been here almost as long as Phil and Rose is Bina. I'll bet she can help us figure it out."

"You trust her enough to tell her about our investigation?" I asked.

"I trust her, but we don't have to tell her. Let's just ask a few innocent questions."

"Sure. That's a great idea. 'Hey, Bina, can you think of any reason why Phil paid Rose for twenty years?' Sounds totally innocent."

Laura frowned at me. "Maybe you should let me do the talking."

WE STOPPED at a liquor store on the way, where Laura selected a pricey bottle of Bina's favorite wine.

"You bought *me* BOGO wine," I muttered.

"But I love you twice as much," she soothed.

I snorted in response.

We left my car at Laura's and walked to Bina's house. Laura rang the doorbell, triggering an outbreak of ferocious barking from inside.

"Cooper! Quiet down." Bina opened the door holding the collar of a large black lab. "Don't mind him. He only sounds vicious." She spied the bottle in Laura's hands and smiled. "Is that for me? Come on in!" She gestured for us to follow her into the kitchen.

As soon as she released the dog, it snuffled up and down our legs. He snorted his approval and followed his owner. She retrieved three glasses and a corkscrew from the cabinet and placed them on the kitchen table. "Have a seat, have a seat." She fluttered her hand at us as she turned to the refrigerator. She bent over, peering inside, giving us a view of her round, muu-muu covered backside. "I've got some sharp cheddar in here that would go great with that."

"You don't need to go to any trouble for us, Bina," Laura said.

"It's no trouble," Bina insisted as she arranged cheese and crackers on a serving plate. Cooper lingered nearby, hoping for a handout.

"Where's Hugh?" Laura asked, filling Bina's wine glass.

"Golfing. I'm glad you stopped by. I was getting tired of having no one but the dog to talk to." She sat down at the head of the table and turned to Laura. "So, what's new with you?"

"I met Rose's nephew the other day. He said he and his mother were cleaning out Rose's house."

"I didn't realize Rose had a sister." Bina stacked a slice of cheese on a cracker.

"How well did you know her, Bina?" I asked while she chewed.

Bina washed the cracker down with a gulp of wine. "She was never a close friend, but when the neighborhood was new, we all got along just fine for a while. Used to rotate houses, having cookouts. But as the developer added more houses, and more people started coming in, that all changed. Rose and her husband didn't like the new people. That's when the complaints started and the cookouts ended."

"What about her husband?" Laura asked. "Did he complain, too?"

"Oh, yes. When we started having public HOA meetings, they took turns complaining and picking fights with the newer neighbors. He and Rose appeared to be in full agreement. That's one reason why their divorce seemed to come out of nowhere."

"What happened when they divorced?"

"He just disappeared. She told us he moved back up North. She got the house. I heard he took the rest."

"What did she do for a living?" I nibbled a cracker while waiting for her answer.

"Some kind of administrator for a mortgage company. Nothing that would make her rich."

Laura sipped her wine before shaking her head. "Looked like she lived pretty well to me. That Mercedes she drove must have cost a pretty penny, even if it was old."

Bina surreptitiously gave a slice of cheese to the dog before continuing. "I wouldn't know about that. But I do remember she always added new things to her house: custom pavers, new stucco, fancy exterior lighting, things like that."

"Was she independently wealthy or something?" I took another slice of cheese while Cooper looked at me expectantly.

"Not to my knowledge. I wonder what her sister is like. Did you meet her, or just her son?"

"We met them both. She seemed very down to earth, but I thought her son, David, was a Mormon missionary when I saw him at my door," Laura said.

Bina chuckled.

"It was the way he was dressed—a white, button-down shirt and black pants. He was extremely neat, except for his head. He had bright red hair, almost orange, sticking up in every direction."

Bina's eyebrows shot up. "Red hair, eh? Must run in Rose's family."

I'd never seen Rose alive, but my memory flashed back to the night I saw her lying dead in a dark puddle of blood with strands of her red hair trailing in it. I shivered.

Laura's mind did not seem to be following mine, because she deftly switched gears. "Didn't you say Phil Mayhew was the other original homeowner?"

"Yes, he and his wife, Christine. They were only here part of the time, though. This was their second house."

"Talk about wealthy." I sipped my wine to steady my nerves.

"Yes, but I believe the wealth came from Christine's side of the family. She was a socialite from Charlotte. They had one daughter. Alice. After she grew up and moved out, Christine spent most of her time in North Carolina. Phil worked in politics. Never made it to Washington, but he was influential in Charlotte's City Hall. I'm sure he benefited from Christine's connections. After he retired, Phil moved down here full time."

"So, they separated?"

"Essentially." Bina held out her glass. "Top me off, would you please?"

Laura complied while continuing to nudge the conversation in the direction she wanted. "And Phil was okay with that?"

"Oh, that poor man. Took it hard, I think. Their daughter took her mother's side. We rarely saw her down here after that. She and my daughter, Tina, used to play together every summer. Got brown as a walnut, always up at the beach. After Phil and Christine split, we hardly saw Alice anymore. 'Course, she was already grown by then. Probably wouldn't have seen her much anyway. But I think Phil took it hard." Bina took a sip from her wine glass, her gaze distant. "Rose stopped visiting him then."

I leaned forward in attention. "Rose used to visit him?"

"Yes. Now that I think of it, he was one of the few people she seemed to like. But when Christine stopped coming down, Rose stopped spending time with him, too. Which is strange, because she used to call on him mostly when Christine went to Charlotte for the social season." Bina turned to look out the window. "Phil's house is right across the pond from mine. Sound travels on the water. I would sometimes hear them out on his patio. Rose had a very distinctive laugh. Could be that it was so memorable because she hardly ever used it."

I tried to keep my expression neutral and avoided eye contact with Laura.

Laura maintained a cool demeanor. "She and Phil used to get along pretty well, huh?"

"That was a long time ago," Bina clarified. "Not long after we all moved here, but after Rose's husband, Paul, took off."

"Didn't they get a divorce?" Laura asked.

Bina shrugged. "I assumed so. We never saw him after that."

The sound of a key in the door, followed by a cacophonous crash in the foyer, interrupted us. Bina called out, "Hugh, is that you? You okay?"

"Yeah, just dropped my clubs," said a voice tinged with a deep Brooklyn accent. A short, wiry man with closely cropped white hair and a colorful golf shirt and shorts clomped into the kitchen.

"Take off your shoes!" Bina scolded.

With a "humph," the man returned to the foyer and dropped the shoes. He returned, padding into the kitchen in pink and green argyle socks that matched his ensemble. He bent to give Bina a kiss on her weathered cheek.

"Hello, ladies. Did I miss wine and cheese hour?"

"Yes, you did." Bina smiled at him with affection. "But I'll make you a snack."

Laura stood. "We won't keep you. It's always a pleasure catching up." She bent to hug Bina.

"You don't have to rush off," Bina said, but she stood to walk us out, and Cooper followed at her heels. At the door, she tilted her head and whispered, "I know you two are up to something. What is it? You can trust me."

We exchanged a conspiratorial look before Laura explained, "We want to figure out who killed Rose so that everyone will stop suspecting me."

Bina nodded. "I see. Okay, then. I'll help."

"I don't want to get you involved in this," Laura said.

"I'll be your adviser. I know everybody in this neighborhood, and I've lived here longer than any of them." She reached up to pinch Laura's cheek affectionately. "Gotta keep you out of trouble, girlie."

Laura smiled. "It's good to know someone's on my side."

"Always," she said, and smiled at me. "And I believe you've got a valuable friend here in Emma." She hugged us both in turn. "Keep me in the loop, okay?"

"We will," Laura assured her.

As we walked back to Laura's house, we discussed the developments of that afternoon. "That sure was interesting," I said.

"Sounded like Phil and Rose were pretty friendly at one time."

"Yes, it did. You feel confident that you can trust Bina?" I asked.

"Implicitly. Maybe I'll have her over for coffee sometime soon and we can chat some more."

"Wine seemed to work better than coffee."

Laura chuckled. "'Wine and cheese hour,' then."

As we turned the corner, Laura's house came into sight. A police car waited at the curb.

Six

LAURA'S FACE BLANCHED. I gave her hand a reassuring squeeze and stayed close by her side as we walked to the front door where two deputies stood waiting.

"Are you the homeowner?"

Laura nodded. "I am."

"We have a warrant to search your property."

"Why? What are you searching for?" She took a step back, her hand groping in the air for support. When I grabbed her hand, she clasped it tightly.

One of the deputies did all the talking while the other stood by, alert. "Your property backs up to a tributary of the Iyola River. A kayaker spotted a knife in the marsh grass at the edge of your backyard. That gives us probable cause to search your property."

Laura's eyes widened. "I have no idea what you're talking about. People leave trash back there all the time."

"Yes, ma'am. We just need to check it out."

"May I see the warrant?"

One of them produced a piece of paper and handed it to Laura. During the exchange, I continued to stand close behind her, stunned and motionless, but I glanced over her shoulder at the document.

I read the word "magistrate" beneath a signature. The text specified that the portion of the property adjacent to the Iyola River could be searched. The description of items to be seized said simply, "knife."

"Is there a gate we can use to access the area, or should we come through your house?" the deputy who seemed to be in charge asked.

"Use the gate." Laura's voice sounded oddly emotionless. "Emma, can you go check if Sam is at home? I think I could use a lawyer. His house is the one with the FSU spear on the mailbox, around the corner, on the cul-de-sac."

I nodded and walked quickly in the direction she pointed, passing by the vehicle with an emblem of the county sheriff's department emblazoned on the door. One of the deputies retrieved two pairs of dark-green rubber boots from the trunk.

Laura opened the gate beside her house. The men pulled on the boots and proceeded to the backyard while I hurried around the corner.

I spotted the garnet and gold mailbox and made a beeline for it. A moment after I rang the doorbell, Sam opened the door.

"Sam." I paused to catch my breath after my sprint. "I was afraid you wouldn't be home."

He wore a dress shirt, a tie, and a confused expression. "I had a meeting that ended early. Is something wrong, Emma?"

I was rattled but pleased that he remembered my name. "There are two cops with a search warrant at Laura's house."

He grabbed his keys off the foyer table and stepped outside. "Let's go." We hurried around the corner. "What's going on? Did you look at the warrant?"

"Yes. They told us a boater reported seeing a knife in the marsh grass behind Laura's house."

"Anybody could have thrown that there."

"But why behind Laura's house?"

He turned his head and examined me with lowered eyebrows, his lips in a tight, straight line. "We'll find out."

As we approached, I noted an additional law enforcement vehicle parked at the curb, this one marked SHERIFF. The cops had called for backup.

The gate beside Laura's house swung freely from the hinges,

creaking in the wind. We passed through it and proceeded into the back-yard. A pathway of tan-hued paving stones led to a matching patio. A stone wall stood around a fire pit in the middle. Two faded red Adirondack chairs faced a scenic view that normally featured a winding creek, wading water birds, and gently waving marsh grasses. At the moment, the view featured two deputies in hip boots.

The sheriff stood planted in front of Laura, looming over her and firing questions at her. She kept shaking her head. From the redness of the sheriff's face and the streaks of tears on Laura's cheeks, it looked like he'd been coming down on her the entire time I'd been retrieving Sam. Now in lawyer mode, Sam rushed to intervene.

Meanwhile, one of the deputies in rubber boots waded out onto a mudflat where something metal glinted in the sun. The tufts of marsh grass parted in the breeze, revealing something silver partially embedded in the mud. A deputy removed a latex glove from her pocket and pulled it on before bending to retrieve the item. It was a broad knife with a silver grip—a kitchen knife.

Laura sat down suddenly in one of the Adirondack chairs. "Oh, my god."

Sam stepped quickly to her side and crouched to face her at eye level. He reached out his hand and placed it on her tightly clenched fists. "Laura, don't say anything. I can take it from here. Okay?"

She nodded mutely.

"Just to make this somewhat formal, I need to ask, do you want me to represent you?"

She nodded again.

"Where's Jack? Can you call him?"

"He went out for a run," Laura replied. "He should be back soon."

Sam stood and gave her shoulder a reassuring squeeze. "I'll take care of this, Laura. Try to be calm. It's best not to appear nervous." He directed his attention to me next. "Emma, you stick with Laura while I go talk to the sheriff."

Sam strode out to where the law enforcement team stood huddled in a scrum on the lower patio. One of them put the knife in an evidence bag. Sam conferred with them in intense conversation. He made quick, firm gestures, pointing to the marsh and then to Laura, who was crying on the phone.

The sheriff accompanied Sam back to the sitting area. "Ma'am, we'd like to talk to you. It's voluntary at this time, but I'd recommend cooperating with our investigation."

"You don't have to do this right now, Laura." Sam turned to the sheriff. "If you need to speak with my client, she can make an appointment to do so at a future date."

The sheriff examined him sternly, but Sam held his gaze. At the bottom of the hill, the search party began trudging back toward them from the marsh. The sheriff gestured at them impatiently, indicating they should head in the direction of the gate. One carried the evidence bag toward the unmarked car.

"Ma'am, is that your decision? Does this man—" The sheriff raked his eyes over Sam and jerked his head. "This *lawyer* represent you?"

"Yes, he does," Laura replied. "I would like to confer with him before being questioned. When do I have to do that?"

The sheriff took a business card out of his pocket, pulled a pen from the other pocket, and jotted something on the card. "Call this number. They can set it up. You'll have to come down to Saint Augustine, though. Sure you wouldn't prefer answering our questions here and now?"

"I'm sure."

After one last grim look at Sam, the detective said to Laura, "We'll be waiting to hear from you." He stalked out through the gate.

Laura let out a long, shaky breath.

"Don't worry, Laura. This is circumstantial evidence." Sam gazed out toward the marsh. "Could have come from anywhere. No fingerprints can survive that environment." He turned back abruptly. "Not that you have to worry about fingerprints, right?"

"Of course, not," Laura snapped.

"Did you get hold of Jack?" Sam asked.

She nodded. "He's on his way."

"Let's go inside and discuss how we're going to proceed."

I MADE coffee while the others sat around the table in Laura's gleaming modern kitchen. Jack arrived, sweaty from his run. Sam stood, and they exchanged a manly handshake.

"I appreciate your help with this, Sam. Are we keeping you from your other appointments?"

"No, I called in to the office. Nothing that can't be moved. My assistant will handle it."

Jack turned to Laura. The tension that filled the air recently whenever they occupied the same room fled at that moment. He opened his arms, and she flung herself into them. He rubbed slow circles across her back. "Can somebody fill me in on what's going on here?"

I brought two cups of coffee to the table. "Laura and I were out shopping today. When I brought her home, there was a police cruiser waiting. The cops told us someone reported a knife in the marsh behind your house. They had a search warrant. I went to get Sam. More cops showed up. They searched the banks of the creek at your backyard and found a knife. They wanted to take Laura in for questioning, but Sam talked them out of it." I returned to retrieve the other two mugs while Sam picked up the rest of the story.

"I didn't talk them out of anything. I just reminded them of Laura's rights. And, incidentally, yours too, Jack. The knife was found on your property, as well."

Jack visibly reacted to the suggestion, jerking his head back. "I guess that's true. But how can they pin this on us? That creek is open to the public. Anybody could have tossed it there."

"You're absolutely right. It's circumstantial evidence at best. But because they can also link Laura to the scene of the crime, that makes her a person of interest. They don't have enough to arrest her, but they want to grill her and find out what they can get."

"Why would I dispose of evidence on my own property?" Laura interjected.

"That's an excellent question. An even better one might be why would someone *else* dispose of evidence on your property?"

The party around the table fell silent.

SAM ARRANGED Laura's appointment to provide a statement to the police and volunteered to drive to the county building. He continued to coach Laura as we headed south in Sam's well-appointed Ford F-150 crew cab. Jack had to go out of town on a business trip, so I offered to come along for moral support. Seated in the full-sized back seat, I could smell leather and a hint of aftershave. Although it was a pickup, it was top of the line.

"Remember," Sam reminded Laura, "stick to your story. Just tell them what we practiced. Don't let them draw you into saying what they want to hear. Don't try to be helpful. Be precise and polite, but don't volunteer."

"Okay," Laura replied in a listless voice. She gazed out the passenger window, staring at the trees and brush as they sped past in a blur.

We arrived at the sheriff's office. I felt my heart race as the memories flooded my mind, replaying the awful night Laura and I had spent there getting questioned incessantly by the police. Regret that I'd offered to return smacked me in the face, followed instantly by guilt. I had to support Laura, no matter how uncomfortable it made me.

Sam circled the squat, tan-colored concrete building and pulled into a spot marked "visitor." He turned to look at us. "Ready for this?"

Laura took a deep breath and nodded. I squeezed her shoulder. We could do this together.

While we waited to check in at the front desk, an officer in a dark green uniform passed us on his way down the hallway. He hailed Sam. "Hey, Turner! Coming to the coaches' meeting Wednesday night?"

Sam raised his hand and nodded. "I'll be there. Squad room, right?"

"You got it. See you then." The officer's rubber-soled shoes squeaked against the laminate floor as he continued down the hallway.

"Coaches' meeting?" I asked.

"Police Athletic League," Sam explained. "I volunteer as an assistant coach for the twelve-and-under league."

I raised both eyebrows. "I'm surprised they let a lawyer participate."

"Hey, I can pass a background check," he replied. "Anyone in the community can volunteer."

"Can we focus, please?" Laura's jangled nerves were evident, and I couldn't blame her. I reminded myself I was there to support her, not flirt with her attorney.

After we checked in, an officer led us to a room with a table and three chairs. Sam and Laura took the two chairs situated side-by-side while I chose to stand beside her, resting my hand on her shoulder. We waited in silence.

A detective entered the room. He was tall and weathered, with closely cropped silver hair and pale blue eyes. He extended his hand to Laura. "Mrs. Benton?"

"Yes." Laura shook his hand. "And this is my lawyer, Sam Turner, and my friend, Emma Stewart."

"I'm Detective Mark Anderson." He shook Sam's hand and then turned to me. "Ms. Stewart, you need to wait outside. The deputy must have assumed you were part of the defense team."

"In a way, I am. I'm here to support Laura."

"I appreciate your loyalty, Ms. Stewart, but we have to abide by the rules here. There are chairs in the hall. You can wait there." He glared at me with a steady gaze that brooked no argument.

Meekly, I exited the room, and Detective Anderson closed the door behind me. I perched on one of the ugly brown chairs and rocked nervously. The cracked leather and bent metal legs of the chair emitted a creaking sound that echoed in the empty hallway. I forced myself to be still and examined my surroundings. One room down from the interrogation room, a door stood open, just a crack. Moved by curiosity and a fondness for detective shows, I peeked inside the doorway and saw an empty chair illuminated by indirect light, like from a TV. I slipped into the room only to find that the light was from a monitor displaying images from a video camera inside the interrogation room. I could see the back of Detective Anderson's head. The authoritative sound of his voice filtered in through the monitor. "Let's get started. I am Detective Mark Anderson, and I am recording this interview. State your name."

"Laura Benton."

"And I'm representing Mrs. Benton. My name is Samuel Turner."

"Mrs. Benton, an investigative team retrieved a potential murder weapon from your property. Deputies Marcus and Webb also found you at the murder scene at 2120 Beach Hammock Road on the night of August eleventh. As a person of interest in this investigation, I need you to answer a few questions." He displayed a photo of a clear, plastic evidence package containing a knife. "Mrs. Benton, do you recognize this item?"

"No. I mean, I saw the deputies pull it from the marsh, but I'd never seen it before that. But it appears to be a common chef's knife. Lots of people have them in their kitchen." Laura twisted her hands in her lap. Sam subtly placed his hand on her arm to calm her.

"Why did you enter the property on August eleventh?"

"The house was going to be listed for sale since the former owner had passed away. I wanted to show it to my friend. She was considering buying it."

"Your friend…" He consulted his notes before continuing. "Emma Stewart."

"You have Mrs. Benton's statement from that night as well, Detective. Is there additional information you need from my client?"

The detective tilted his head in Sam's direction. "I believe a representative of the sheriff's department attempted to get Mrs. Benton's statement at the time the evidence was discovered, but she chose to delay. But, yes, I would like to ask you something. Do you have any idea how this knife came to be on your property?"

"No idea. We see kayaks, canoes, and people fishing back there all the time," Laura said.

"I see. When were you last inside the house, prior to the night of August eleventh?"

"I don't recall. I know I've been in there before when the former owners had parties, but that was before Mrs. Mayhew died."

"Mrs. Mayhew, former owner of the house?"

"That's right."

"This knife matches a set of cooking tools from the Mayhew home."

Sam said, "Fingerprints?"

"No fingerprints could be found on the knife due to exposure to mud and water in the marsh," said the detective. "However, the manufacturer name and style match that of a set found in the Mayhew home."

"That same knife can be found in many homes, Detective," Sam interjected. "Looks like the kind you can find at any department store."

"Actually..." The detective paused to consult his notes. "This is a chef's knife made from a single piece of high-quality stainless steel, valued at approximately two hundred dollars. Not the kind of thing a fisherman would toss in the creek."

Sam was not intimidated. "That is circumstantial evidence. What are your intentions for my client?"

"As I said, Mrs. Benton is merely a person of interest. She has not been charged with a crime. I am simply collecting her statement." He turned back to Laura. "Mrs. Benton, what was the nature of your relationship with the deceased, Rose Martin?"

"She was a neighbor. We both served on the homeowners' association board of directors."

"How would you describe your interactions with Mrs. Martin?"

Laura paused. "She was an abrasive woman with many complaints. She didn't get along with anyone."

"What was your role on the board?"

"President."

"And what was Mrs. Martin's role?"

"She was the president before me. She left her position on the board when a neighborhood vote made me the new president."

"So, your relationship was antagonistic?"

"You're putting words in my mouth," Laura protested. "I wasn't—"

Sam reached out to stop her. "Detective, I believe you are attempting to lead a witness."

Anderson held up his hands. "This isn't a courtroom. I was merely attempting to clarify. Mrs. Benton, did you ever argue with Mrs. Martin?"

"Yes. The entire board of directors argued from time to time. Neighborhood associations often have to resolve conflicts."

"So, none of the arguments were directly between you and Mrs. Martin?"

"She often disagreed with my stance on issues concerning neighborhood regulations. She wanted the association to enforce the covenants with higher penalties for rule infractions."

"And that's all you argued about?"

"Yes, I believe so."

"You believe so." He repeated, scribbling on the form in front of him. He was silent for long enough to make Laura squirm.

"What about that threatening note I received? I turned it in to your department."

Anderson looked up. "As we told you when you turned it in, handling the paper contaminated it as evidence." He shuffled through some papers on his desk. "The only fingerprints we found on that note belonged to you, Mrs. Benton."

"Well, I touched it when I took it out of the mailbox, but—"

"The note was a dead end, but we appreciate your cooperation, Mrs. Benton." Abruptly, he stood, causing Laura to jump. The detective opened the door and gestured for Laura to exit. "We'll be in touch if we need anything more from you." Before he came out of the room, I stepped quickly into the hallway.

Sam escorted Laura out of the room with a reassuring hand on her back. I stepped forward to join them, and we hurried out of the station.

Once we were outside, Laura took a shaky breath and released it with a sigh. "I'm glad that's over."

"I think it went well. Hopefully, that will keep them off your back temporarily." Sam opened the passenger door of the F-150, activating the power running board that lowered automatically. He offered each of us his hand as we stepped up into his truck.

"I didn't think lawyers drove pickups," I said. "Shouldn't you have an Audi or something?"

"I used to," he replied as he climbed in the driver's side and turned the ignition. "Got rid of it when I quit the big firm and opened my own office. I needed the space in my garage for my fishing boat."

"All about priorities," I replied.

"I need a truck to pull the boat. I go fishing more often than I drive clients around." He turned to wink at me. "Besides, I'm a Georgia boy. A truck is a requirement." He pulled out of the parking lot and headed north out of Saint Augustine. "There's an English pub up here, practically out in the middle of nowhere. Y'all feel like making a stop?"

"A drink sounds marvelous to me," Laura said.

"They also make a great shepherd's pie," Sam said. He turned and grinned at me over his shoulder. I observed that his demeanor had changed since we left the police station. During the interview, he was all business. His posture and mannerisms commanded respect. In his truck, he was once again a good ol' boy. His left arm rested on the window ledge, and his right hand draped casually over the wheel.

After a short drive up the state highway, Sam pulled into the gravel parking lot of a pub with little else around it. It was a small Tudor-style building with two Union Jack flags flying over a pair of bay windows. A sign bearing a portrait of Henry the Eighth declared it to be the King's Head Pub. A pair of stone lions guarded the front door, and a traditional red English telephone booth stood isolated out front.

"Well, that's random," I said, taking in the sight of a double-decker bus in the parking lot. "I never noticed this was here."

"I normally don't even come this way," said Laura. "I take A1A whenever I go to Saint Augustine."

"I come by here on my way to the courthouse," Sam said. He held the door open. Above his head, a sign proclaimed, "There is no place like this place anywhere near this place, so this must be the place." He gestured for us to enter ahead of him.

My eyes struggled to adjust from the Florida sun outside to the dimly lit interior of the pub. Dark, wooden beams crossed the ceiling overhead. Brightly colored flags danced from the beams, with England, Ireland, and Scotland represented most prominently. A line of copper kettles dangled from another beam, and images of castles and suits of armor lined the wall above the bar. Sam led us to a small round table surrounded by short wooden stools with well-worn velvet cushioned seats.

A waitress approached wearing a T-shirt that suggested we should "Keep Calm and Drink On."

"What can I get for you?"

After the waitress listed the daily specials, Laura ordered a hard cider.

"I'll have a Guinness," I said.

Sam eyed me appreciatively. "I'll have the same. And can we have one of those plates of Scotch eggs?"

"Sure thing, sugar." She departed with what I thought was an unnecessary swing of her hips.

I returned my attention to Sam and cocked an eyebrow. "*Sugar?*"

He responded with a sheepish look, but his gaze hadn't followed the waitress out of view.

"What's a Scotch egg?" Laura asked, seeming oblivious to the exchange.

"It's a hard-boiled egg cooked inside a big ball of deep-fried sausage." Sam laughed at Laura's reflexive grimace. "Give it a try."

The waitress returned bearing a tray of drinks. With thanks, I accepted a pint of dark brew with a layer of creamy foam.

Laura picked up her pint of cider and took a long drink. She placed it back on the table and said, "Sam, be straight with me. How bad is this situation I've gotten myself into?"

"So far, they've got nothing but circumstantial evidence. But I would be careful in the days to come. They might start monitoring you, hoping they've scared you into showing your hand. Stay away from the Mayhew house for sure."

Laura and I looked guiltily at each other.

"What?" he asked.

"Right before the police showed up, we were at the Mayhew house for an estate sale."

Eyes narrowed, Sam sipped his Guinness. When neither of us elaborated, he prompted, "May I ask why?"

We glanced at each other again.

"Quit it, you two," he said. "Stop with the guilty looks, and 'fess up."

"We're trying to find the real killer," Laura said.

At that moment, the waitress returned, giving Laura a sideways glance. She placed a plate of brown, white, and yellow orbs cut into quarters on the table.

"I'll just give you a minute to look at the menus," she said and darted away.

"Why would you do that?" Sam asked. "Try to find a murderer?"

"The police aren't looking at anyone but me," Laura said.

"You don't know that." Sam stuffed a large section of Scotch egg into his mouth.

Laura wrinkled her nose. "That looks disgusting."

"Don't knock it 'til you try it," Sam replied.

I reached for a smaller section of egg and took a tentative bite. As I chewed, I pondered the universal truth, or at least the truth as we knew it in the South, that frying anything made it tasty. Sam was watching me, so I gave him a thumbs-up. I washed the egg down with more Guinness.

Sam appeared to approve of my actions, as if I had passed some sort of test. He leaned back and eyed Laura. "If you really think we ought to investigate further, I'll give it a shot. But you need to steer clear, Laura. They've got you in their sights."

"Sam and I can take over the investigating."

At my declaration, both of my companions turned to me. Laura smirked knowingly, while Sam looked pleased.

"I believe that's a great idea." He smiled and raised his glass to toast.

I clinked my pint against his, feeling the warmth of a blush creeping into my cheeks. Avoiding Laura's eyes, I proclaimed, "Let's do it."

SEVEN

SAM DROVE us back as the sun was going down over the Intracoastal Waterway. Crossing the bridge, I pointed out the small row of townhouses where I lived. The Spanish-style tile roof glowed red in the sunset.

"Looks nice," Sam said. "Convenient to get downtown. Do they have a boat dock?"

"They do, for an extra fee."

"That's handy. How come you let Laura talk you into looking for another place?"

"Laura could always talk me into anything," I said, but my smile softened the words, and I reached over the seatback to pat my longtime friend on her shoulder.

"I just wanted to have her closer," Laura said. "And there is the whole living-at-the-beach thing."

"True," Sam said. "I'm on the water every chance I can get. Fishing, surfing, and, of course, swimming." With a mischievous look on his face, he said, "But Emma already knows about the swimming, since we ran into each other at the pool."

"Really? When was that?" Laura asked.

"It was so brief, really." I quickly changed the subject. "So, Laura, when does Jack get back from his business trip?"

She gave me a look that expressed *we'll talk about this later* but allowed the change of subject. "He should be back tonight."

When we reached Laura's house, Sam got out and walked around to the passenger side. "Let me just walk you ladies in. Now that Harbor Shores is a hotbed of criminal activity, you can't be too careful." He opened the double doors, helped Laura out, and then held out his hand to me. As I climbed down from the vehicle, he took my hand.

As Laura fiddled with the keys, the door opened abruptly from inside. Jack appeared, looking rumpled from the plane but happy to see Laura. He hugged her tightly.

"How did it go? I'm so sorry I couldn't be there. Lucky you have a friend like Emma to back you up. And I appreciate your help, Sam. Would you two like to come in? Have a drink?"

"No, I'll let you two catch up," Sam said. "We can discuss business another time."

"I'm going to head home," I said.

Laura hugged me tightly. "Thanks for being there for me."

"Always," I replied.

Jack nodded and said, "Well, good night. Thanks again," before pulling Laura to his side and inside the house.

Sam and I walked back along the pathway toward my car. "Maybe we should get together soon to discuss our investigation," he said.

"Sounds like a reasonable idea," I agreed, looking straight ahead and trying to appear casual.

"How about dinner tomorrow night?" he said.

"I think I'm available."

We reached my car and turned to face each other. Sam pushed a few buttons on his phone and handed it to me. "Would you mind giving me your number? I'll give you a call tomorrow, and we can make a plan."

"Sure." I typed in the number and handed it back to him, like I did that sort of thing all the time. Actually, I hadn't gone on a date in years. I unlocked my car, and he opened the door for me, watching with a smile as I slid into the driver's seat. "See you tomorrow, then."

"See you tomorrow." He gently closed the door.

I backed out of Laura's driveway, put the car in gear, and drove away. Before I turned the corner, I checked my rearview mirror.

He was still watching me.

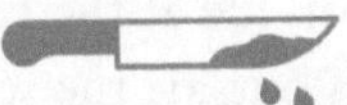

THE NEXT MORNING at eight o'clock, the phone rang. It was Sam. "Hey, Emma. Hope I didn't call too early. Did I wake you?"

I cleared my throat. "No, no, it's fine. How are you?"

"I'm doin' just fine," he said. The twang of his voice brought to mind an image of Matthew McConaughey. "I was just calling to find out if you were still interested in getting together tonight."

"To discuss Laura's case?" I asked.

"Sure," he replied. "If that's what you want."

"I'm available," I responded without taking the bait.

"Do you like seafood?"

"Love it," I said.

"How about the Silver Marlin?"

"Sounds good. What time?"

"How about seven? I'd like to pick you up, if that's all right with you."

Alright, alright, alright.

I STOPPED by Laura's house to check on her later that afternoon. She immediately asked about my dinner with Sam. "What time is the date tonight?"

"It's not a date. We're meeting to discuss the investigation."

"Right. Thank you for your invaluable assistance. And you're welcome for the introduction to your new boyfriend."

"He's not—"

Laura made a calming gesture. "Fine, fine. Let's change the subject. I need to show you something." She led me to her dining room, where Rose's binder lay open on the table.

"I've been reviewing the binder that Rose's nephew gave me. I thought it was strange that Rose kept her own records, when most of this information should be on file at the HOA management office. Of course, she kept information outside the scope of typical management, as I noticed immediately. Data on house prices, homeowners, and extraneous occupants and pets. So, many things were odd in this binder, but one list stood out."

"What is it?"

Laura flipped to a section near the end of the book. "This appears to be a list of people that violated HOA covenants."

"What's odd about that? From what I've heard, Rose filed a lot of complaints."

"As the current president of the HOA, I have access to the official files at the HOA management office. I compared the information in Rose's binder with the official record, and Rose's list doesn't match up."

"Does it say which rules they broke?"

"No, and that's another thing that feels wrong about it. An accurate record would include the violation letter, the response letter, and a list of dates when they notified the resident, when the resident responded, and when they complied. Rose's binder doesn't have any of that. It's a list of names and a record of fines." She flipped a page. "Here's the financial record of the fines paid. Look at the account number." The box from the estate sale sat open on the table next to the binder. Laura pulled out one of the slips and held it up beside the binder.

Skepticism heavy in my voice, I said, "But Phillip Mayhew isn't on the list. There has to be some other explanation for all those payments to Rose. There is no way the HOA fined Phillip Mayhew for twenty years."

Laura pointed at the rows of figures. "But what about all of these? I still say she used the fines as a cover for her extortion."

"But what was she blackmailing them for?" I asked.

"I have no idea," she said. "We have no evidence of anything except the payments themselves. There are a lot of them. Too many to be explained as fines."

"*If* you're right," I pointed at her and qualified the statement by adding, "and I'm *still* not saying you are, that would at least explain the reason why she got so pissed when you dethroned her as president. You interfered with her scam. And without the protection of her position, she couldn't continue extorting money from these people."

"The increased chance of exposure certainly must have made it riskier, but I doubt she ended the scheme. She probably depended on that money."

I nodded at her, but when my gaze met her eyes, they darted away. She chewed her lip.

"Is there something else?" My gaze returned to the binder, but she snapped it shut.

"No, not right now. I'll keep looking." With a furrowed brow, she continued to stare at the closed binder.

"We should tell Sam about this."

"Already did. He said he'd look it over and come up with a plan of action. Maybe he'll discuss it with you tonight at your date—I mean meeting."

I rolled my eyes. "Quit it."

"Want me to come over and help you get ready?" A mischievous smile wiped the serious look from her face.

"Absolutely."

With Laura's assistance, I prepared for my evening with Sam. She helped me do my makeup, applying smoke-colored eyeshadow that enhanced my gray eyes. Then, we went through the contents of my closet and selected a flirty sundress and sandals with kitten heels. After she left, I decided to use the flat iron on my hair.

I'd asked my dogwalker to take Hopper to the park for a while. I didn't want him to jump on Sam the moment he walked in the door. I checked my reflection in the hall mirror before answering the door.

Sam looked good enough to eat, with his curly brown hair casually mussed, and his white shirt with the sleeves rolled up, accentuating his tan. A slow smile crept up his face and warmed his brown eyes.

"You look pretty as a picture, Emma," he drawled.

"Thanks," I said. "You clean up pretty well yourself."

"Ready to head out?"

"Sure, as soon as I grab my bag." I locked up and followed him to his truck.

He offered his hand to help me up. "Nice place you have here. Close to the Intracoastal. Maybe sometime I could pick you up in my boat and take you on a sunset cruise."

"Sounds scenic," I said. "I'd like that."

When we arrived at the Silver Marlin, Sam gave his keys to the valet and escorted me inside with a warm hand on my lower back. The hostess greeted us, aiming her smile at Sam more than me. She seated us at a table by the window with a view of the water.

"This is pretty scenic, too," I commented. The late evening sun set the water ablaze with rosy light. An egret patrolled the water's edge, intrepidly hunting for a fish dinner.

I studied the menu, hunting for my own dinner. "What do you like to eat here?"

"I usually go with the catch of the day. Whatever's freshest. What looks good to you?"

You, I thought, before reminding myself that we weren't on a date. We were supposed to be discussing the investigation.

A waiter arrived and took our drink orders. Sam chose a local craft beer, while I opted for white wine. Once I had a glass in hand, I decided it was time to get back on track.

"What are your plans for the investigation? I feel like the police aren't considering any suspects other than Laura."

He narrowed his eyes at my directness. "Ready to talk business, huh?"

"That was the plan."

"Okay." He leaned back in his chair and took a sip of beer. "First off, I want Laura to steer clear of the scene. I'd appreciate your help with that." He waited for me to nod before he continued. "Then, I want to go down that list she found in Rose's binder and talk to everybody on it. I think it's our best lead yet."

"I agree. How well do you know the people on the list? Can you get them to open up to you?"

"I think so. I've met pretty much everybody in the neighborhood at some party or another. They're a friendly bunch, for the most part."

I raised one eyebrow at him. "For the most part?"

The waiter returned, preventing any specifics. We each ordered the catch of the day—mine grilled and his blackened. I sipped my wine and waited for our server's departure before I said, "So, you're pretty confident about getting them to confide in you."

He shrugged. "Just speaking from experience. You'd be surprised what people tell me. Guess it's better than being a dentist, though. People talk to them at parties and start opening up about problems with their teeth."

"I guess I can relate to that. Because I majored in Computer Science, all my friends and family ask me to solve their tech problems."

His eyebrows lifted. "Maybe we can use that. How are you at hacking?"

I crinkled my nose. "See what I mean? You're doing it right now."

"Sorry," he said, making a calming gesture with his hands. "Just a thought. Sure would be sweet to get a look at Rose's financial information. Ah, well. I do have a professional investigator I use for tough cases. A former police detective."

"What kind of information can the detective dig up for you?"

"All kinds of stuff. Usually, we begin with basic surveillance, but my investigator can access information that only the police have. Reports, criminal background, stuff like that. I'll give Taylor a call and get it started. I'll introduce you. So, no hacking? We sure could use a peek at that protected information. Other information is accessible by anyone. Public record stuff. You and I can go over that when we have a computer in front of us. What are you doing Saturday?"

"Nothing, I guess. Why?"

"You mentioning FSU gave me another idea. There's a game-watching party at Ed and Mindy's on Saturday night. You should come.

We can tag-team people there. Ed's on the list. I'll try to talk to him, and you can find out if Mindy knows anything. What do you think?"

I smiled. "Put me in, coach."

One side of his mouth quirked upward in a satisfied smile. The waiter returned with our salads. "I think that's enough business for now." He leaned forward, placing his elbows on the table. "I'd like to investigate *you*, Emma Stewart."

"Me?"

"Yes, you. Tell me more about yourself. I know you're a 'Nole and a technology expert, but how about some personal details? Have you ever been married?"

"I have, but not for long."

"How long?"

"Not quite two years, right out of college."

He gave a low whistle. "That was quick. How did he let you get away? What happened?"

"He cheated."

"Oh." Sam leaned back. "That'll do it. Must've been an idiot."

I nodded. "I came to that conclusion eventually. How about you? Ever married?"

"Nope, I never found the right girl. Kept myself too busy, I guess. First, there was law school, and that took all my focus. Then, when I graduated, I took a job with a big law firm that expected eighty or ninety hours a week. Did that for a few years before I finally wised up and opened my own practice. It's small, but I set my own hours. What's the sense of living at the beach if you never have time to get out on the water?" He dug into his salad.

I followed suit, managing to spear a cherry tomato without shooting it across the table. Even if it wasn't a date, I felt self-conscious. "So, you quit your old job to have more time for fishing?"

He shrugged and grinned. "Have to admit, it was a factor. I also didn't enjoy the kind of law they practiced there. I wanted to choose my own clients. Criminal lawyers get a bad rap, but I'd like to think I can help the innocent folks who get caught up in the rush to convict."

"Like Laura," I said.

He nodded. "But let's not go back to business. What do you like to do in your spare time?"

"I like to get outdoors. Ride my bike, walk on the beach. Sometimes, I take my dog."

"What kind of dog?"

"He's a bulldog mix. A rescue. I take the Chuckit down to the beach, and he chases the ball until the sun goes down."

"Chuckit?"

"A stick with a cup on the end that holds a tennis ball. Makes the ball fly farther."

"What's your dog's name?"

"Hopper." I smiled proudly and showed him the screensaver photo on my phone. "He's my guy."

"A handsome fella," he said in his Southern twang. "Looks like a good watchdog."

"You'd think so, but he'd probably let a burglar in for a scratch behind the ears. When you arrived, he was at the park with his dogwalker—a teenager that lives nearby. Otherwise, he would have been all over you. He likes company."

"How 'bout you introduce us later? I love dogs."

I smiled and nodded. He'd better like dogs. That would be a deal-breaker.

AFTER DINNER, Sam pulled into a spot near my house. Releasing my seatbelt, I said, "Well, counselor, that was a productive meeting."

He grinned. "All business again, eh?" He put his warm, calloused hand on top of mine and gently squeezed. "How about I walk you to your door? Then, I could meet that pup of yours." When I nodded, he leaped out of the truck and came around to open my door.

Hearing me at the front door, Hopper gave an impatient howl from inside. "Prepare to be greeted." Hopper welcomed me with ecstatic leaps and wet kisses. "He always acts like I've been gone a year."

Sam followed me inside and stood in the foyer looking all around. "Nice place."

"Thanks." I rubbed Hopper's ears, but he was too excited to sit still. He ran up the hallway and back again, nails clicking on the hardwood floor, then skidded to a stop in front of Sam. "Be a good boy," I said sternly.

"I'll try," Sam said with a sideways grin. He bent down to Hopper's level and extended his hand, knuckles first, for the dog's inspection.

"I was talking to Hopper." I watched Hopper sniff Sam's hand and receive a thorough scratch near the base of his tail. "You found his favorite spot."

Sam peered up at me from where he crouched, now rubbing the furry belly Hopper presented to him. "I like to think I have a knack for that."

I felt my cheeks grow warm. "He probably needs to be walked."

Sam stood. "Mind if I come along?"

"Not at all." I bent down to hide my still-flushed cheeks as I secured the leash to the loop on Hopper's collar.

Sam opened the door. "After you."

Hopper pulled impatiently as I closed the door behind us.

"Don't you lock it when you go out for a walk?" Sam asked.

The deadbolt emitted a whirring sound behind us. "It's a smart lock. I enabled the auto-lock feature with a time delay, so it locks automatically when I leave. There's an app that I use to let the dogwalker in and lock up remotely." I held up my phone. "It uses Bluetooth."

"Ah," Sam nodded. "You and your technology."

"Yep," I agreed, slipping my phone back in my pocket. "I do like my gadgets."

We walked side by side beneath the streetlights lining the road. "You ever worry, living here by yourself?"

"I've got Hopper." My guard stopped abruptly to sniff a suspicious bush. He marked it and moved on.

"He looks ferocious, even if he is friendly," Sam said. He looked around at the mock-Spanish style townhomes. "How long have you lived here?"

"Five years," I said.

"You like it?"

"It's all right." I nodded my head toward Hopper. "I wish I had a decent backyard for this guy sometimes."

"Are you still thinking about moving to Harbor Shores?" he asked.

"I'm not sure." I turned my head toward the nearby highway and the sound of traffic. "This place has its drawbacks, but at least I've never stumbled across a dead body here."

"That was pretty unusual." His white teeth flashed in the dim light. "Do you and Laura have a history of getting into trouble?"

I smiled reluctantly. "A little bit, but usually nothing like that. We used to sneak into bars at college when we were underage. Wasn't all that hard, though, once Laura fluttered her eyelashes at the bouncer."

"I'm sure the bouncer was checking you out as well." His brown eyes held my gaze. "I sure would have."

The potentially romantic moment was interrupted when Hopper squatted and left a souvenir. Ruefully, I pulled out a plastic baggie from the roll attached to the leash and packaged up his little gift. "Dog owner-ship has its drawbacks."

He chuckled, but the moment was broken. As we turned back in the direction of my house, he said, "Litter boxes are worse."

"I agree." I stopped walking. "Wait—do you own a cat?"

"No," he said. "Just an observation. We always had dogs when I was growing up. I miss it sometimes."

"You could get one."

"I've thought about it. It wasn't that long ago I was working long hours at the firm. Now that I have my own business, I guess I could even bring a dog to work with me sometimes if I wanted to."

"A legal beagle?"

"Something like that." We reached my front door, and Sam bent to pat Hopper on the head.

"Well, thanks for dinner," I said awkwardly, having never before considered the difficulties of flirting while holding a bag of dog poop.

"I had a great time with you tonight," he said. "Can I pick you up tomorrow before the game-watching party?"

"No, that would be silly. The party is in your neighborhood. I don't mind driving."

"Okay. Want to meet at my place around six o'clock?"

"Sounds good." The automatic lock buzzed and clicked open.

Sam examined me for a moment before leaning in and brushing a feather-light kiss on my lips. "Goodnight, Emma." He put his hands in his pockets, grinned at me one last time, and walked away.

I SHOWED up at Laura's house the following morning with two cups of coffee and a bakery bag.

Laura greeted me with a double kiss and took one cup from my hand. She nodded at the bag. "I hope you have something keto-friendly in there."

"Yeah, I brought you a bag of meat cuts." I rolled my eyes at her. "Of course not, goober. It's bagels and cream cheese."

She led me to the kitchen. "If you keep bringing me carbs, I'll force you to join me at Francesca's boot camp again."

"Not on your life." I sat down and applied a thick layer of cream cheese to half of a poppy seed bagel. "Once was more than enough."

She sat down across from me, elbows on the table, and rested her chin on her clasped hands. "So," she purred, "tell me all about the date last night."

I filled Laura in on all the details of my date with Sam. Indeed, I had to admit it had a decidedly date-like feeling. "He took me to the Silver Marlin for dinner at sunset."

"Sounds romantic."

"It was, surprisingly. He's easy to talk to. He asked a lot of getting-to-know-you questions. We didn't actually talk about your case that much."

"You're fired."

"Very funny. After dinner, he walked me to my door, and then came in and met Hopper."

"And did Hopper approve?"

"Whole-heartedly. Sam accompanied me on our evening walk."

"Did he give you a goodbye-kiss?"

I held my forefinger and thumb up and pinched the air. "A little one."

"Nice. Not too pushy." She smiled, looking pleased with herself for having introduced us, and nodded once. "This one seems like a keeper. You've been single too long."

"It's too soon to say that, Laura. Besides, even Ryan seemed like a good guy at first."

"I never liked him." She broke off a bit of bagel and added a dab of cream cheese.

"You say that now, but at the time you thought he was all right. You said he was hot."

"Being attractive is not the same as being a good guy."

"Seemed like it when I was twenty-two." I removed the lid from my coffee and breathed in the scent of hazelnut. "Plus, he seemed so confident."

"Cocky, you mean."

"What can I say? I have a type." I felt a smile tugging at the corners of my mouth. "I always preferred Han Solo to Luke Skywalker."

Laura shook a packet of sweetener and shot me a sideways glance. "You're speaking geek again." She tore it open and dumped the contents into her cup.

I slurped my coffee, earning another censorious glance. "Anyway, why are you so sure Sam's a good guy?"

She counted her arguing points on her hand, starting with the pointer finger: "He's smart, he has a good job, he likes dogs, and he's keeping me out of jail," she concluded on her pinkie.

"Those are all valid points, I must admit." I smeared cream cheese on the other bagel, broke it in half, and handed a piece to Laura.

She accepted it without complaint. "So, when do you plan to see him again?"

"He invited me to an FSU game-watching party Saturday night at Ed and Mindy's house. We're going to investigate your neighbors while watching football. You want to come?"

Hands outstretched as if warding off an unwanted advance, she said, "Wouldn't want to be a third wheel. Besides, you know I never really cared about football, even when we were at FSU."

"Bless your heart," I drawled. "It's against the rules to be Southern and not at least pretend to care about college football."

"What do I know? I'm a military brat. The only football my dad cared about was the Army-Navy game."

"Speaking of your dad, have you heard from him lately?"

She sighed. "Mom called me. Apparently, word of my brush with the law somehow got back to her military wives' club at The Colony. She was mortified."

"How on earth—"

"I don't know. Word gets around." She stuffed the remaining bite of bagel in her mouth and chewed aggressively.

I reached across the kitchen table and squeezed her hand. "You're a model daughter. Give her a grandchild, and she'll forget all about it."

"Don't even joke about that. She mentioned that her neighbor has a new grandson." Laura rolled her eyes. "It's too much pressure being an only child. Sometimes I wish I had a sibling to take some of the load off me."

"Me, too," I replied quietly.

She squeezed my hand. "Oh, I'm sorry, sweetie. That was thoughtless of me. Let's get back to talking about this party you're going to."

"Where do Mindy and Ed live?"

"Catty-corner from the Mayhew house, across the street. You can see it from there."

"All roads lead back to the murder house, don't they?"

"Well, we do live on a circle, so..." She raised both hands in the air, palms up, and shrugged. "Yes, they do. Maybe you'll hear some juicy gossip while you're there."

"That's the plan," I replied.

eight

THE NIGHT of the big game, Sam opened the door wearing a garnet-colored golf shirt with a Seminole spear embroidered over his heart. He greeted me with a boisterous, "Hey, beautiful!"

"Hey, yourself." I pointed at his shirt. "Nice threads."

"I like yours, too," he said, pointing at my vintage-wash T-shirt emblazoned with the sentiment, "Love My 'Noles."

"Ready to go?" I asked. "The game starts at eight."

"I need a minute." He took a step back and extended an arm. "Please, come in."

I stepped into his home and looked around. It was one of the smaller stucco houses in the neighborhood. I guessed it had three bedrooms instead of four, but I didn't ask for a tour. The furnishings appeared comfortable and decidedly masculine. Two brown leather sofas huddled around a massive flat screen TV—the focus of the room. He gestured toward the sofas. "Have a seat. The appetizers need a couple more minutes."

I settled into the buttery leather cushions. "You cooked?"

He relaxed into the seat beside me. "Sort of. Nothing fancy. Just pigs in a blanket."

"Now I feel bad I didn't bring anything."

He grinned. "I'm happy to share my blankets."

"Behave." I couldn't help but return his smile, though I tried to remain focused on the underlying plan for our evening. "We've got to find the killer, Sam. It's got to be someone else on that list."

"Not necessarily, but it's the best lead we've got."

"Tonight, at the party, you need to talk to Ed."

He gave me a mock-salute. "Yes, ma'am. I haven't forgotten."

"And I'll talk to Mindy. And we can tag-team if we find anyone else there who had something against Rose."

"That could take a while. Can I watch the game?"

"I guess so." I laughed, and some of the tension left me. "I'm just worried about Laura."

He rested his hand lightly on top of mine. "Just remember, Laura is innocent. The cops couldn't find enough evidence to pin this on her. They are going to be out there looking for the real murderer. You've got to trust them to do their job."

"Trust is not my strong suit."

"We'll just have to work on that." An oven timer buzzed in the other room. "That'll be the pigs in a blanket."

He led the way into a small but modern kitchen. After grabbing a spatula from a utensil canister on the counter, he began scraping sausages off the tray.

I held a foil-lined plate ready to catch appetizers as he scooted them off. "I'm impressed that you can cook."

"This is nothing. I can cook fish seven different ways."

I wrinkled my nose. "Yum. Fish every night of the week."

He grinned. "Don't worry. I spread them out."

"That's reassuring." I covered the snacks with another sheet of foil. "All set?"

He nodded. "Teamwork makes the dream work."

As we walked up the street in the fading light, Sam pointed out the homes of some folks I'd met at the previous party. The majority clustered around an inner circle, shouldering out the rest of the world, but there were a few side streets and cul-de-sacs sticking out here and there. Sam lived on one of the cul-de-sacs. We turned off his road and strolled toward Ed and Mindy's.

Thanks to Daylight Savings Time, the sun would be up for another hour. However, the evening light was softer, and the Florida heat had abated slightly. Despite the recent arrival of September, we would still be dealing with summer for a few more weeks, along with the added threat of hurricanes that tended to strike in fall.

Laura lived a few houses to the right of the entrance so, when I visited her, I only passed a couple of homes. Laura had accused me of being "lost in my own world" and not very observant of my surroundings. Now on foot, I looked around more than ever before. The uniformity of the houses was noticeable. Most were some version of tan, ivory, or gray. Some homes were plain stucco, or the more textured coquina with small shells dotted through it, with a few exceptions displaying brick enhancements or lap-siding. Somehow, they blended into a sameness that might be soothing or bland, depending on your perspective.

Once we rounded the corner, I spotted a house with all the lights blazing and figured we had reached our destination. I was unprepared when I also recognized the Mayhew house. It stood catty-corner to the home of Ed and Mindy. In comparison to the party site, which was blazing with lights, the "murder house" loomed dark and ominous.

The sweet scent of jasmine wafted from trellises flanking the front door. Sam pushed the doorbell with his free elbow while carefully balancing the tray of appetizers.

Mindy answered it. "Hi, Sam..." Her eyes swept from him to me and back again. She smiled. "And Emma. Glad you could join us."

A referee's whistle pierced the hum of many voices inside. Sam looked suddenly concerned, awkwardly attempting to consult his watch without upsetting the tray of appetizers. "Are we late?"

Mindy rescued the platter from Sam. "Not really. Just missed the kickoff."

I followed Mindy to the kitchen while Sam winked and hurried away to join the others in the TV room. Ed and Mindy's home had a different layout from Sam's. The kitchen didn't overlook the living room, so it was quieter. But, when the team scored, the partygoers roared.

"Sounds like Sam made it just in time," Mindy said. She eyed me with open speculation. "You two make a cute couple."

"Oh, we're not a couple."

She examined me while arranging a tray of cheese and crackers. "Not yet, maybe."

"Can I help with something?"

"Sure. I have another block of cheese that needs to be sliced over there on the counter."

The crowd in the TV room cheered again. "Sounds like you've got a good turnout tonight."

Mindy nodded. "Yes, a lot of Seminole fans in the neighborhood. Or at least they're fans of free food and beer."

"Always a sure-fire combination," I agreed. The wire on the cheese slicer suddenly came loose. "Mindy, the wire-thingy broke. Do you have a knife handy?"

She made an exasperated sound and handed me a paring knife. "This is the best I've got that's clean. Things are always breaking around here faster than Ed can fix them."

I resumed slicing. "Is Ed pretty handy?"

"Yes, that's his business. We run a handyman service, and I'm his bookkeeper. I take care of invoicing and such. But I have a hard time getting him to fix things in his own house because he gets so much work from people in the neighborhood."

"What kind of work?"

"A lot of small repairs, but he also does kitchen and bath remodels. I think Miranda asked him to put up some shelves or something. He wasn't real specific about what he was doing over there." Mindy began spearing meatballs with toothpicks. "These houses were all built twenty to thirty years ago, and some of them are beginning to show their age. We have a lot of elderly neighbors who can't manage the upkeep."

"What about the houses that are coming on the market? Has he worked in either of those?" I quickly added, "I might be looking to buy one soon. He can tell me what kind of shape they're in."

"Rose never hired him. She probably thought our business wasn't good enough for her. I've heard she's actually discouraged some neighbors from using our services. But Phil's daughter, Alice, asked him to fix a few things for her before she put the house on the market. Mostly little things like cabinet doors that didn't line up, a closet door that wouldn't slide—stuff like that. He does quality work."

"Of course." I tried to keep my voice casual. "When did Alice ask him to fix those things?"

"Let me think." Mindy scrunched her lips to one side. "Alice was here, sorting through Phil's house a few weeks ago. She told me she had to finish up quickly, so that the estate sale company could do an inventory. But she left town right before the estate sale. Flew home to Charlotte. Seems like she'd have wanted to stick around and supervise."

"Are you close friends with Alice?"

"We used to be close. I haven't seen as much of her since her parents' marriage broke up. That was such a shame. I just stopped by Phil's house that day to give her my condolences and see if she needed anything. I offered to help her sort it all out." She held out the plate of decorated meatballs. "Would you mind carrying these out?"

"Sure." I set out the platter of meatballs and hurried back to the kitchen. Mindy was slicing celery sticks for a vegetable tray, so I grabbed the paring knife again and began to help. Mindy sure had a lot of good information, and she liked to talk.

"Don't you want to watch the game?" Mindy asked. "I appreciate the help, but you don't have to stay in here with me."

"I don't mind," I assured her.

Ed's voice boomed from the living room. "Mindy, bring me a beer!"

She dropped the knife and immediately retrieved the beer from the refrigerator. Without another word, she scurried off to make her delivery. When she returned, she picked up the knife and continued her chopping. She spoke to me again as if nothing had interrupted. "It didn't take them very long to reschedule the estate sale. Did you find anything good?"

"No, just did some browsing. The Mayhews had unique taste, didn't they?"

"They certainly did. Alice let me look around, but that was before... I was curious to see what the house looked like after." Mindy dried her hands. "Let's bring this stuff out and actually watch some of the game, shall we?"

I took the vegetable tray, and she gave the ranch dip one last stir before picking up the football-shaped bowl and leading the way out of the kitchen.

Sam's eyes followed me as I entered the room. He scooted over and patted the seat beside him. When I sat down, the cushion sank beneath me and tilted me toward him. He murmured, "Get any juicy details?"

"Yes, as a matter of fact. I'll tell you all about it later. How about you?"

"Um, I got a little caught up in the game."

I huffed impatiently. "So, who's winning?"

"Seminoles, seven to three."

"That was quick. Sounds like it might be a high-scoring game." I caught the scent of his aftershave. It was difficult to stay irritated with him for long. Resigned, I settled back into the deep seating and felt his arm creep around behind my shoulders.

At half time, Ed stood up from his recliner and stretched his massive frame. "I'm gonna go check on the smoker." He strode out to the patio.

I turned to Sam. "Maybe you should check the smoker, too."

"That's a good idea." He grinned. "But I am awfully comfortable here."

I gave his leg a playful slap.

"All right, I'm going." He stood and followed Ed.

I scanned the crowd for anyone else I recognized. There were quite a few faces familiar to me from the last social event. I spotted Miranda at the beverage table, so I joined her.

"Hi, Miranda. Remember me? We met at the community party." Selecting an open bottle at random, I poured myself a drink.

"Of course, I remember you. Anna, right?" She raised a glass of white wine to her lips.

"It's Emma, actually. Are you an FSU grad as well?"

She mustered a thin smile. "No, I just enjoy a party. I live next door to Ed and Mindy."

"Is that so?" I glanced out the darkened window of the dining room. "What's back there? Do both houses have the same view?"

"Yes, they both have a marsh view."

"That sounds lovely," I said. "Must be so peaceful."

"Except for the occasional snake in your backyard." She gazed out into the darkness and took another sip. "You still thinking about moving here?"

"I might take a look at Rose's house."

"That's a fancy one. Lots of upgrades. You should ask Sophie to show it to you. She can get you in anytime with her realtor's key."

"That sounds like a good idea. I'll talk to her." *Realtor's key?* Laura's decision to sneak me into a house at night seemed worse every day.

Miranda's gaze wandered. "A pleasure seeing you again, Anna."

"Emma," I corrected, but she had already sashayed away, headed for the patio.

Sam returned holding a steaming plate of barbecue. He waved it under my nose. "You have to try this."

I inhaled the smoky, sweet scent with my eyes closed. "You convinced me. Point me at it."

"Ed's pulling smoked pork on the patio table. You want this one?"

"No, that's okay. I'm not sure I want that much. You go ahead. Halftime's almost over."

"Okay," he said and ambled away.

I headed for the patio. As I approached the sliding glass door, I heard angry voices.

"Not now. Not here," Ed said in a hard voice. I stopped where I stood, unwilling to intrude on what sounded like a marital disagreement.

Another voice whined at Ed, but it was not Mindy's. "I'm sick of this."

I peeked around the doorway, trying to see without being noticed. It was Miranda. When she turned abruptly, I slid into the nook between a cabinet and the wall. Miranda stormed past without a glance in my direction.

Back in the TV room, the second half of the game had started, but Ed's recliner remained empty. I resumed my spot beside Sam.

"Where's your plate?" he asked.

"I forgot to get any. I got distracted." The close call had raised my adrenaline, and I tried to appear calm.

"Distracted by what?"

"I'll tell you later."

He raised his eyebrows questioningly but stopped pushing. "You want some of mine?" He held out a forkful of meat.

I hesitated, but then I leaned to accept the bite from his fork. "Mmm. That's delicious."

"Told ya," he said, holding my gaze.

Nearby shouts from the other guests interrupted the moment. "Unbelievable! I can't believe he made that catch!"

Sam smirked, a bit ruefully. "Hope they show an instant replay."

When the game ended, the guests filtered out. Before leaving, I stopped to thank Mindy for her hospitality. She seemed distracted, and I wondered if she might have overheard the same exchange I witnessed earlier.

I walked back to Sam's house, still pensive.

"I can't wait to find out what you heard that's got you so bothered," Sam said, glancing over at a nearby couple walking home. "But I guess it'll have to wait until we have more privacy." He wiggled his eyebrows suggestively, making me laugh so loudly the couple turned in my direction.

"It was an interesting party," I said.

"We know how to throw a shindig around here."

When we reached his house, I hesitated next to my car, suddenly nervous.

"You are coming in, right? I need to hear the details."

"For a little while," I said, and followed him inside.

"You want anything else to drink?" he asked.

"Maybe some water." While I waited, I glanced around his living room. On the wall, there was a framed glass display of what looked like bugs. I walked over to get a closer look.

He returned holding two glasses of water and noticed me trying to make sense of his wall art. "They're fishing flies. Those belonged to my dad. He used to make them." He handed me one glass and began pointing to the fuzzy insect things. "That one's a black gnat, and that one's a blue bottle—they're designed to mimic the insects that trout like to eat."

I leaned closer and spotted the hook hidden inside each elaborate tangle of feathers and string. "These are just for display, or are they real?"

"They're real. I just don't go fly-fishing much anymore. Used to go with my dad when I was a kid." He became very focused on one of the flies and didn't say anything more for a minute. He cleared his throat and took a sip of water, then gestured toward the sofa. "Why don't we sit down?"

I settled into the deep leather cushions and angled to face him. "That was some game, wasn't it?"

He stretched out one arm along the back of the sofa. "Sure was. I forgot about our reconnaissance mission. Did you pick up any new information?" A phone rang in the other room, and he held up one finger. "Hold that thought." He hurried away. I heard him talking in a serious voice for a couple of minutes before he returned.

"Everything okay?"

He settled back beside me on the sofa. "Just an update on some work stuff. I turned off my cell phone, and the calls are being routed here."

My eyebrow shot upward. "You have an actual landline?"

"Yes, I'm an old-fashioned guy. I keep it for work purposes. When I don't want to be bothered on my mobile number, I set all my calls to come here. But enough about business. What upset you during halftime?"

"I overheard Ed and Miranda arguing outside."

His forehead wrinkled. "Ed and Miranda? That's an odd pair."

"Yes. He said something like, 'Not here,' and she said, 'I'm sick of this,' then stormed off."

"Sounds like old Ed might have been a little more than neighborly with Miranda."

"It did sound that way. Poor Mindy. She was an excellent source of information in the kitchen."

"What did she say?" he asked.

"Ed worked for Alice Mayhew as a handyman."

"Ed does odd jobs for a lot of folks around here."

"He had a way into the house, and he was there frequently during the days leading up to the murder. That's opportunity," I pointed out.

"But what about motive?"

"He's on Rose's list of violations."

"We don't know what that list means."

"Think she knew about him and Miranda?"

"I suppose it's possible. Creepy, but possible. She was awfully nosy." He shook his head. "But I don't know if she was nosy to the point of actually spying."

I shivered. "It would feel awfully strange, knowing that someone could be watching you."

He sidled up closer to me and put his arm around my shoulder. "Are you cold?"

I rubbed my arms, feeling tingling goosebumps. "I guess I was just imagining Rose peeking through the window at me or something. The only time I ever saw her was when she was dead."

He reached over and pushed a lock of hair behind my ear. "That must have been traumatic." His fingers trailed through my hair, down the side of my neck, and along my shoulder.

I squinted at him. "Are you using my traumatic situation to make a move on me?"

"Is that bad?" he asked, but his chocolate brown eyes didn't look sorry, and his hand didn't leave my shoulder. "Would you mind if I was?"

I nervously licked my lips. The tingling had moved from my arms into other regions of my body. "I don't mind."

He smiled a slow, wide smile. "Good. Then, I'm definitely making a move on you." He bent to kiss my shoulder, tracing a reverse path from the one his fingers had taken, upwards. He trailed soft, warm kisses up my neck, behind my ear, and, finally, brushed my lips with his own. He wrapped his other arm behind me, embracing me as we kissed. The kisses started out tender, almost teasing, but they increased in intensity. My fingers worked their way under his shirttail and found the smooth, warm skin of his back.

When he started to tug on my shirt, however, I stopped him. "I can't."

"Why? What's wrong?" He squinted at me, confused by my mixed signals.

"I have to get home. I pay a neighborhood kid to walk Hopper in the afternoons, but she'll be off-duty at this hour. I need to go home and walk him."

"I'm sorry." Sam blew out a long breath. He reached up and stroked my cheek with his thumb. "Maybe I was moving too fast."

I chewed my lip. "Possibly. But I really should get home to Hopper."

The corner of his mouth tugged up in a half-grin. "Next time, I guess I'll just have to invite Hopper to come along."

nine

THE NEXT MORNING, Laura showed up while I was still in my pajamas. In contrast, Laura wore patterned leggings, a matching tank top with a saucy crisscross design on the back, and simple thong sandals in lieu of athletic shoes. I guessed she'd come straight from yoga.

She made a beeline for my coffeepot, poured herself a cup, and sat down at my kitchen table, an avid look on her face. "Tell me everything."

I retrieved the sweetener from the pantry and handed her a spoon. "I gathered some great intel at the party at Ed and Mindy's."

"I meant about you and Sam." She stirred her cup and pouted.

I refilled my cup and sat down. "Aren't you interested to hear the information pertaining to the murder we stumbled upon?"

She lifted one shoulder, then dropped it. "I guess so, but the romantic parts are more fun. So, what did you find out?"

"Mindy was a font of information. Apparently, she's friendly with Phil's daughter, Alice. She told me Alice hired Ed to fix some things over at Phil's house the week before the murder. He's also been in Rose's house and Miranda's house."

Laura's eyes widened. "That gives him opportunity and potentially places him at the scene of the crime!"

"Exactly. But why would he be working on the house at night? And why was Rose there that night?"

"I guess those are both valid points." She propped her chin on her hand.

She looked so disappointed, I decided to share the juiciest bit of gossip next. "I think something hinky is going on between Ed and Miranda."

She sat up straight. "Mindy told you that?"

"No, but I overheard them arguing."

"Mindy and Ed?"

I obviously wasn't telling the story right. "No, Ed and Miranda."

"Ed and Miranda? I never would have pictured those two together." Laura closed her eyes, then moved her hand as if erasing the image from her mind. "Tell me exactly what they said."

"She said, 'I'm sick of this,' and he said, 'Not here.'"

"That's it?" Her avid expression fell away. "I was hoping for something more."

"Well... Miranda sounded pretty angry. And Ed's tone of voice wasn't exactly something you'd use with a casual neighbor relationship, either."

Her eyes narrowed. "If that's it, then let's get back to you and Sam."

I sighed and relented. "I went inside his house." She gestured for me to continue. "He showed me his flies."

Laura slapped the table. "Emma!"

"Not *that* kind of fly. Fishing flies. He has a collection."

"You have that in common." She nudged the saltshaker toward me. "Maybe he'd appreciate your kooky collections."

"I found out he can cook. I helped him wrap up an appetizer to bring to the party. He cooked pigs in a blanket."

"What did you bring?"

"I didn't know I was supposed to bring anything."

"Emma!" She lightly smacked me on the arm. "Have I taught you nothing? You should never show up to a party empty-handed. It's my mother's second-most important rule, right after sending thank you notes promptly."

"Sorry. I was focused on the investigation, not the party. Anyway,

Sam snuggled up to me on the sofa to watch the game. Practically did the yawn-and-stretch move. Then, afterward, we went back to his place."

She tilted her head. "Did he show you his flies again?"

"Tried to."

Her eyes widened.

"He made a move, but I put him off. I told him I had to get home to walk Hopper."

She leaned back in her chair. "I guess that was the right way to handle it. It's still early. You wouldn't want to appear over-eager. But..."

I raised an eyebrow. "Yes?"

"You're not getting any younger."

"Now you really do sound like your mother."

"I'm fairly sure that Mom wouldn't approve of the third-date rule. But if you two do start spending more time together, it makes sense you would get there eventually."

"I don't know." I stood up and took my cup to the sink, washing it and drying it with excessive care, as if handling fine china instead of a free mug with a software logo.

Laura continued in a gentle tone, "Emma? Don't you think it's time to consider another relationship? You seem to be attracted to him."

"He's attractive, all right." I gave up polishing the mug and returned to the table, bracing myself for a counseling session.

Laura leaned forward. "Then give him a shot, Emma. And let yourself have some fun, for a change. There's more to life than software." She sat back, then added, "Speaking of which, don't forget we have tickets to see The Whigs in concert Saturday night."

I had forgotten. "What time?"

"Doors open at eight, but there's an opening band. No need to be punctual. Let's meet at my place. And, while I'm here..." She pushed her chair away from the table and stood. "Let's go pick out what you're going to wear."

"Do you know who the opening band is?" I asked as we headed south on A1A the night of the concert.

"Nobody I recognized. It'll give us time to get some drinks and hang out on the deck." When we reached the Costa Verde Concert Hall, she followed the waving flag of a parking attendant into an adjacent field that became a parking lot on concert nights.

Outside the building, we stood in line waiting to be scanned and searched for contraband, making conversation while we waited. Laura gestured at my outfit. "You look amazing. I should pick out all your clothes."

I tugged at the hemline of my skirt. "Normally, I wear this as a tunic over leggings. Feels a little exposed."

"You'll be thanking me when the crowd fills the room and the air conditioning can't keep up." She glanced up at the faded façade of the stucco building. "This old church has seen better days."

Costa Verde Concert Hall was formerly a place of worship until the enterprising congregation sold the building and built a new megachurch near a growing community populated by young families. The new owners remodeled the building and turned it into a music venue, removing the old wooden pews for standing-room concerts. Off to the side of the former sanctuary, two full bars served hard liquor, beer, and wine—not of the communion variety. The facility hosted country and folk singers, jazz and blues musicians, and popular bands from past decades.

I turned to Laura. "Remember the last time we saw The Whigs?"

As I expected, the memory elicited a broad smile from Laura. "That time when we drove all the way to Chicago for Lollapalooza?"

I nodded. "Come to think of it, that was the last time we had a brush with the law."

"That's right!" Laura briefly covered her eyes with one hand. "When we got kicked out of the park for climbing into Buckingham Fountain!"

"Well, it was hotter than the devil's armpit. Who knew it got hot like that so far up north?" At the head of the line, I dumped my keys and phone into the bowl and proceeded through the metal detector.

On the other side of security, Laura declared, "I'm ready to jump into a fountain right now. Let's get a drink." She linked her arm through mine and, together, we navigated the crowd to reach the bar.

"First round's on me," I said and caught the attention of the bartender. "One Longboat IPA and my friend here will have a vodka cranberry, please."

"With a lime," Laura added.

I smacked my forehead. "How could I have forgotten the lime?"

We pointed at each other and shouted in unison, "You're out of lime!"

"No, you're out of lime!"

"No, you're out of lime!"

The bartender gave us a quizzical look as we dissolved into laughter at an old private joke that nobody else appreciated. We collected ourselves and our beverages and moved aside. Heavy velvet curtains divided the bar area from the auditorium, doing little to muffle the sound.

Feeling uncertain about the opening band, which sounded heavy on drums, I asked, "You want to go in?"

She hesitated. "Let's hang out here for a while." She neatly snagged a high-top table away from the curtains. "We can talk about your love life."

I groaned. "Why *my* love life?"

"Because I'm a married woman, and I have to live vicariously through you. Have you agreed to another date with Sam?"

"You're assuming he asked me." I spotted a familiar face in the crowd and used the distraction to divert the conversation. "Hey, isn't that Mindy?"

Laura turned to look. She waved and caught Mindy's eye. As we watched them approach, Laura muttered, "Wouldn't have pegged her as a Whigs fan."

"Laura! Emma! Funny running into you here!" Mindy chirped, waving her arms with enthusiasm. The cup of wine in her hand sloshed dangerously.

Laura put her arm around my shoulders. "Emma and I are big fans of The Whigs from way back."

"Is that right? To be honest, I'd never heard of them." Mindy covered her smile in mock embarrassment. "I'm here with Sophie. Miranda bought the tickets, but she's not feeling well tonight, so she gave me hers. I don't normally spend money on frivolous things like concert tickets."

"That's a shame," I replied awkwardly. "I mean, for her. Not for you."

"Yes, I guess her loss is my gain." Mindy giggled.

"Where's Sophie?" Laura asked, looking around.

"Bathroom," Mindy said. She downed the rest of her drink and said, "I might head there, too, before the next band starts. You girls have fun tonight!"

"You, too!" Laura replied, lifting her cocktail.

"Do you think Ed's business isn't doing well?" I wondered aloud as we watched her dash away. The opening band had finished, and the house lights were up while they swapped out equipment. "Sounded like Mindy was worried about money."

Laura's lower lip protruded in a pensive pose. "I doubt that's it. Maybe Mindy just counts pennies. She's a bookkeeper, after all."

After sipping my beer, I said, "That's right. She probably manages their household finances. But I would have pegged Ed as one of those over-controlling types who gives his wife an allowance."

Laura rolled her eyes. "Such a high opinion of men."

"She seems submissive." I shrugged. "But I guess looks can be deceiving."

Laura rested her forearms on the table and leaned forward conspiratorially. "Do you think she suspects about Ed and Miranda?"

"In a neighborhood like Harbor Shores, I would think it would be difficult to keep a secret like that. If, in fact, they are having an affair. Have you heard any other gossip?"

Laura leaned away. "You imply that I gossip."

I raised my hands, palms toward her. "No, I imply that your *neighbors* gossip, and you might have innocently overheard them."

She narrowed her eyes but let it pass. "I haven't heard anything. But I do know that Steve, Miranda's husband, travels a lot. His company has another office in Miami, and he travels back and forth."

"Drug dealer?" I asked innocently.

She slapped my arm. "Hardly. Some financial job."

"Money launderer?" I continued.

Finally, she laughed. "Enough! All of our detective work has given you an overactive imagination."

The lights dimmed. "My detective skills tell me we'd better get in there. The show's about to start."

ten

THE NEXT MORNING, I felt the effects of my late night out with Laura, reminding me that I'd aged a bit since Lollapalooza. I crawled out of bed, knowing Hopper would be upset with me for delaying his morning walk. I got dressed, walked the dog, and made myself breakfast. I spent the late morning and early afternoon catching up on housework and laundry. When my phone rang, I figured it was Laura calling to chat about the night before. Instead, I saw Sam's name on the screen and felt a jolt of pleasure. "Hello?"

"Hey there, beautiful. How's your day going?"

"Not bad. How's yours?"

"Can't complain, what with the weather being so nice. I got an idea that maybe I could take you for that boat ride? We could go down to Vilano Beach for dinner."

"That sounds amazing. What time?"

"How about four? I can have her gassed up and ready to go by then. Think we can use that boat dock by you?"

"I've never used it before."

"No problem. If you don't mind meeting me over at my place, we can put in at a public access boat ramp."

"I don't mind."

There was a pause in the conversation. "Do you think Hopper might like to come?"

I felt a smile tug at my lips. "I'm sure he would."

"There's a great little place called Beaches at Vilano that has a boat dock and allows dogs if we sit outside. Sound good to you?"

"Is that the restaurant under the Vilano Bridge? I've been meaning to try that place."

"That's the one. You're going to love it. Can you meet me in an hour? That'll give me a chance to get the boat ready."

"Sure. See you then."

What would I wear on a boat? After examining my closet, I decided to keep it simple. I heard somewhere that you were supposed to wear rubber-soled shoes on boats, so I wore white sneakers with a pair of shorts and a crisp, sleeveless button-down shirt. I grabbed a sun hat from the hall closet and tossed it into a bag, along with some sunscreen, bottled water, and a couple of bowls with some bagged food for Hopper. I probably over-prepared, but I didn't know how long the boat ride would last.

When I pulled up, Sam was in the driveway tinkering with the boat. The moment I exited my car, he wrapped his arms around me and kissed me thoroughly. "You ready for a ride?"

I felt my cheeks grow warm. "Ready as I'll ever be." Hopper wriggled in between us.

Sam obligingly petted him. "So that's how it's gonna be, huh? You think I'm trying to steal your girl?"

A big grin tugged at my cheeks. Sam had figured out the quickest way to my heart. "He just wanted some attention."

He squatted down to give Hopper a thorough belly rub. I began to feel jealous before he grinned up at me. "This ought to be fun. The ramp is a couple of miles from here. I'll lock up, and we can hit the road."

He helped me up into the truck and we drove toward the boat launching area. We followed the coastal highway south through a nature preserve. To the left, I caught glimpses of white caps dotting the dark waters of the Atlantic Ocean. On my right, the slow-moving Iyola River wound between tall grasses and mudflats. I rolled the window down so Hopper could stick his head out.

Sam gave us a sideways glance and a grin. "Now this is a real truck. It's got a dog hanging out the window."

When we reached the public boat ramp, Sam expertly maneuvered the trailer backward until it sloshed into the brown water. He put the truck in park and opened the door.

"How do we do this?" I asked, clueless about boats.

"How 'bout you hop out, but let's leave Hopper in the truck for just a minute. You'll need both hands."

"What?" I felt my heart race, but patted Hopper reassuringly before climbing out and closing the door. He didn't like it any more than I did.

Sam was already behind the truck, fiddling with some straps securing the boat to the trailer. He turned a crank on the trailer and guided the boat down a series of rollers. When the boat floated free of the trailer, he attached a sturdy rope securely to the boat before handing the end of the rope to me.

"What am I supposed to do with this?" I asked.

"Just hold it. I'll move the trailer and bring Hopper." He winked. "Don't let go."

I stood there feeling useless while he pulled the truck forward. The hull of the boat was deep enough to float, and the trailer easily rolled back up the ramp, dripping wet and empty.

Sam parked the truck in the adjacent lot and returned to me with Hopper. He looked at Hopper and then back at me. "Think he'd mind if I pick him up?"

"He's comfortable with you."

He lifted Hopper close enough to allow him to jump into the boat. Then, he offered his hand to me and grinned. "I could pick you up, too."

"I think I can manage it." Awkwardly, I climbed in.

Sam had carried my backpack from the truck, and he passed it to me before leaping in beside me with athletic grace. He stroked the railing lovingly. "This here's a twenty-four-foot Sea Chaser with twin Suzuki one-fifties. A hybrid fish and cruise."

"If you say so." Observing his look of pride, I asked, "Has it got a name?"

He cocked an eyebrow. "*She*. I call her Lola."

"Would you prefer I left you two alone?"

"No way. In fact, I bought you something." At the rear of the boat —aft? stern? whatever—he flipped a latch and opened a compartment from which he drew two life jackets plus something that looked like a big, puffy, orange handbag.

"What's that?"

He called Hopper and arranged the puffy orange thing on his back with the handle sticking up. Then, he secured it with straps under Hopper's belly while stroking his fur reassuringly.

"You bought him a life jacket?"

He smiled up at me, shading his eyes from the sun with his hand. "Safety first. But let's not forget about you." He stood and held out a life jacket.

"Thanks." I lifted it over my head and attempted to secure the straps.

"Allow me." He stepped close to me so he could wrap his arm around me and secure the strap around my back. I smelled his woodsy aftershave. He maintained our proximity longer than necessary and held my gaze with his own. "Does it feel too tight?"

I shook my head mutely.

He stepped back and donned a vest of his own. "All set?" When I nodded, he gestured at a padded bench to the rear of the boat. "Then, make yourself comfortable."

Hopper settled on the floor beside my feet while Sam took the helm. I felt the engines rumble behind me as he maneuvered the boat into the Intracoastal Waterway.

I watched the marsh rush past us in a blur, and when I turned to smile at him, I saw the same view reflected in Sam's aviator sunglasses. His broad smile and relaxed posture, one hand draped over the wheel, made it clear that he was in his element out on the water. The sun picked up reddish highlights in his ruffling hair.

We left the waterfront homes behind and traveled south into an area that was a wildlife preserve. When the ride smoothed out, I grasped the railing and moved to stand beside him. He put his free arm around me and pulled me closer.

The roar of the wind combined with the motor's rumble made it difficult to hear, so he spoke into my ear, "Having fun yet?"

I nodded, feeling his hair tickle my cheek as I did.

Sam slowed the motor, and we coasted peacefully for a while. Snowy egrets stalked the banks in search of fish, and a silver mullet breached the surface of the water with a splash nearby.

"One of those jumped into my kayak once, when I was fishing. Damn near scared me to death. At first, I thought it was a snake." He chuckled.

"What did you do?" I asked.

"Nothin'. It jumped back out again. Turned out to be the only thing I caught that day. Well, almost caught. A day on the water is never wasted, though." His eyes scanned the water as he guided the boat past mudflats and marsh grass. I saw his shoulders lift as he inhaled deeply and appreciatively. "I love that smell."

Hopper appeared to love the experience. Once he became accustomed to the feel of the boat, he stood on his hind legs and placed his front paws on the bench, lifting his nose into the breeze. I supposed it wasn't all that different from hanging out of the car window for him. Sam occasionally reached out to give him a quick pat on the head.

Immediately after we passed under the Vilano Bridge, Sam steered the boat toward a floating dock. As he tied off multiple lines from the boat to the dock, I surveyed the area. Previously, I'd viewed this spot only in passing as I breezed over the nearby bridge. I spotted the distinctive metal archway with three leaping dolphins and a cartoonish-looking bird sculpture with the words "Happiness is Vilano Beach, Florida" painted on a blue background.

Reggae music emanated from a cerulean-blue building. Sam helped me onto the dock and passed Hopper over to me. He took my free hand in his and escorted me to the Caribbean-themed restaurant. Instantly, I felt like I was on vacation. There was a small sandy beach lined with a string of colorful chairs and a rough-hewn tiki hut topped with palm fronds.

Once we sat down and Hopper settled beneath our table with a water bowl, Sam scanned the drink menu. "Would you care for a Naked Mojito or a Naked Turtle Rum Bucket?" He wiggled his eyebrows comically.

"I'm sensing a theme." I tapped my lips with my finger and tilted my head. "Maybe just a margarita, though." I scanned the restaurant for our server. A familiar figure standing at the bar caught my eye. "Is that Francesca?"

Sam glanced in the direction I pointed. As he did, the woman turned and caught my eye. It was indeed the perky exercise instructor. She waved, picked up her tropical drink, and headed our way. I sat up straight and sucked in my gut.

"Hello there!" she said with her exotic accent. "So pleasant to bump into you two!" Her voice suggested that the drink was not her first.

"Hey there, Francesca," Sam said. "How's Adam?"

She waved her hand dismissively. "He's fine. I left him at home with the kids. Carly and I are having a girl's night out." She indicated the bar where Carly stood waiting for her drink. Francesca pointed a finger at me. "When will you to try another class with me?"

"I think I need to be in better shape before I can keep up with you," I said sheepishly.

Her chin jutted forward. "No, no, you must come to class in order to get in shape. I can help you."

Not a chance, I thought, but tried not to let my face show it. "Francesca, I've been meaning to ask you, how did you get the HOA off your back so you could keep teaching classes?"

She pulled up a chair and joined us without being asked. "It's all about who you know."

"Can you give me some advice? I might decide to move to the neighborhood, and I need to know what to do if I want to run my own business there."

She removed the umbrella from her drink and took a swig. "The only person who would give you any trouble is gone now." She pointed the tiny umbrella at me for emphasis. Her accent seemed to grow more exaggerated with every sip. "You should move to our neighborhood. It is the best place."

Sam voiced his agreement.

She waved the umbrella in his direction. He swiftly dodged as her gesture nearly endangered his eye. "He is a smart man. You should listen to him."

"I don't know," I said. "It worries me the way the HOA hassled you. I'm thinking I should move somewhere without a neighborhood association."

"It was only Rose Martin. She forced the HOA to fine me. When I got back from my vacation and heard that she was gone, it was like a gift."

"You were on vacation when the murder happened?"

"Yes, visiting family in Italy." She pulled out her phone and scrolled, looking for something. Finding it, she held it up to show us a picture of her in a bikini on a yacht floating on cerulean waters with an Italian-looking coastline in the background. "Portofino," she added. A motion at the bar drew her attention, and she glanced over her shoulder where Carly was waving madly. Francesca stood. "I believe our table is ready."

"Are you and Carly driving home tonight, or are you staying somewhere down here?" Sam asked.

"We took an Uber," she answered, waving the tiny umbrella again. "Going to have a good time tonight!"

Sam chuckled. "Stay safe."

She nodded. "Enjoy your dinner." She pointed at me once more. "And come back to my class."

"All right, I'll try." I watched as Francesca swished away. "I wonder if she ordered the Rum Bucket?"

"Sounded like it," Sam agreed. "But at least it made her oblivious to your investigative questioning."

"Too obvious?" I asked.

"Possibly. But you can scratch her off your list now."

We shared a double order of steamed clams, soaking up the buttery sauce with hunks of garlic bread. "At least we'll both have garlic breath," I commented. "Will you still kiss me later?"

"I'll kiss you now," he said, and leaned toward me. His lips were slippery with butter, and I pressed mine against them, prolonging the kiss.

"Mmm," he moaned. "Aren't clams supposed to be an aphrodisiac?"

"I think that's oysters," I murmured.

"Too bad," he said. "Did you save room for dessert?"

We shared a slice of key lime pie before heading back.

"You did promise me a sunset cruise," I said. The September sun emblazoned the water with pink and orange hues as we made our way back up the Intracoastal.

"I aim to please." Back at the access point, he skillfully maneuvered the boat onto the trailer. When he pulled the truck back into his driveway, he asked, "Can you come in?"

I nodded at the dog in my lap. "If you don't mind Hopper being in your house."

"No, I don't mind at all. In fact, I specifically invited him, if you will recall."

"Yes, I guess you did." Once we were all inside, I unhooked Hopper and retrieved his food and water bowls from my tote. After eating, he investigated the room, sniffing everything before settling down on the couch right in between Sam and me.

"Oh, is that how it's gonna be?" Sam ruffled the dog's ears.

"Should I make him get off the furniture?" I asked.

"He's fine, as long as he shares you." He leaned over the dog's head and gave me a kiss. Hopper jumped down, and Sam immediately scooted closer to me. "Let's see. The other night, we were right about here—" Sam put his arms around me and leaned me back on the couch.

"Sounds about right." My voice caught in my throat.

"And I was doing this." He began stroking my lower back and kissed me deeply while his fingers worked their way beneath the edge of my shirt.

"I'm beginning to understand why you invited the dog," I said.

"Just thinking ahead," he admitted.

THE NEXT MORNING, I awoke to the smell of bacon. After gathering my clothes from the floor, I hurried into the adjoining bathroom to get myself together. Toothpaste on my finger had to do as a makeshift toothbrush. After checking my reflection and deciding there wasn't much I could do about it under the circumstances, I went to find Sam.

He was standing at the stove with his back to me, wearing a pair of low-slung pajama bottoms and nothing else. Hopper waited at his feet, hoping for a handout. Sam removed the bacon from the pan with a fork and placed it on a nearby plate already stacked with strips resting on a paper towel. As I watched, Sam broke off a bit of bacon and blew on it to make sure it was cool before handing it to Hopper.

I walked up behind him and rubbed his smooth, muscular back. "Should you be frying bacon without a shirt on?"

"I like to live dangerously." He turned and bent to kiss me.

"Do you make breakfast for all the girls that spend the night?"

He grinned at me. "No, I usually kick them out the night before."

"Well, then I guess I'm lucky."

"No, I think I'm the lucky one." His arm slipped around my waist and gave me a squeeze. "How do you like your eggs?"

"Scrambled."

"The coffee should be ready by now if you want some. Mugs are in the cabinet above the microwave."

I filled my mug and leaned back against the countertop to drink it while savoring the hot guy cooking for me. I could get used to the sight. Hopper nudged his nose against my leg, reminding me that he needed his breakfast. I filled his bowls, which looked right at home in Sam's kitchen. Sam dropped another small piece of bacon in the bowl when he thought I wasn't looking.

When breakfast was over, Sam asked, "Got any plans for today?"

"Not really." I smiled. "Did you have something in mind?"

"I was thinking we might hang out at the beach. It's Labor Day, after all. Got to enjoy every last bit of summer."

"That sounds wonderful, but I'm going to have to run home first. I didn't come prepared for a sleepover, you know."

He smirked and leaned forward to give me a peck on the lips. "I'm glad things worked out the way they did. How about later today, then?"

I smiled again. I was doing a lot of that. "Tell you what—why don't I go home and get changed, maybe pack up a few things for the beach.

Then, I can run by the store and pack a lunch for us in the cooler before I come back?"

"Sounds like a solid plan to me. Hopper can stay here with me if he wants. I've got a fenced-in backyard, and I'd be happy to toss a ball with him."

"Are you holding my dog hostage?" I looked down at Hopper, who sat at Sam's feet, gazing at him adoringly. "One slice of bacon, and suddenly, he's man's best friend. I guess if you don't mind." I started to gather our plates.

Sam stopped me. "Don't worry about that. I'll get it."

"Full service around here, huh?"

"Only for you."

"I guess I'll get going, then, so I can come back for more."

He grinned widely.

"I meant lunch!"

He shrugged. "That, too."

He walked me out to my car and kissed me goodbye. I guessed the neighbors would get an opportunity to gossip about us. The thought made me drive to Laura's instead of driving straight home.

As I walked up the path to her door, I glanced down at my outfit—the same clothes I had worn the day before. I hadn't done the walk of shame since college, but Laura had been there. I knocked quietly on her door.

She answered promptly, fully dressed, with her hair neatly done. I smoothed my hand over my own tangled locks. She surveyed my rumpled attire and cocked her head. "What do we have here?"

"Laura, you won't believe what happened last night."

"What." Laura's tone and expression were strangely flat.

"I slept with Sam."

"That's amazing. I'm so happy for you." Again, she spoke without any expression on her face.

Panic seized me. "Laura, what's wrong? Do you know something about Sam that I don't? Why aren't you happy for me?"

"Oh, I'm sorry. I am so happy for you. I just got back from Ageless Medical Spa. They have a Labor Day Botox special going on today." She patted her face gently with her manicured fingertips. "My face is still numb." She hugged me to prove her happiness. At least her arms still worked. "Want to come in for coffee?"

"No thanks. He made me breakfast."

She whistled. "He's a keeper."

"I'm supposed to be heading home to get ready for a picnic at the beach with Sam."

"You're spending the day together? It must have been good." She wiggled her eyebrows and smirked.

"Your face is moving again," I pointed out.

"Excellent. I was starting to get worried." She patted her face. "You'll probably run into people you know at the beach. There's a private access gate for our neighborhood."

"Maybe that will give us more opportunities for detective work."

"I doubt you will be paying attention to anything other than your handsome lawyer. I think I'm going to need another partner in crime."

"Don't worry. I'll always have your back."

"Yeah, but he has your front."

I swatted her arm before hugging her goodbye.

EVEN THOUGH SAM saw me wearing nothing at all the night before, in the light of day, the prospect of a bathing suit felt daunting. In the heat of passion, I failed to consider what had or hadn't been waxed, moisturized, or exfoliated. It was fortunate I had put off Sam's invitation until lunchtime because there was a lot to do.

I did the best job possible without the help of a professional and trusted my gauzy, white cover-up to blur whatever was not toned or evenly tanned. A pair of Audrey-Hepburn-inspired sunglasses and a white broad-brimmed hat completed my ensemble. It wasn't quite up to Costa Verde standards, but it would have to do.

I filled a small cooler with ice and stopped by the New York Deli on my way to Sam's. When I pulled up in his driveway, the garage door was open, displaying a wall of fishing gear worthy of a sporting goods store. Off to the side, a large rack supported three surfboards of varying lengths. A two-seater golf cart occupied one half of the garage, and a fishing kayak occupied the other half. I spotted Sam loading the golf cart with beach chairs and an umbrella. Hopper sat in the passenger seat, ready to ride shotgun. It looked like I'd be riding in the back.

"I thought this neighborhood was supposed to be within walking distance of the beach?" I teased.

"Not when you're hauling fishing gear. Besides, I wouldn't want to make my lovely companion walk in the heat." He grinned, white teeth flashing in the tanned skin of his face. He wore turquoise board shorts slung low enough on his waist to expose the slant of his hip muscles. He sauntered over to me and planted a kiss on my cheek that slowly meandered its way over to my lips.

"I missed you," he said.

"Since breakfast?"

"Mm-hmm." He kissed me thoroughly. I wondered if we might not make it to the beach. "You look good enough to eat." He took the cooler from my hand. "But I'll pack this for backup." He loaded the cooler in the golf cart with the other things. "Ready to go?"

I nodded and climbed into the golf cart, which was burgundy with a Seminole spear on the hood, of course. He backed out, closed the garage door, and sped up the causeway.

On the oceanfront road, there was an empty lot across from the beach gate. Sam parked the golf cart beside two others already there and began unloading the gear. He slung the umbrella and a backpack chair over his muscled shoulder and carried the cooler in his free hand. I took the remaining chair and my beach bag and followed him to the gate. Luckily, another resident had left it open, so we didn't have to worry about the key.

I followed Sam along the sandy path lined with wild beach sunflowers, Hopper frolicking along beside us. As we crested the dune, I saw a few colorful beach umbrellas marking the spots already claimed by neighbors. We headed for an open area, and Sam shrugged off his load. He expertly set up the umbrella in record time.

"I can never do that right," I commented. "Mine always blows over."

"Well, today you have your own cabana boy." He set up my chair and gestured to it. "Milady."

"Thank you, kind sir." I settled in the chair, slipped off my sandals, and wiggled my toes down into the sand. "This is the life."

"This life could be yours as a resident of Harbor Shores." He sat beside me and opened the cooler, retrieving two bottles, one containing beer, and the other water. "Ready for refreshments? Take your pick."

I accepted the water bottle, chilled and wet with condensation—a welcome gift on a humid Florida afternoon. I opened it and drank deeply while gazing out at the ocean. "I could get used to this."

He flashed a charming smile. "That is my plan."

I inclined my head at the nearby umbrellas. "Are those all neighbors?"

"Some are from Harbor Shores," he said. "But we share the beach access gate with that condo building. Some residents, some renters. Usually not crowded around this stretch of sand, at any rate."

He was right. In the distance, hotels and public beach access points funneled in dozens of families with tents, coolers, and boomboxes, but down here on the south end, fewer than ten people shared the wide stretch of sand with us. In the steel blue ocean, a lone surfer sat astride his board, feet dangling, waiting patiently for a wave to come along, but the waters were calm. On the sand directly to our left, a striped umbrella stood atilt, blocking our view of all but the smooth, tanned legs and pink manicured toenails of the woman languishing in its shade. At the shoreline, a paunchy, gray-haired man stood ankle deep in the surf, reeling in a fishing line.

"Anyone you know?" I asked Sam.

He squinted out towards the waterline. "That's my neighbor, Steve. Don't think you've met him. He's married to Miranda."

"Miranda?" I asked incredulously in a voice that was a tad too loud.

The occupant of the umbrella emerged and lifted her sunglasses. "Oh. Hello, Anna," she said. Her head turned toward Sam and then back to me. In a warmer tone of voice, she said, "Hello, Sam," and smiled like a cat with a dish of cream.

"It's Emma, actually."

"Of course. Did you enjoy the party?"

"Yes, I did. Everyone here has been very friendly to me."

Her eyes raked over Sam as she said, "They certainly have." She lowered the sunglasses once more. "Time to turn over. I hope you two enjoy this lovely day." She withdrew behind the umbrella and rolled over so that her pink bikini bottom and the backs of her legs gleamed beneath the sun.

I turned to Sam with wide eyes. He just shrugged and took a swig of his beer. I reclined my chair and turned my gaze outward, where a formation of pelicans glided in unison over the breaking waves. From the corner of my eye, I saw Miranda's husband recasting his line. He appeared much older. I wondered what the attraction was.

Sam opened the cooler and retrieved two sandwiches. "You ready to eat?"

"Sure, I'll take one. I got turkey and provolone. Hope that's okay."

"Sounds tasty to me. I'm easy to please," he drawled in his good-ole-boy voice.

As we ate, I gazed at the water and watched a surfer navigate a small wave. "I noticed the boards in your garage. How often do you surf?"

"Not that often. Work keeps me busy, and when I have time, I usually spend it fishing instead."

"What kind of fish do you catch here?"

"Pompano, redfish, whiting. Sometimes, I'll even hook a small shark."

"A shark? What do you do then?"

"Cut the line!"

"I'd like to see that!"

We finished our sandwiches and stuffed the wrappers back in the cooler.

"Want to take a walk?" he asked.

"Love to," I said retrieving the sunhat I'd tossed aside earlier and took his outstretched hand for a lift from my low chair. He kept the hand I'd given him and held it as we walked along the shoreline. South of the beach access gate, enormous mansions lined the beach like expensive seashells. He pointed out the ones owned by prominent local figures and football players.

Once we were half a mile down the beach, I brought up the question that had been lingering in the back of my mind. "So, what's the deal with Miranda and her husband?"

"Trophy wife," he said. "He's an investment banker. She's wife number two."

"Oh, I see. So, she didn't marry him for his looks, I guess."

"I'm guessing the answer to that is 'no,' but I'm not an expert on male attractiveness."

The sun glinted off his curly hair, revealing blond highlights normally hidden in the brown locks. His muscular, tan body gleamed with sunscreen, and his crooked smile contradicted his words. He knew very well what women found attractive, and he knew he had it.

Eleven

Monthly meetings of the homeowners' association of Harbor Shores took place in the offices of Leview Management, the company that provided oversight for business matters and regulations enforcement. Laura informed me that a quorum of homeowners rarely bothered to show up for HOA meetings. Turnout increased for the annual meeting, particularly once word got out about the controversial vote concerning Laura's future on the board. Selecting seats near the back, Jack and I flanked Laura.

At the head of the room, six people sat at a long table facing the audience. In front of each dignitary was a sign showing the person's name and board position. Neighbors occupied about ten rows made up of eight chairs each.

A woman with a helmet of gray hair, seated front and center, cleared her throat. "I'm going to call this board meeting of the Harbor Shores Neighborhood HOA to order. I am Vice President Ginger Davis. Because of the nature of certain business at hand, I will be directing this meeting."

The hum of voices continued to buzz in the audience. Two elderly women picked over the snack table. I spotted one slipping cookies into her purse.

"May I have your attention? Let's hold all conversations until after the meeting. Thank you. The first item on our agenda is the manager's report from Tom Johnson of Leview Management."

"Thank you, Ginger," said a balding man with a tonsure of brown hair circling his head. "First off, we've had some issues with failure to request approval from the architectural committee prior to performing exterior home alterations. I'd like to remind you that any changes to the exterior of your house require approval. Reputable contractors should be aware of this policy. An architectural approval form is available on the neighborhood website. Submit requests no later than thirty days prior to construction." Tom consulted his notes. "Next, we have received complaints about neighbors who consistently neglect to pick up dog feces."

An elderly man in the front row harrumphed. "I'll say! Damn dogs always crapping in my yard. I'm going to get a BB gun and take care of the problem."

"Mr. Bennett, please reserve your comments for the open forum portion of the meeting," Ginger reprimanded the man with the red hat seated in the front row. "Please continue, Tom."

"Thank you, Ginger. As I was saying, there've been a number of complaints. We plan to include a reminder to all neighbors in our monthly newsletter."

"Like that's gonna help," said Bennett.

"Other issues that continue to plague the neighborhood include premature placement of yard waste on the curb and garbage cans left out too long after trash pick-up. Some neighbors have been storing their trash cans in plain view. This is against HOA covenants. Stow garbage cans out of sight within twelve hours of trash pick-up. We will also be sending out a reminder to all residents to place yard waste and trash on the curb no earlier than the prior evening." Tom tapped his stack of papers on the table.

"In light of frequent disregard of this rule, the board will vote on a fining schedule tonight. There is a list of recommended fines in the meeting agenda each of you should have received at the door. Does anyone need a copy?" He scanned the room and nodded. "Good. First, I will go over the plan, and then we will open the floor for discussion. For the violation of placing yard waste and trash receptacles out too early or leaving them on the curb more than twelve hours after trash pick-up, a fine of fifty dollars—"

A murmur from the crowd threatened to derail the explanation, but Tom held up his hand to quiet them. "Please allow me to finish. Violation of lawn maintenance guidelines warrants a fine of fifty dollars forty-eight hours after issuance of a warning letter. Failure to submit a proper request for proposed changes to property warrants a fine of one hundred dollars. We will now open the floor for discussion." Voices erupted around the room.

"Are you kidding me?"

"Fifty dollars for a trash can?"

"What about the dog crap?"

Tom held up his hand. "Please, one at a time. Raise your hands, and we will hear from each of you in turn."

Mr. Bennett raised his hand.

"Yes, Mr. Bennett?"

"How about the fines for leaving dog crap on my yard?"

"It would be difficult to impose fines on pet owners when there is no proof regarding the origin of the, um, fecal matter."

"A neighborhood in Atlantic Beach requires all pet owners to have their pet's DNA sampled. Then, when pet deposits are found, they can be tested to determine ownership," said a blond woman in the second row.

"Are you kidding me?" A white-haired woman in the front row turned around to face her. "You want them to test dog poop for DNA?"

The blonde tossed her mane of hair. "I only mentioned it as an example."

The neighborhood manager intervened. "At this time, we are not considering fines for this matter. Let's confine discussion to the violations previously mentioned." He pointed to a middle-aged man in a shirt and tie. "Please state your name and house number."

"Alex Marcus, unit three-oh-one. I'd like to go on record and say that fining residents fifty dollars for leaving a trash can in sight seems extreme, Mr. Johnson."

"Thank you for your input, Mr. Marcus. We will make a note of it. Next comment." Tom pointed. "The young lady in the back row."

"Tiffany Farley, house number one-fifteen. Since you mentioned proof, I'd like to know who is going to monitor these violations. Are you planning on patrolling the neighborhood on trash day?"

"As I mentioned, the fining procedure is contingent on approval. We propose forming a neighborhood committee."

"Oh, great. Neighbors reporting on neighbors. How fascist." The woman sneered, leaned back in her chair, and put her feet up on the empty chair in front of her.

Another young woman waved her hand laden with an enormous diamond ring. I was surprised she could lift it. "My neighbors just got a dog, and I'm almost positive it's a pit bull. Don't we have rules against vicious breeds?"

A silver-haired woman on the aisle nudged her husband with one bony elbow. "I don't think so, Margot. When your husband divorced his ex and married you, we let you stay."

Margot huffed, grabbed her Louis Vuitton handbag, and stomped out of the room. An older man in a business suit followed her meekly.

"Man, is he whipped," said Bennett.

"Please, everyone, let's keep this civil," said Ginger. "I think we should postpone a decision on this matter for another time. Direct any further input to Tom at Leview Management. I make a motion to table this discussion."

The board member to her right raised his hand. "I second the motion."

"Let the board vote. Those in favor?" All hands lifted except for a scowling man with a monobrow at the far end. Ginger nodded with satisfaction. "Motion carried. Let's move on to the next item on the agenda. Due to recent unfortunate events in our neighborhood, some neighbors and board members have suggested a change in board leadership. I move to hold a vote of no confidence regarding our current HOA president, Laura Benton."

Laura grabbed my arm and squeezed. I patted her hand, and Jack put his arm around her shoulders.

A pink-cheeked woman at the front table caught Laura's eye. I thought I remembered her from the community party. It was Ellen, the one with the Tinker Bell bun. She cleared her throat. "Before any voting takes place, I move for a discussion."

"Very well," said Ginger. "Since I made the motion, I will begin the discussion. The current president is under investigation for a serious crime. While I am not accusing her of guilt, I propose that her focus must be directed toward her own defense, leaving little time for her duties as a board member and president. Furthermore, it reflects poorly on this board to continue with leadership that has been tainted by potential criminal activity. That is why I propose a vote of no confidence. Any further discussion?"

Laura stood and cleared her throat. "I have something to say."

Ginger said in a grudging tone of voice, "Proceed."

Laura stepped out into the aisle and walked toward the front before turning to face the audience. "Friends and neighbors, I want you to know I am innocent. My involvement in the incident in question was purely circumstantial and accidental. I am fully committed to this neighborhood, and I will continue to devote myself fully to the role of president. If I may point out a few of my contributions as your president, I'd like to remind you that my efforts directly brought about the neighborhood-wide update of all mailboxes. The project improved the uniformity and appearance of Harbor Shores. I also chaired every holiday party in the neighborhood for the past two years: Christmas, Halloween, and Memorial Day, as well as the newly added End of Summer block party. Under my leadership, we repaired the causeway and the entry monument. If you examine my record, you will see I have been an effective and fair president. Thank you." Laura's voice had intensified as she spoke, and with her concluding words, she raised her chin and strode confidently back to her seat.

I squeezed her hand as she sat down and whispered into her ear, "You were great. Really picked up some steam there at the end." She smiled at me as Jack put an arm around her and hugged her.

"Any further discussion?" Ginger asked.

Ellen stood. "I can confirm that Laura has indeed acted professionally and effectively as president. She also encourages a friendly attitude between neighbors and the board. I have full confidence in her abilities." She nodded at Laura and returned to her seat.

The exterior door opened and closed with a thud. The noise drew the attention of most of the audience, with the exception of a few aging neighbors suffering from hearing loss. Bina entered the room with her dignified waddle. Hugh followed behind, dutifully carrying her purse. Bina jerked her chin in Ginger's direction. "I hope I'm not too late to add my two cents."

Ginger pursed her lips as if tasting something sour. "I was just about to close the floor discussion."

"Just in time, then." Bina proceeded to the front of the room and faced the audience. "I served with Laura on the board for two years. During that time, she carried out her duties with great attention to detail, and perhaps even more remarkable, great concern for her neighbors. She never approached neighborhood matters with a punitive mindset as others on the board pressured her to do. Instead of spending hours nitpicking rules, she spent time planning enjoyable activities that provided opportunities to bring us all together as neighbors. If Laura's removed from the board, I would expect the tone of the HOA to become more austere and disciplinary. I urge you to place your vote based on facts, not rumors and unsubstantiated accusations." Bina took an empty seat in the front row and lifted her chin.

Ginger peered down her long, aquiline nose at Bina before addressing the general audience. "If there is no further discussion, I move that we take a vote. Along with tonight's agenda you will find a ballot. Fill it out and deposit it into the box on the refreshments table. Tom Johnson will be monitoring the vote on behalf of Leview Management. We will tabulate the results tonight."

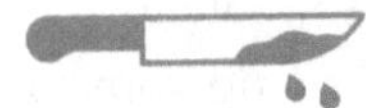

As we drove away, Laura buzzed with elation. Her green eyes met mine in the rearview mirror. Lit intermittently in the passing headlights, they blazed with triumph. "Bless that sweet, dear Bina. I really owe her one."

I edged up closer to the driver's seat. "Yeah, I think her speech really swayed them. But it was nice of Ellen to say something, too."

Laura turned in her seat to face me. "Ellen is the queen of nice. I'll never figure out how she got looped into Miranda's circle."

"Would you two like to stop somewhere to celebrate?" Jack asked.

"I could use a drink after that meeting." Laura pointed to a sign ahead. "How about the bar at Calypso's? What do you think, Emma?"

"Maybe just one. I hate to be a spoilsport, but I have to go home and walk the dog."

Jack nodded and turned into the parking lot, stopping at the valet stand. A young man in a blue polo shirt opened our doors. We climbed the staircase to a second-floor open-air bar overlooking a small lagoon. Discreetly placed speakers played steel drum music, adding a Caribbean vibe. We claimed a high-top table overlooking the water. A waitress with a bouncy ponytail and short shorts arrived to take our order.

"Did that meeting warrant a Painkiller? And, if so, was it worthy of one, two, or three shots of rum?"

"Worthy of a three, for sure, but I think I'll have a chardonnay."

"Well, I'm going for a Painkiller. Number two for that pile of hooey we just witnessed."

Jack ordered a soft drink. After watching the waitress leave, he spoke. "I'm surprised Sam wasn't at the meeting."

"He had a hearing down at the courthouse and couldn't make it back in time," I explained. "He asked me to stop by his office tomorrow and fill him in. I'm sure he's sorry he missed the fun. Are your board meetings always like that?"

"The annual town hall always is."

"I don't understand why you want to continue serving as president." I accepted my drink from the returning waitress.

Laura drank before replying. "I like to think I am a positive force in a sometimes-harsh environment."

Jack smirked. "She also doesn't like to lose."

Laura swatted his arm. "Thanks for your support."

He raised his arms in surrender. "Hey, I like your competitiveness." He tilted his head toward me. "She's vicious whenever we play doubles."

I eyed her skeptically. "Despite knowing you for over a decade, I continue to find ways that we differ."

She raised her glass. "It meant a lot to me that you came tonight, Emma."

I clinked my glass against hers. "You know me. I've always got your back."

Laura's phone rang. She set her glass down and began digging in her designer satchel while the phone cheerfully played marimba. At last, she located it. "Hello?"

I watched her face as she listened. After only a moment or two, her expression brightened, and a huge grin spread across her face.

"That was Ellen. It's official. They voted to keep me! I won!"

Jack leaned over and kissed her. "Congratulations, honey."

I couldn't remember the last time I'd seen him kiss her in public. I reached out and took Laura's hand, which she squeezed tightly. I slung my arm around her in a side hug. "You did it!"

"I did!" She glowed with her victory.

twelve

My INAUGURAL VISIT to Sam's office yielded many surprises. First among them was the lavish décor designed to impress visitors and sway potential clients the minute they crossed the threshold. It was all such a contrast to Sam's good-old-boy, easygoing, pickup-truck-driving persona. A deep-pile rug woven in jewel tones covered the hardwood floor in the reception area. Leather furniture with deep seating beckoned visitors to sit awhile, and fine art adorned the walls. A dark, gleaming mahogany desk stood sentinel in the back.

Aware of Sam's gaze on me, awaiting my reaction, I gave a low whistle. "I think I might not be able to afford your services, sir."

Sam ducked his head and waved off the observation with his big, work-roughened hand. "It's all rented. Come on back." He opened the door behind the reception desk and led me further into his domain. At the last door in the short hallway, he gestured for me to enter. "After you."

I took a seat in a comfortable-looking leather armchair. "Am I on the clock?"

Sam perched on the edge of his desk and crossed his arms. His tan forearms stood out against the crisp white shirt he wore with the sleeves rolled up. "No, I'll never charge you by the hour. Unless you're into that sort of thing."

I snorted but let it pass. "That HOA meeting was something else. Definitely re-thinking my house hunt."

He pushed his lower lip out in an adorable pout. "Not everyone in the neighborhood is bad."

I kissed his pouty lip. "I second that motion. Bina was awesome last night, too. And Laura's speech went flawlessly."

"Sorry I missed it." He reached over and squeezed my hand. "Maybe we can grab lunch after this?"

"Sure," I agreed, squeezing him back. "When is your investigator going to be here?"

He glanced at his wristwatch—a rugged, waterproof-looking contraption with a big dial around the face. "She should be here shortly."

"Wait—she?"

"Yes, Taylor is a female as well as a former JSO detective." He crossed one nut-brown ankle over the other knee.

I absently noted that he'd chosen to go sockless that morning. "You didn't mention that fact when you suggested I should meet your investigator."

"That she used to work for the sheriff's office?"

I cocked an eyebrow. "Funny."

"I didn't think it was relevant. I wanted you to meet Taylor so we can all discuss a legitimate investigation."

"But Laura's not here."

"You're my partner investigator now." He winked and gave me his most charming smile. "You can fill her in. Besides, I was hoping to take you out to lunch afterward."

"That can be arranged." Our eyes met and held briefly before his flitted away over my shoulder. I turned to see what had distracted him.

It was a woman, slim but muscular, wearing a blue button-down dress shirt that made her blue eyes stand out. She wore her long, shiny black hair pulled back into a low ponytail. I immediately regretted my decision to go with the dry shampoo that morning in lieu of actually washing my hair.

"Am I late?" she asked in a voice more suited to a spokesmodel than a hardened detective. Her blue eyes, fringed with dark lashes, scanned the room.

"Not at all," Sam said. He'd risen at her entrance and gestured to the vacant seat. Then, he moved behind his desk and took his place in the creaking desk chair.

"Emma, I wanted you to meet Taylor Evans. She's a talented investigator. Because of her connections with the JSO, she will be able to obtain information that we wouldn't be able to access."

She pulled a notebook and pen from her bag and smirked at Sam. "Not to mention my advanced interrogation techniques." To my ears, her voice sounded husky and suggestive. With a start, I realized why she instantly unnerved me. She looked exactly like Thea, the woman my ex-husband cheated with.

Sam chuckled. "All right, all right. Let's get down to business. I need background checks for the people on this list." He passed a copy of the page from Rose's notebook to Taylor.

I examined her while she scanned the page, her dark lashes down swept. *It's not her,* I reminded myself. *It's not Thea.*

Sam's professional voice resumed. "I also want to get a look at the police reports. Something has been bothering me. Emma, how long were you and Laura at the house before the police showed up?"

Jolted from my inner turmoil, I replied, "Only a couple of minutes."

"How'd they get there so fast?"

"They said someone called them to make a report. The neighbor either saw something or heard something that prompted them to call. We just happened to be in the wrong place at the wrong time."

"I want to find out who called the police." He turned to Taylor. "Can you get that information for me?"

"Shouldn't be a problem." She jotted the request in her notebook.

"Once that's been determined, we can interview them and ask what exactly they saw or heard. Unless the police already did that. They should have, but I find as a criminal lawyer that once the police set their sights on one suspect, they don't look around much after that. They had Laura on the scene, covered in blood. Then, later, they found the knife on her property." He turned to Taylor again. "That's the other thing that bothers me: the anonymous tip that led the police to find the knife. Track down anything you can about that tipster."

"It seems likely that whoever called in the tip also planted the knife," I speculated.

"Not necessarily," Sam said. "It could have been a random guy in a boat. There's some good fishing back there. I've been back there in my kayak."

"Maybe you planted it." I raised an eyebrow at him.

He grinned devilishly. "Anything's possible."

"Obviously, someone wanted to put the finger on Laura, away from the real killer," Taylor interrupted. "Sounds like we need to find out how the knife got there, and who planted it."

"Good luck with that," I said gloomily.

"Anything else?" Taylor asked. When Sam shook his head, she stood. "I guess I've got my assignment. I'll get on it." She strode across the room with authority. When she reached the doorway, she turned. "Great to meet you, Emma."

I nodded. "Nice to meet you."

When she was gone, I speared Sam with a look. "You also forgot to mention that your female investigator could moonlight as a model." I heard the bitter edge in my voice and winced.

Sam shrugged. "It's purely a business relationship. Taylor is a talented investigator, and she has a lot of law enforcement contacts." He stood from the creaky chair and approached me, putting both hands on the arms of my chair and bending toward me. He spoke quietly so close to my face I could feel the warmth of his breath. "You have nothing to worry about." He pressed his lips to mine before I could formulate an argument.

THE NEXT DAY, I returned to Sam's office to share the results of some internet digging I'd been working on, but when I arrived, I found Taylor seated at his desk, typing on a laptop. Her shiny black hair hung across her forehead like a curtain. At the click of the door closing behind me, she looked up, blue eyes wide and full lips parted in surprise.

"Oh, Emma! You scared me. I thought Sam locked the door on his way out. What are you doing here?"

Something about her tone irked me. Actually, everything about her irked me. "I just stopped by to see Sam. Is he in?"

"No, he left for court."

"I was just going to show him some public records information I dug up on the internet. Do you have any idea when he'll be back?"

"Probably not any time soon. I'm only here because I needed to turn in some receipts and fill out a time sheet. How's Laura holding up?"

"As well as can be expected." Her concern for my best friend made me soften toward her. "Got any new information?"

"I haven't had time to discuss it with Sam yet. He had to rush off. I'll let him fill you and Laura in." Her voice was cool.

So much for softening, but I told myself she was just being professional. "Oh. Okay."

"What did you find in public records?" she asked.

"I guess I'll wait until I can tell Sam and let him fill you in." *Touché.*

One black eyebrow arched as Taylor's lips pinched tightly together. "Look, Emma. I understand that you are Laura's best friend, but I don't think that means I should have to report to you. I also don't believe you have any business investigating this on your own. I am a professionally trained detective. Leave the investigating to me."

I raised my hands in surrender. "Fine. Whatever. Can you tell Sam I dropped by?"

The words she spoke were, "I'll be sure to do that," but her manner suggested I'd better not hold my breath.

I turned to leave. "Maybe you ought to lock the door behind me, *Detective.*" I let the door slam shut. As I walked to my car, I felt my hands shaking. I never liked confrontation. Hated it, in fact. Tears threatened to form in my stinging eyes, and I quickly climbed into my car and drove off before I could embarrass myself further. As I drove home, all the things I could have said ran through my mind far too late to say them.

A FEW DAYS LATER, Sam called Laura to share newly discovered information, courtesy of his intrepid investigator. He requested that both of us stop by his office. I tried to get out of it, but Laura dragged me along. We all took our places in his stuffy office. The air conditioning, a necessity of life in Florida, couldn't keep up with the heat. Thanks to the dress I wore at Laura's insistence, my legs stuck uncomfortably to the leather sofa cushions. My reluctance to be there was due to the presence of Taylor. She perched on the corner of Sam's desk, flipping through a small notebook.

Sam sat beside her and crossed his arms. "Taylor tracked down the neighbor who made that nine-one-one call."

"That's right." Taylor sounded like a newscaster taking her cue from the anchorman. "The neighbor that called was on the south side of the Mayhew home, a man named Walter Clark."

"That's the old guy who keeps calling the cops whenever someone's dog is off leash," Laura said.

Taylor nodded. "He has gotten a reputation down at the station for being a, shall we say, 'alert and attentive neighbor.'"

"I'll say," Laura agreed. "He doesn't miss a thing. This nice family that lives two houses down from him has a big dog. Mr. Clark called the police on them when the dog got out. Said it was aggressive." She opened her arms. "That dog is as gentle as a lamb... to everyone else."

Taylor nodded. "The guys at the station were happy to fill me in. Seems he reported someone lurking outside a vacant house. Then, he said he thought he heard the sliding glass door opening. It was enough to get a nearby patrol car to stop by and check it out." She glanced at me briefly before settling on Laura. "Seems like bad luck that you two happened to be there when they arrived."

Laura nodded. "I'll say."

"I stopped by Mister Clark's house yesterday and asked him about it. After he told me all about his neighbor's unleashed Labrador retriever, I finally got some details about the night in question. He said he saw someone creeping around behind the house the night of the murder. He told me he stepped out back to investigate, and that's when he heard the slider. Shortly after that, he heard voices arguing inside and decided to call the police."

"So now we know why the cops were there so quickly," Sam said. "It raises more questions than it answers, unfortunately. Guess that explains how they got in, but we don't know who was in there or what they were arguing about."

Taylor said, "Because of the source of the information, I think the cops have put it on the bottom of the list. They dusted the place for fingerprints, but they didn't find any solid leads. Dozens of people came in and out of that place, getting it ready for a property liquidation *and* a real estate listing."

"What about the person who reported the knife behind Laura's house?" I asked.

Taylor shook her head. "No leads there either. Anonymous tip submitted on the county sheriff's website. Pretty convenient."

Laura added, "From my perspective, it's pretty inconvenient."

Sam tossed me a crooked smile. "Can we revisit the possibility of your hacking skills?"

"Are you suggesting I break the law?" I arched an eyebrow.

Sam narrowed his eyes. "Wouldn't want to suggest anything illegal. Let's hold off on that, shall we?"

I shrugged. "You're the boss."

Taylor stood. "Well, *boss*, I've got to run. I'll touch base with you later."

Sam nodded and waited for her to leave before asking, "Can I take you ladies out to lunch?"

Laura started to speak, but I cut her off. "Thanks, but we have other plans. I'm sure you have a lot of work to do. I'll let you get back to it." I strode to the door before he could reply.

Laura tottered behind me on her designer high heels. "What was that all about?"

"Nothing. I need to catch up on some work." I gave her a quick hug. "I'll call you later." I got in my car and drove away. In my rearview, I saw Laura still standing there, watching me in confusion.

While I drove, I came up with an idea for an investigation that Laura and I could handle on our own, with no involvement from Taylor. In my home office, I dug through the items in the top drawer of my roll-top desk—an antique, purchased at an estate sale not long after I bought the townhouse. Apart from being one of my favorite pieces of furniture, it also hid all my mail and junk. Laura never succeeded in making me more organized when we lived together in college, though she did try.

Finally, I found what I needed: Sophie's business card. I dialed the number and listened to the voicemail message. "You have reached Sophie Wilson at Apex Realty Group. Please leave your name and number and I'll get back to you as soon as possible."

I left a message requesting an appointment for a viewing of Rose's house. No more breaking and entering for me. Sophie quickly returned my call and arranged to show Rose's house that evening. I called my partner in crime, who agreed to meet me there.

WHEN I PULLED into the driveway that evening, Laura stood outside waiting for me, checking her watch and pacing. She wore an ensemble in shades of pink with a matching handbag. "You're late."

"Bad traffic. Nice to see you, too." I fell into step beside her. Sophie was already inside. The lights were on.

Laura shifted her bag on her shoulder nervously. "I've never been inside Rose's house."

"That makes sense since you hated each other," I said.

Laura shot me a reproachful look. "She never hosted parties. Most of the neighbors have *something* at some point: an open house for Christmas, a barbecue for Independence Day, a football championship party. Not Rose Martin. She even turned off the porch light on Halloween, the old witch."

"From what I've heard, I wouldn't let my kid eat any candy that came from her," I said.

"Candy? I'm sure she would have been the type to give out pencils or toothbrushes." At the doorway, Laura hesitated, staring into the house as if it were haunted. "There's an aura of evil in here."

I sniffed. "Actually, I think that's a scented candle."

Sophie fluttered through the rooms, turning on all the lights. "Rose's sister hasn't gotten everything cleared out yet, as you can see. I convinced her to give us an early peek." Boxes stood in clusters and stacks around the edges of the living room.

Laura picked up a framed photo from the top of one of the boxes. "Who keeps an eight-by-ten portrait of themselves on display?"

I took it from her hand. "I've never seen her—alive, I mean." The woman in the photo posed in a style I remembered from the old days of portrait studios, with her chin resting on one hand. She had long, strawberry blond hair that fell over one shoulder. On her wrist dangled an engraved silver bracelet.

"Probably had it taken at Glamour Shots," Laura muttered. She looked around for Sophie, but she was in the other room, turning on more lights. Laura whispered, "You stay with Sophie. I'm going to do a little digging."

I lowered my eyebrows and gave her a concerned look, which she ignored. She slipped out a side door into the garage. I placed the photo back in the open box a moment before Sophie swished back into the room, making expansive hand gestures.

"Rose added a lot of nice upgrades to the place. You're going to love her bathroom."

She led me through the spacious and light-filled bedroom featuring a high tray ceiling. Large picture windows framed a view of a carefully manicured backyard. Rose's sister had already removed all the bedroom furniture except for the mattress and box springs. I made a mental note to tell Laura that there would be no drawers for her to ransack. I opened the closet door and scanned the shelves in search of some overlooked item like Phil's box of receipts but found nothing.

Dutifully, I followed Sophie into the bathroom. Halting at the threshold, I admired the enormous garden tub, frameless glass-enclosed shower, and wide marble vanity with double sinks. "Wow."

"I know, right?" Sophie replied. "This place is going to go fast. If you decide to make an offer, we should act the moment it hits the market."

"Any guess when that might be?"

"Rose's sister told me she'll be back in town this weekend to finish clearing out. I'd guess sometime early next week."

"I'll give it some thought."

"Well don't think too long. It's important to move quickly." Sophie swiveled her head with concern. "Where did Laura get to?"

"Let's take a look at the kitchen," I suggested. Whatever Laura was doing, Sophie probably wouldn't approve.

The kitchen, like the rest of the house, was full of upgrades. "The island cook top has a built-in downdraft vent," Sophie pointed out.

"Rose really invested some money into this place," I commented. Whoever lit the candle had also left a few bottles of chilled water on the counter, so I helped myself.

"Yes, she did. She must have made out all right in her divorce settlement."

Just then, Laura popped into the kitchen from the garage. She had a smudge of dirt on one cheek. When she noticed Sophie, she furtively hid something in her handbag. "So? What do you think?"

"Have you been in the garage this entire time?" Sophie asked.

"Well, I was, um, measuring. Yes. Emma needs storage for her... kayak."

"Thanks, Laura." I gave her a look. *Kayak?* Then, I turned to Sophie. "I like this house. Maybe I'll consider making an offer."

"Great!" Sophie said. "Just let me know. I'm here whenever you're ready, but I'd advise you to act fast. This one won't last long."

ONCE OUT OF earshot and walking back to Laura's house, I asked, "So, what were you doing in the garage?"

"Going through the trash," she answered.

I stopped walking. "Are you kidding?"

Laura pulled a pair of latex gloves from her purse. "I came prepared."

I eyed her, no longer surprised by anything she did. "I wondered why you brought a handbag to a house-showing. Find anything?"

She withdrew a stack of folded papers. "I found some old mail and a pocket calendar. Who keeps a paper calendar these days?"

"Old people." I looked up and saw that we had arrived back at Laura's house. "Let's examine it inside."

We spread out the papers on the floor, since they had been in the trash can prior to discovery, and sat cross-legged on the rug, digging through the pile. I flipped through the paper calendar and read aloud, "Tuesday: broom tune-up. Wednesday: eat small children."

"I don't doubt it," Laura said.

"Hey—this is interesting. She had an appointment with a lawyer the week before she died."

"Could be useful. Wonder if Sam can find out anything about it."

"Because all lawyers know each other?" I asked.

"Exactly. Hey, look—" Laura held up an envelope. Along the top, there was a ragged tear where it had been opened, but the document had been stuffed back inside. "I found a bank statement."

"Bingo," I said. "We can match it to those deposit slips. Any other suspicious-looking deposits?"

Laura held up the paper and examined it closely. "A lot of cash deposits. Guess nobody pays off a blackmailer with a personal check and writes 'blackmail' in the memo line."

"Sure would be helpful if they did."

The whir of the garage door opening made Laura jump. She hastily gathered all the papers into a stack and snatched the calendar out of my hands.

"What the—"

"Jack's home." Laura shoved all the papers inside an oversized basket beside the couch and replaced the throw blankets it held on top of them.

Jack walked in. "Oh, hi, Emma." He surveyed us quizzically. "What are you two doing down there?"

"Yoga," Laura said brightly. She put one arm up in the air and did a side bend. "How was your day?"

"It was fine. I'm going to go make a phone call in the study. Looks like I missed a call from the office while I was driving home, and I want to follow up on it."

"Sure, honey," Laura replied.

After Jack was gone, I said, "What was that all about?"

"I don't want Jack to find out I'm still investigating. He'll fuss at me and tell me to let Sam handle it."

"He has a point. Why don't we take the papers over to Sam's house?"

"You just want an excuse to go visit your boyfriend," she said with a smirk.

"That's just a side benefit. Give me a plastic bag or something, and I'll take them over."

She dug around in a cabinet under the kitchen sink and retrieved a shopping bag labeled "Victoria's Secret."

"No way! I'm not showing up at Sam's house carrying that. Don't you just have a plain, brown grocery bag from Publix like a normal person?"

Laura snorted in amusement. "I was just messing with you. It was too good to pass up. Here's your boring old bag." She shoved a crumpled plastic bag into my hands.

I moved the blankets in the basket and retrieved the paperwork. "I'll head over there right now."

"Fine," Laura said. "Give him a kiss from me."

"No way," I replied. "He's all mine."

Before Jack had time to emerge from the study, I let myself out of Laura's house and walked down the road to Sam's place. I wondered if he'd even be home yet, but when I rounded the corner, I saw an unfamiliar car in his driveway. I started up the walk but stopped when I heard voices coming from the backyard. One was female.

I crept around the side of the house and peeked around the bushes, my heart thumping in my chest so frantically I wondered if it might alert them to my presence. Sam was sitting on the patio with Taylor. They each held a bottle of beer. I watched Sam laugh at something Taylor said. She reached out and touched him on the arm. He covered her hand with his own. I backed away and quietly crossed the grass back to the road where my car was parked. Still clutching the plastic bag, I got in my car and drove home.

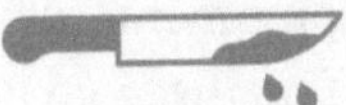

THE NEXT MORNING, I realized I might have been hasty and decided to give Sam another chance. He deserved the benefit of the doubt. I picked up my phone and saw that it was eight o'clock. Maybe I could catch Sam at home before he left for work.

His home phone rang seven or eight times, and I figured I must have missed him. I was about to hang up and try his mobile number when I heard a female voice answer.

"Hello?"

I froze, unsure of what to do.

"Hello?" the woman said again.

I stammered, "Sorry, I must have dialed the wrong number."

"This is Sam Turner's residence," she said.

"Sorry," I repeated and hung up.

The voice sounded like Taylor. I checked the time again. What was she doing at Sam's house at eight in the morning, after she was just there last night?

Then, the truth hit me. *Taylor had never left.*

I HAD to go into the office that day for a meeting and decided to grab an empty cubicle and work from there, hoping it would help me focus. It turned out to be a waste of time. I was completely useless. My helpful mind replayed the scene I'd witnessed the night before—the touch on the arm and the playful, laughing pair. Yes, they'd looked like a couple. I kept rehashing the phone call in my mind, trying to find any other conclusion than the one I'd drawn. It was useless. By late afternoon, it was clear that nothing productive would come of the day, so I decided to call it and head home.

As I drove, I talked to myself. "You've got to get over this, Emma. Whatever you had with Sam was just a fling," I reasoned, but my bruised heart and wounded ego indicated otherwise. "Besides, we never said we were exclusive." My drive was momentarily halted by a stoplight, but my self-talk continued. "In fact, I ought to go home and dress up. I'll put on some makeup. That'll make me feel better. Then, I'll go out somewhere." I glanced around and saw a man in the next car next looking at me strangely. I swiveled my head back, eyes on the road. "Nosy old man. So what if I am talking to myself like a crazy person? I might be on the phone. Ever heard of Bluetooth?" The light turned green, and I sped off, leaving Mr. Looky-loo in the dust.

That gave me the idea of calling Laura. "Hello! What are you up to?"

Her voice barely exceeded the roar of my SUV. "Why are you yelling? Are you in the car?"

"Yes," I hollered.

"Did you stay over at Sam's?"

"No. That didn't work out. What are you doing tonight? I need a wingman."

"I was about to heat up a couple of frozen dinners, but I can stick mine back in the freezer. Where'd you have in mind?"

"Dos Gatos. It's ladies' night."

"Why not someplace closer to home? Is something wrong?"

"We'll talk about it later. Can you pick me up? I'm going to need a designated driver."

"This is sounding less and less like fun, but I can be over there in twenty minutes."

THIRTY MINUTES LATER, Laura and I were sitting side-by-side at a bar. I caught the eye of the bartender.

"Margarita," I demanded. "And give me a shot on the side."

Laura turned to stare at me. "Maybe we should order some food."

The bartender asked her, "And what are you having?"

"Club soda, apparently. And some chips and salsa, please."

"Coming right up," he said, and hurried away.

I followed his retreat with my gaze. "He's not bad."

"What is wrong with you?" Laura asked. "Spill it."

Our drinks arrived, and I slammed the shot. "I can't do this relationship thing with Sam. You can't trust men. Open yourself up, and they turn on you."

"What on earth happened?" She took a sip of her soda without taking her eyes off me.

"I went to Sam's after I left you and found him drinking in the backyard with Taylor. Hot, raven-haired Taylor. They were laughing it up, and she was pawing at him like a bear digging for honey."

"You're kidding!" She sounded suitably offended on my behalf, exactly like a best friend should. "What did you say?"

"Nothing. I walked away before they could spot me."

She had begun to raise her drink to her mouth again, but upon hearing my explanation, she set it down with a thud, sloshing soda over the rim and onto the bar.

"That's it? You walked away?"

"I was too humiliated."

Laura gaped. "You should have confronted him. You could have just walked in there like you own the place, and Taylor would have backed off."

"How can you be so sure?" I asked before taking another gulp of my drink.

"Emma, you always sell yourself short. You are every bit as attractive as Taylor. Anyway, Sam was acting crazy about you before all this."

"I don't know about that. I have no desire to compete with anyone over a man. Especially not with someone who could have played Sandra Bullock's role in *Miss Congeniality*."

"She's not all that."

"Please! Compared to me, she's a supermodel."

Laura held up her hand. "Stop it. Just stop. We need an intervention here."

"No, no, no." I waved my hands to swat away her words like so many pesky flies. "Not that. Anything but that."

"Yes, that. Emma, you haven't had a serious relationship since that short-lived marriage of yours right out of college."

"Which was a mistake."

"I'll say. But it was a bigger mistake not to get back on the horse after you fell off."

"I've been back in the saddle." I wiggled my eyebrows suggestively.

"That's not what I meant. You avoid commitment."

"This is way too deep of a conversation for ladies' night." I signaled the bartender for another drink. "Besides, I didn't tell you the entire story."

"There's more?"

"I was actually going to give him a chance to explain, so I called him this morning. Early. And guess who answered the phone?"

A wrinkle formed between Laura's eyebrows, but she didn't answer.

I gave her the answer anyway. "It was Taylor. Taylor answered Sam's home phone at eight in the morning. She never left last night."

"Are you sure it was Taylor?"

"I recognized her voice."

"Did you confirm it was her?"

"No, I pretended I had the wrong number. Who else could it be? And why does it matter? Any woman answering the phone would still be proof that he's a dog. A lying, cheating dog." I held up a finger. "No, that's an insult to dogs. He's a snake." The bartender slid me a shot of tequila, and I downed it in one gulp.

She pushed the basket of chips toward me. "I think you need to eat. Did you skip lunch?"

"I'll be fine as soon as I get another margarita. And forget about Taylor."

Her expression tightened. "We need to work on your self-esteem."

I squinted at her. "What is this, *Dealing with Feelings*?"

"You are a smart, beautiful woman with a lot to offer."

"You sound just like my little sister." I reluctantly accepted a chip and nibbled.

"Sarah?"

"Yeah." Rather than helping, the alcohol was making me more melancholic. I felt tears threatening at the thought of my baby sister, taken away too soon. "I wish you could have gotten to know her."

"I met her when we moved into the dorm. I remember she looked sadder to leave you than even your parents did. And I remember she used to call you all the time."

"I should have gone home to visit more. She was always asking me to come to her basketball games. I never did. And then she died."

"You couldn't have known that would happen. Nobody knew about her heart."

"She depended on me. I wasn't there for her." I worried that if I started crying, I wouldn't stop. "Next month will be the anniversary of her death—fourteen years."

"Emma, I'm genuinely worried about you." She put her hand on my arm.

I trusted Laura, but even more than a decade later, it was difficult to talk about Sarah. I shook off her hand and decided to change the subject. "What we need is to dance it out." I tilted my head and let the thumping bass wash over me—wash away all those maudlin feelings. I didn't want to think anymore. "Come on. Let's go dance. They're playing 'The Thong Song.'"

She frowned and shook her head, so I left her at the bar and went to the dance floor alone. The bass thumped, and I shook my body in rhythm, or what I thought was rhythm. I attempted to twerk while I sang along about moving my butt.

Laura covered her eyes.

I decided to ignore her and mindlessly continued my gyrations. A pack of girls joined me on the dance floor when the DJ began to play "Truth Hurts" by Lizzo. Their voices could be heard over the music, singing along, and I joined in with all the enthusiasm a heartbroken drunk girl could muster.

When music shifted to deep house, most of the crowd on the floor drifted back to the bar, but I remained. Closing my eyes, I began to sway. When my head started to spin, I opened them again. A swarthy guy with a five o'clock shadow loomed over me. I stumbled, and he reached out to steady me.

"Need a partner?" His hand moved to my waist.

I was feeling good, and a man was paying attention to me. Even if he did look a little greasy, I didn't mind. *Screw Sam.* I wanted to lose myself and forget everything. The stranger's lips moved, but I couldn't hear what he said, so I just smiled and kept dancing.

When the song ended, Laura approached me and took my hand. "I need to steal her for a minute."

"I'll be waiting," he said, but his eyes immediately scanned the room for my replacement.

Laura pulled me toward the exit. "I think we need to go home," she said.

"You're a lousy mingwan, I mean wingman," I said.

With an exasperated huff, she dragged me out the door.

thirteen

THE NEXT MORNING, I didn't feel empowered, I felt empty. I glanced around and realized I was in Laura's guest room. Hopper was spread out on the bed beside me.

There was a tentative knock on the door before Laura pushed it open and poked her head around to check on me. "You're up! How're you feeling?"

"Like crap," I said, clutching my forehead. "Do you have to speak so loudly?"

"Sorry." She plopped down beside me on the edge of the mattress.

I cringed as the movement jostled my head, which felt in danger of falling off my neck. I peered at Laura through gritty eyes. "How badly did I embarrass myself last night?"

"Not too much," she lied. She held a neatly folded stack of clothing on her lap. "I brought you something clean to wear. When you're ready, I made coffee."

"Coffee. Yes. Thanks, Laura. You're the best."

"You've taken care of me more than once. That's what best friends do." She patted my arm and left, closing the door gently behind her.

A shower and a change of clothes went a long way towards

improving my outlook. Some ibuprofen from the medicine cabinet also helped. I shuffled to the kitchen in search of caffeine.

Laura stood at the dining room table, folding laundry. After letting Hopper out into Laura's backyard, I poured myself a cup of coffee and refilled hers before sitting down across from her. "I've made a decision."

"What decision is that?"

I raised my mug in a toast. "I am a strong, independent woman, and I am not going to forget that fact from now on."

She tapped my mug gently with her own, careful not to slosh. "Whatever you say."

"I'm serious," I said. "We are intelligent women. We are problem solvers."

"Yes, we are." She resumed folding laundry. Evidently, Jack was a boxers man.

"We can figure out who killed Rose," I continued. "We always made a good team."

"That's true. But are you referring to situations like a campus scavenger hunt? Because I'm not sure that applies to our current situation." She folded a white T-shirt into a perfect little square.

I paused, momentarily distracted by her precision. "Actually, I think the same principles apply."

When she lifted a lightweight floral jacket from the pile, something fluttered out of a pocket onto the tile floor.

"What's that?" I bent to retrieve the object. At first glance, I thought it was a credit card, but upon closer examination, I determined that it was a customer loyalty card. The teal background of the card contrasted with the white logo: *ParkCLT* crisscrossed with a swooping airplane graphic. "This looks like a repeat-use parking card. I think CLT must be the code for the Charlotte airport."

Laura took it from my hand. "Oh, I found that during the estate sale at Phil's house. It must have gone through the wash in my pocket."

I raised an eyebrow at her. "How did it get in your pocket?"

Laura met my gaze with wide, innocent eyes. "Well, I had just spotted this card-thing on the floor in the master bedroom closet when that mean woman asked us to leave, so I stuck it in my pocket. I have no idea if it means anything. It just looked out of place. I forgot about it until now."

I narrowed my eyes. "You say you found this in Phil's closet?"

"Yes, on the floor. Actually, it was in his former wife's closet."

I opened the sliding glass door to let Hopper back in. "Did Phil travel frequently to Charlotte?"

"No, his health was poor. But his daughter did."

"Alice?"

"Yes. She works in sales and marketing, I think."

"A job like that might require frequent travel," I speculated. "Do you think this card belongs to Alice?"

Laura took the card from me and turned it over in her hands. "Could be, if she was going through clothes in her mother's closet."

I tried to envision the scenario. "Sounds plausible. She might have been trying things on, deciding what to keep, and this fell out of her pocket."

Laura handed the card back to me. "Okay. But why is this significant?"

"Something about what Mindy told me at her party has been bothering me ever since. She mentioned that Alice left abruptly—sooner than planned."

"Why did she leave so abruptly?" Laura paused before adding, "And why would it matter?"

"If Alice was in town, she would make a good suspect. We need to find out if Alice was truly gone or if she was still in town at the time of the murder. Maybe she found out about Rose and her father. That would give her a motive. We want the police to investigate someone other than you, Laura. If we can throw another suspect their way, that might help your case."

"Okay, but Mindy said she was gone. Alice must have told the police she was in Charlotte," Laura said.

I pointed at Laura. "What's the first thing you do when you fly home?"

"Rehydrate."

I covered my forehead with one hand briefly before continuing. "No, I mean, after you land, you collect your luggage, and then what?

You retrieve your car. But Alice left her valet ticket here. I want to call the parking company and ask them about it." I held it up. "I could call, pretending to be Alice, and claim I needed a receipt for my business records. Tell them to check their records and see if they recorded my exit from the parking lot."

"I like it," said Laura. She consulted her wristwatch. "Think we could call now?"

"Let's give it a shot."

"I should be the one to call," insisted Laura. "Alice Mayhew is a rich, corporate executive, and I can cultivate that type of voice."

"A money voice?"

"Exactly."

"If she's such a bigwig, why wouldn't her assistant be making this call?" I pointed out.

"I guess you're right. Let's decide together what to say. We need a script." We sat down at the kitchen table, and Laura grabbed a long, skinny notepad. At the top, someone had scribbled "toilet paper."

I handed her a pen. "Cross that out. We don't want you getting confused."

Laura rolled her eyes. "Be serious. First, I'll identify myself as Alice Mayhew's assistant. I'll say that I want to find out if they have a record of my boss's recent visit, because I'm compiling her travel receipts."

"Why wouldn't she know that information already?" I asked.

"Maybe Alice travels so much, she lost track. She's obviously a bad record keeper. I'll put it on speakerphone." Laura flipped the card over and dialed the number on the back. She tapped zero to bypass the automated menu and speak to a real person.

A customer service agent with a deep Southern accent said, "Thank you for callin' Charlotte Douglas Parking Services. My name is Rebecca. May I have your first and last name, please?"

Laura's eyes widened. We hadn't planned for that. I shrugged, and she stammered, "G-good morning. My name is..." She glanced at the notepad with our script. "Tully Piper."

I covered my eyes with both hands.

"Hello, Miz Piper. How may I help you today?"

"Yes, I'm the executive assistant for Ms. Alice Mayhew. I'm

attempting to reconcile her travel receipts, and I don't seem to have a record of her parking expenses for her August trip from Jacksonville International to Charlotte. I wonder if you could look up the charges for her parking time. I have her ParkCLT account number here."

"May I have the account number, please?"

Laura flipped the card over again and read the digits on the front aloud.

A silence fell, broken only by the tap-tap-tap of a keyboard. "We have a record here for long-term parking from August first through the twenty-third. My! That was a long stay, wasn't it?"

"Quite." Laura scribbled down the dates on her notepad.

"The total charge was one hundred sixty-two dollars. Is that all the information you needed?"

"Yes, thank you."

"Is there anything else I can help you with today?"

"No, thank you."

"Well, then. You have a nice day." The way she said it sounded like "nass day."

"Thank you." Laura hung up and looked at me. "Alice could have been here when the murder took place."

"That's nass."

"Be serious."

I started thinking, and something didn't add up. "All that tells us is that her car was parked in Charlotte. She could have been anywhere. Maybe we could try calling the airline."

"Which airline? We don't know anything about her travel plans."

"Some executive assistant you are, Tully Piper."

Laura sighed at my pathetic attempt at humor. "Let's get back to the facts. Alice did not retrieve her car from Charlotte Airport until August twenty-third, which means she could have still been here."

"But Mindy told me that Alice left abruptly instead of staying until the estate sale as planned. So, where did she go?"

"Wherever she went, it wasn't the airport." Laura said. "All we know is that she wasn't in Charlotte on the night of the murder. It doesn't tell us where she actually was."

I sighed. She was right. "Let's put a pin in this and focus on your neighbors. Let me read that binder. We are going to figure out this mystery and clear your name one way or another."

Laura retrieved the book and angled it so that I could look at it with her. "I've been going over the list of names. Some of the people on this list had actual violations of the neighborhood covenants. I compared Rose's list with this printout I got from our neighborhood management company."

"What kind of violations?"

Laura ran her finger down the column. "This person had more than seven potted plants in front of her house."

My eyebrows knitted together, and I inspected the column her finger indicated. "That's a real rule?"

"Yep. Right in the covenants. Most board members would never think of enforcing it. Leave it to Rose to actually count the plants in someone's yard."

I shook my head. "That's crazy."

"That's Rosie."

"Have you found any discrepancies?"

"I found a long list of dates beside Ed and Mindy's address, but no specific violations indicated. Just a list of dates. That's not according to procedure." She held up the official printout. "The neighborhood management company keeps a record of the date a violation notice was sent, any follow-up notices sent, the resident's response, and the date the violation was corrected. Rose's list only includes the names. We might be heading down the wrong path by assuming these are all HOA related."

"So, there's no way to tell what they did to end up on Rose's list?" I asked.

She crossed her arm and exhaled. "No. I was certain Rose had a scheme of some sort."

"Keeping a list of names is sketchy, but it's not proof of anything. It doesn't tell us if they were fines or just people she didn't like."

"I could talk to Mindy," Laura suggested. "Ask her if she was aware of any violation notices or fines."

"Wouldn't she think that was unusual?"

She shrugged. "I'm detail oriented. It's part of the job."

I rested my hand on her shoulder. "Why does this position mean so much to you? It's a pain-in-the-ass, thankless job."

"I don't expect you to understand," she said, and returned her attention to the binder. "So, we've got Ed, Mindy, Miranda, and Steve. What about the rest of these names? Were they all paying Rose? Was she really blackmailing them?"

I examined the list. "That seems like too many names. Can you guess what their connection might be?"

"There's no way of knowing." She rested her chin on folded hands. "But maybe I can come up with something."

"What about Ed and Miranda? Remember, I saw them arguing at the game-watching party."

"They live next door to each other. Maybe they were arguing about whatever next-door neighbors argue about. Maybe Miranda's annoying little accessory dog pooped in Ed's yard."

"Accessory dog?"

"Yes, Miranda has a yippy little Chihuahua that she carries around in a designer handbag."

Leaning back in my chair, I pictured it. "Somehow, that fits her image perfectly."

Laura nodded in agreement. "I'm sure she thinks so."

"I still can't get over how old her husband looks," I said, shaking my head.

"Yeah, she's a trophy wife. But they have a prenup."

"More neighborhood gossip?"

"From a reliable source. The point is that Miranda's husband is old but rich, and she can't leave him without giving up her lifestyle."

"And Ed lives next door. Could he be visiting her to borrow a cup of sugar?"

"You could call it that. He and Mindy don't exactly resonate happiness," Laura said. "So, we've got two unhappy couples on Rose's list. If she somehow found out through her spiderweb of intrigue that Ed and Miranda were cheating on their spouses, she could get them to buy her silence."

"Miranda wouldn't want to risk breaking up her marriage. And I guess Ed wouldn't either, although I'm not sure why. He treats Mindy like a servant."

"Good servants are hard to find, and Mindy's probably a lot easier to live with than Miranda ever would be." Laura shook her head. "Not that she'd ever marry a handyman, no matter how handy he was."

"How are we going to find out anything more? The cops need evidence."

"Ed's house backs up to the same creek as mine. He could have thrown that knife out in the marsh. Wish it had some fingerprints on it."

"Do you think Miranda could have stabbed Rose? The first night I met her at that neighborhood party, she sounded like she hated her."

"I wouldn't put it past her." Laura tapped her lips with a finger. "We should do some surveillance of Miranda and Ed."

"Surveillance?" I squinted at her suspiciously. "That wouldn't require disguises again, would it?"

"No, we could just follow her."

"Mindy said Ed did some handyman work at Miranda's house."
Laura snickered. "I'll bet."

"One of us could pretend we're going to hire Ed and ask Miranda for a reference," I suggested. "She could show us the shelves he built."

"But he probably didn't actually build any shelves," Laura pointed out.

"Guess you're right. But we could ask anyway. She doesn't realize we suspect anything."

"Worth a shot," Laura said. "If I see her out walking that bedazzled rodent she calls a dog, I'll ask her."

"That's harsh, Laura. It's not the dog's fault."

"You might be right, but the little rat is awfully noisy for such a small creature."

I checked the time. "Guess I'd better scoot." I stood and bent to hug Laura. "Thanks for taking care of me last night."

She walked me to the door. "I'm always here for you. But maybe you could consider giving Sam another chance? Or at least talking to him about what you saw?"

I crossed my arms. "No way. I'm going home. I'll keep digging for useful information about our suspects. I am a strong, independent woman—remember?"

She gave me a condescending pat. "Of course, you are, sweetie."

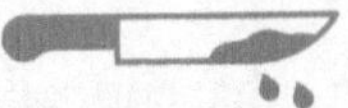

THE NEXT MORNING, Laura arrived with a bakery bag in hand. After letting herself in and helping herself to coffee, she peered at my laptop, surrounded by notes. "Is this the research you said you were going to do, or are you working?"

"Yes, I'm working for you. I'm doing a public records search on the principle suspects you found in the binder."

She peered at the computer screen. "Sure you shouldn't ask Sam to help you with this?"

"I don't need his help," I said indignantly. "I'm going to put my considerable talent with technology to work on your behalf."

Laura claimed the chair beside me. "All righty, then. Let's get to it. Why don't you Google 'real murderer'?"

"I doubt that will lead us to anything we want to see."

"So, what is it that we are looking for?"

"Public records. Amazing what you can learn on the internet."

On a website called "Florida Parcels," I found the sales date, price, name of occupants, as well as the occupants' birthdates and political party affiliations.

"Creepy," Laura said. "Guess all that information Rose kept wasn't actually hard to come by."

"It would have been less accessible back when she began keeping records. At present, however, personal information is only a click away."

I went to real estate sites and found dates of sale, sale prices, and tax information.

"I'm going to check out property tax records."

"Enter Rose's address and see what you can find."

"Thanks. That's helpful," I deadpanned. I typed in the street address and found the taxable value of Rose's house, the amount paid for it, and the dates on which it changed hands. "The first owners are listed as Paul and Rose Martin. Then, in 1995, ownership changed to Rose Martin alone."

"Guess that's when they got the divorce."

"No, it says 'deceased,'" I said.

"Paul is dead?"

"Just a rumor. I listened to that entire Beatles album backwards."

Laura looked confused. "What are you babbling about?"

"I thought—never mind. So, Rose's husband, Paul, died in 1995?"

"Looks that way."

"I didn't realize that. Guess Bina didn't, either."

"That surprises me. She seemed to know more about Rose than most folks around here."

"Hey—look up Phil's address."

"What is it again?" I asked.

"It's 2120 Beach Hammock Road. I would think you'd remember the place we got arrested."

"Fair point. Let's check it out."

When I entered the address into Google, the first thing that popped up was the real estate listing, followed by the estate sale. All the pictures of the ugly furniture showed up as well. I followed the link to the real estate listing.

"It says 'highly motivated seller.' Wonder what that's all about?"

"Probably just real estate lingo. Thinking about making an offer?"

I snorted. "Doubtful. Still feels like the Murder House to me."

"Look at the sales and tax records."

I scrolled down to where it listed the owners and sellers. The only transaction was in 1989 when the original developer sold the house to Phillip Mayhew.

"Let's go to the county tax collector website and enter the street address."

We scrolled through the page until reaching the bottom, where a big red box caught our eye. It read "Prior Years Taxes Due."

"Looks like Phil owed some back taxes." Absently, I reached for the bakery bag, dipped my hand inside, and pulled out a muffin. I took a small bite before jerking my face away in disgust. "What *is* that?"

"It's their new keto muffins," Laura said. "I'm watching my carbs."

"I'm pretty sure there's no carbs in sawdust," I said, taking a swig of coffee to wash away the taste in my mouth.

"You could watch your carbs, you know," she said.

"What for?" I asked.

"For Sam?" she said. "Have you considered that you might have jumped to conclusions about him and Taylor?"

"It doesn't matter. I've come to my senses. I don't need the headache."

Laura raised her hand to stop me. "You're doing it again, Emma. Every time you get close to having a relationship, you find something wrong with the guy."

"I do not."

"Do too." She reached for a muffin and peeled off a third of the wrapper. "What about that guy from work?"

"Bad idea. You should never date a coworker."

She peeled away another third of the muffin cup. "And the one you met at the library?"

"He had bad breath."

"And the guy from the gym?"

"Body odor."

"Of course, he did. He was at the gym." She pulled the last bit off and tossed it on the desk.

I eyed it warily. She must be upset if she was littering. "I didn't realize you were keeping such close tabs on my social life."

"I'm your best friend. It comes with the job." Evidently unable to let trash lay on the table for more than five seconds, she folded it up into a tiny square. "How about that great-looking guy from Jack's office? The one with the hair."

"He was a cat person."

"Heaven forbid," Laura exclaimed, fanning herself like a shocked spinster aunt. "Why is that a problem?"

"Everybody knows that cat people and dog people are incompatible."

Laura grabbed my hand and gave it a gentle squeeze. "Emma, Sam is a handsome man with a solid job, his own home, and no cats. And despite what you saw or think you saw, he's crazy about you. What is it going to take to convince you?"

"A sign from God," I said.

Laura sighed. "Good luck with that."

I turned back to my computer. "Can we get back to work, please?"

Laura stood. "I'll leave you to it. Text me if you find anything." I watched as she walked toward the door with Hopper following at her heels. She bent to scratch him behind his ears. "I'm wondering if you might have jumped to conclusions. Like when people don't know Hopper, and they assume he's vicious because he's part pit bull."

"That's completely different." I glanced at Hopper, who was now laying on his back with all four legs in the air, angling for a belly rub.

"Not really. They're judging based on preconceived notions. Just because one dog bites doesn't mean other dogs will."

I put my hands on my hips. "What are you saying? Is this a metaphor?"

She looked up at me from where she crouched, obligingly rubbing Hopper's belly. "Ryan hurt you, but that doesn't mean all men can't be trusted."

I flinched, feeling as if I'd been struck. "There is no comparison. Besides, I'm fine the way I am."

She stood to her feet and smiled sadly. "You know, Emma, if you never take any chances, nothing will ever change."

"That's what I'm counting on," I said.

THE NEXT TIME I got in my car, I spotted the bag full of envelopes Laura collected from Rose's house lying forgotten on the floorboard. We needed to look through them. Reluctantly, I admitted that we also needed to turn them over to Laura's defense attorney, despite him being *persona non grata*.

I picked up the phone and dialed Sam.

"Hey there, Emma," he said in his Southern accent before I'd even spoken.

Damn. I was a sucker for that drawl. *Be strong.* "Hi, Sam. I'm just calling to tell you that Laura might have some evidence. We asked Sophie to show us Rose's house, and Laura collected some mail from the trash. It's a bunch of bank statements."

"She stole Rose's bank statements?" he said incredulously.

Though I didn't always agree with Laura's actions, I felt the need to defend her. "They were in the trash. Laura compared them to the binder Rose's nephew gave her and found a match."

"Have they ever heard of a shredder? I guess I'll swing by her house after work." He hesitated, and then the drawl returned. "Will I see you there?"

"I'm not sure. Gotta run." I ended the call without waiting for a response.

As I DROVE to Laura's house later that afternoon, ominous clouds were gathering on the horizon before me. Florida residents could depend upon almost daily afternoon thunderstorms during the late days of summer. Glancing in my rearview mirror, I saw the sky behind me was clear and brilliant blue. Weird. Even the weather confirmed that turning around would be a more pleasant option than showing up at Laura's and confronting Sam.

I arrived late for the meeting to find them already gathered around Laura's kitchen table. Ever the polite hostess, she had set out fancy napkins and a plate of cheese straws, as if we were having a party instead of meeting with her lawyer. Nevertheless, I was hungry. There was no need to let perfectly good cheese straws go to waste.

Sam, on the other hand, got right down to business. "Emma said you found something while you were snooping around Rose's house."

"We weren't snooping. We were investigating," Laura said. She gave me an unhappy look, as if I were the one who used the objectionable word. I held my hands up, one holding a half-eaten cheese straw, demonstrating my innocence.

"I'm sorry," Sam said, but his voice didn't sound sorry. He sounded tired. "What did you find when you were *investigating*?"

Laura said, "*Hmph,*" but she obliged him with an answer. "The recycling bin was full of old paperwork Gwen had cleaned out of Rose's house. Some of them were bank statements, so I slipped them in my handbag."

Sam shook his head. "Maybe you should keep my services on retainer if you plan to continue in this life of crime."

I snorted in laughter before remembering that I was mad at Sam. *Mr. Turner,* I mentally corrected.

Laura placed the box of deposit slips on the table. "We found these at the Mayhew estate sale."

"Found them?" Sam said.

"Yes. In the closet. The account number matches the bank statements I collected at Rose's house," Laura said in a business-like tone.

"Collected?" Sam repeated.

"Stop that," Laura said, giving Sam a reproachful look. "Yes, collected."

"The fact that the numbers match proves that Phil paid Rose regularly. We don't know why he was paying her, however," I said.

"Could have been blackmail," Laura interjected. "There are other names on her list that don't match up with official HOA records of covenant infractions."

"What are the other names?" Sam asked.

"Ed Rivers and Miranda Fox are on the top of the list," Laura said.

Sam looked at me. "Emma saw those two arguing during the FSU game."

"That's right. Mindy told me Ed had been doing some work at Miranda's house, but she didn't say what," I said.

"I bet I can guess what kind of work Ed is doing over there," Laura said, her green eyes twinkling with amusement.

Sam snorted. "Ed and Miranda?"

"She's got that wrinkly, old husband," I said.

"But, Ed?"

"He's conveniently located right next door," Laura said. "Also, he's extremely muscular."

"Let's get back to the point." Sam tapped his finger on the stack of ripped-open envelopes. "Phil paid Rose hundreds of thousands of dollars. But Phil's dead. How does that get us any closer to Rose's killer?"

"How did Phil die?" I asked.

"Heart attack," Laura said. "At least, that's what I heard."

"Let's confirm that," Sam said, starting a list on his legal pad. "And look into Ed Rivers and Miranda Fox. I'll put Taylor on it."

"That Taylor sure is handy," I said bitterly.

Sam searched my face in confusion.

Thunder rumbled outside. Out the window, I could see the trees behind Laura's house swaying in the wind, and the sky had turned a threatening shade of gray. Abruptly, I stood up. "I've got to go. I don't want to get caught in that storm." I grabbed one more cheese straw for the road, hugged Laura's shoulders, and headed for the door.

I heard the shuffling of papers behind me. "I'd like to study these some more, Laura," Sam said. "Mind if I take them with me?"

I heard her say, "No problem," before I slammed the door behind me.

I was desperately searching for my keys in my purse, but the wind kept blowing my hair in my face. Behind me, I heard Sam's voice. "Wait up, Emma."

Where are those damn keys? "What?" I felt the first sprinkles of rain on my face.

"What's wrong? Did I do something?" he asked.

"No. I just wish you'd be honest with me."

"About what? I have been honest."

"About Taylor." I dropped my purse on the hood of my SUV with a thump so that I could dig through it with both hands. I really needed to upgrade to something with keyless entry.

"What about Taylor?"

"You two seem pretty cozy." *Ha!* I found the keys at last and jammed them into the lock.

"Cozy? Taylor and I are coworkers. That's all."

I opened the door and attempted to close it, but Sam grabbed it firmly and stopped the motion. "Let go," I demanded. The rain started falling harder.

"Not until you tell me what's wrong." Rain streamed down his face unheeded.

"What's wrong? I'm getting soaked. I need to go home now. Good night, Sam."

He raised his hands in surrender. I slammed the door and drove away.

THE NEXT MORNING, my phone rang. I looked down at the caller ID and saw it was Sam. I didn't feel ready for a confrontation, but I answered anyway. "Hello?"

"Hey there," he said. "I wanted to talk about what happened last night."

I inhaled deeply and launched into the speech I had rehearsed as I lay awake into the wee hours of the night, staring at the ceiling fan. "Sam, I think it's better if we take a step back. I think you need to concentrate on Laura's defense, and I need to focus on helping my friend."

When he didn't respond for a moment, I prompted, "Sam?"

He cleared his throat. "I'm here. Where did this come from? I'm doing my best for Laura. You know that. I thought we had the beginnings of a good thing. What did I do?"

"Nothing. I want to keep our relationship on a professional level only."

"Geez, Emma." I heard him exhale sharply. "Don't you think it's a little late for that?"

"I'm sorry."

"I am, too." He was silent for a moment, and I thought he'd hung up.

"Sam?"

"Goodbye, Emma."

I dropped the phone, rested my elbows on my knees, and covered my face with my hands. Hopper approached me and nudged my elbow with his big, wet nose. I reached out and stroked his smooth head. "It's okay, boy. You're all I need." I bent down and buried my face in his fur.

fourteen

WHEN I FINISHED with work for the day, I headed to Laura's place for a listening ear and a shoulder to cry on. I was relieved to see that Jack's car wasn't in the driveway. I needed some girl talk.

She immediately wrapped her arms around me. "I'm glad you called me, sweetie. I made something to cheer you up."

She led me to the kitchen where a plate of chocolate cupcakes waited. "You made me carbs?" I put both hands to my cheeks and gaped in shock. "I can't believe it."

She shrugged. "You sounded pretty down on the phone. Chocolate seemed in order."

We sat across from each other at the table. I chose a cupcake and began to peel off the paper liner. "Sam called today. I told him I wanted to keep things on a professional level."

Laura picked a small chunk off the side of her cupcake. "Professional?"

"We still need to be able to work together on your team." I licked the creamy vanilla frosting off the top.

Laura handed me a napkin. "What was his response to that?"

"He wasn't happy, but the call didn't last very long after that."

"You did it over the phone?"

"I thought I'd better get it out of the way, since he's supposed to come over here tonight and I'll have to face him."

"I still think you should have confronted him about what you saw."

"I hate confrontation."

"I know, but you could be wrong. It has been known to happen." Laura stood. "I'm going to get some water. Want some?"

"Sure. Thanks." I popped the last bite of cupcake in my mouth and chewed pensively. "I can't think of another explanation for what I saw."

She handed me a glass of water and sat back down. "That's why you'd ask for one."

"What does it matter? If he were to come up with some alternate story about what happened, how would I know it was the truth? I saw what I saw. Eyes don't lie."

She pushed the plate toward me. "Want another one?"

I held up my hands. "No, I'm good."

"Then, I've got something else to show you. Something I've been working on. Might take your mind off things." She pushed her chair out. "It's in the laundry room."

"The laundry room? Why there?"

She led me down the hallway. "I didn't want Jack to see it, and that's one place he never goes."

The washer and dryer were in a narrow room connecting the house to the garage. She flipped the switch, illuminating the space with cool fluorescent light. A corkboard hung on the wall opposite the washer and dryer. A large map of Harbor Shores dominated the board, and string connected photos and other slips of paper tacked up with thumbtacks on the periphery.

"Oh my god—you made a murder board." On closer inspection, I noticed that a sculpted daisy topped each of the pushpins, and in lieu of the red string shown on TV detective shows, the connections were formed by a quarter inch floral ribbon. I stepped back, amazed. "You went with a floral theme?"

She straightened one of the photos. "There's no reason my *investigation* board can't be pretty."

I examined her "investigation board" more closely. Along the east border of the neighborhood, a wavy blue curve on the map represented the creek running behind Laura's, Miranda's, and Ed's houses. Beneath this, Laura had pinned a photo of the knife. "How'd you get an evidence photo from the police?"

She followed my gaze and shook her head. "Oh, it's not. They said what kind of knife they found, so I looked it up on the internet and printed out a stock photo."

At the center of the board—dead center, if you will—was an enlarged map of Harbor Shores. Photos around the periphery were connected to the neighborhood map by a ribbon leading to their house. I traced a line with my finger, following the trail. "Who are all these people?"

"Photos of the people on Rose's list." She looked quite proud of herself.

I touched the photos. The texture of inkjet paper told me she had printed them at home as well. "Where'd you get them all?"

"I lifted most of them off Facebook. Miranda's was on Instagram." Laura rolled her eyes. "You wouldn't believe how many selfies that woman takes! And when she's not posting selfies, she's posting pictures of her dog, that little Chihuahua rat."

"And the map of Harbor Shores came from?"

"The HOA office, of course."

I crossed my arms and leaned back against the washing machine. "So, give me a tour. What connections have you found?"

"Right away, by looking at the photos lined up like that, I noticed that most of them were elderly."

"Seems mean of Rose to pick on them."

"That's just it; I don't think she did. I talked to each of them, pretending I was doing some kind of informal survey, asking them about their experiences with the HOA under my direction and Rose's. Nobody had any complaints. It was weird."

"I thought everybody hated Rose."

She shrugged. "Maybe it's just the younger residents."

I made a rolling gesture with my hand. "Continue, please."

"Oh, right. So, I asked them questions like how they like living here, when they bought their house, and most of them had lived here for fifteen to twenty years."

"Did you carry a clipboard?" I asked.

"Don't interrupt. I talked to Walter Clark. He's such a grump. All he does is complain, complain, complain. Anyway, he mentioned that things were starting to need repairs around the house, since he'd lived there so long. I told him Ed Rivers runs a handyman service, and he said he already knew that because he'd hired him, but he wasn't pleased with the work."

"Mindy said a lot of the neighbors use his services. Miranda, for one." I snickered. "Which services, she didn't specify."

Laura looked ready to burst. "That's the connection."

"What?"

"These people all hired Ed to fix something in their house."

"Why's Ed on the list, then?"

She pointed to the copy of the original list tacked to the bottom right of the board. "Well, he's at the top of the list. Maybe his name is the header."

"Did you ask what kind of work they were having done?"

"After I talked to Walter, I backtracked and asked people about the condition of their houses. Besides the small things, many of them were doing kitchen or bath remodels." She pointed out the hot pink sticky notes attached beneath each photo designating which repair each resident had paid for written in large letters.

I pointed to one of the photos. "Why is Phillip Mayhew on here? Why not Alice?"

"Rose was killed before Alice Mayhew hired him. If Phillip's on the list, he must've hired Ed before he died."

"Hired him to do what, specifically?" I tapped the photo of Phil. "Is there a way to find out what he had done?"

"I looked at the real estate listing." Laura indicated a piece of paper tacked beneath the photo of the recently deceased Phillip Mayhew and read aloud. "It says 'updated kitchen.'"

I noticed she'd also tacked a printout of Mr. Mayhew's obituary. There was also a news clipping from a Charlotte newspaper. Recalling that Mr. Mayhew had been a retired government official, I leaned in to read the newsprint. Cause of death was reported to be pulmonary disease.

The rumble of the garage door caused Laura to jump. With a tug of two ribbons, a length of color-coordinated fabric rolled down to cover the corkboard.

Stunned by her ingenuity, I asked, "Is that a Roman shade?"

She made a shooing motion toward the door. "Let's get out of here before Jack comes inside."

We scurried out of the laundry room and settled back in the kitchen. Jack shuffled in, taking no notice of us. Dumping his laptop bag in a chair, he rolled his shoulders and rubbed his stubbled chin.

"Long day?" Laura angled her cheek up to receive a kiss.

Jack put his arm around her and complied. "It was tiring. Lots of meetings."

"Oh?" She pursed her lips to one side. "Well, we've got one more meeting tonight. Sam's coming over soon."

The doorbell rang before she'd even finished the statement. Jack loosened his tie. "Guess I'll go."

Laura picked up the laptop bag and hung it on a hook near the door.

Nervousness flooded through me at the thought of facing Sam. I needed something to do. "How about if I make some coffee?" I hurried away from the table and huddled in the corner where Laura kept her coffee making accoutrements. I sensed his presence the moment Sam entered the room.

"Evenin', Laura." He paused before adding, "Emma." Sam's demeanor towards me was cool, but I could tell his grave expression was due to something more serious than relationship problems. Whatever he had to say, it couldn't be good.

I glanced over my shoulder and muttered, "Hello," before returning my focus to scooping coffee into the basket of Laura's fancy coffee maker. Once I'd filled the reservoir with water, there was little to do but wait. I busied myself with gathering mugs, spoons, and sweetener. I arranged them on a tray while I eavesdropped on the conversation at the table.

Chairs scraped against the floor as Jack and Sam joined Laura. "Would you like a cupcake?" she asked.

"No thanks. I think we'd better get right down to business. I have a buddy over at the DA's office that says the cops have new evidence."

"What kind of evidence?" Jack asked.

"They have some kind of witness," Sam said. "Any idea who that might be, Laura?"

"Witness to what? I didn't do it." Laura's voice sounded high-pitched and panicked. I briefly considered that coffee might not have been a good idea, but by then it was too late. The machine gurgled and beeped to signal the brew was ready.

I carried the tray to the table, deeply inhaling the fortifying smell of coffee. A rumbling sound outside made me glance out the window as I crossed the kitchen. Dark, ominous clouds were forming above the picturesque setting of Laura's backyard. Another Florida thunderstorm was on its way. I handed Laura a mug which she clutched tightly, as if it could somehow give her strength along with the warmth.

Sam waved off my offer of a cup. "Could be someone who over-heard you say something. Who knows? Anyway, together with the murder weapon and your arrest report, they think they have enough to get an indictment. According to my source, they're presenting it to the prosecutor soon. You should be prepared for the possibility."

"Soon?"

"If the state attorney thinks the sheriff's department has a good case, they're going to take it to the grand jury."

"Why?" Laura asked.

"The grand jury doesn't follow the same rules of evidence as a regular trial. The prosecutor can introduce only the facts and scenarios that they want the jury to hear. You can't be present, and I can't defend you there. They have the advantage."

Laura looked down at her shaking hands, causing the coffee in her mug to slosh like stormy seas. She set down the cup with an audible *thunk*. "That's not fair."

"That's just how it is." Sam reached out and placed his hand over one of hers.

"How long do I have before this happens?" she asked in a whisper.

"The grand jury meets in two weeks," Sam said in a low tone of voice.

"Two weeks?" I interjected loudly. "We need to identify the actual killer."

"I have my investigator working overtime, trying to dig up stuff on Rose and whoever she might have run up against. It's a long list. The woman had a lot of enemies."

"Overtime, huh?"

Sam turned to me with a questioning look.

"Never mind," I said. "Let's focus on Laura's defense."

He wagged his head as if to clear it and went on. "I stopped by the property management company's office yesterday and spoke to Amy, the liaison for Harbor Shores. She's always friendly, and she wanted to chat. So, I was just there, sitting on the edge of her desk, shootin' the breeze. I had to drop off an architectural approval form for some new land-scaping I'm fixin' to put in. Anyway, Amy said some detectives stopped by the office recently. They asked for copies of the minutes from the meetings of the Harbor Shores board of directors. They specifically asked for the period of time when Laura and Rose's terms overlapped. I didn't like the sound of that." He focused his gaze on Laura. "Can you think of anything they might find in there?"

Laura bit her lip the way she always did when she was deep in thought. "Towards the end, we did a lot of verbal sparring. Arguments over small stuff, like what kind of mailboxes everyone should have, or her insistence that we should fine residents fifty dollars every time they leave their trash can out too long."

"I can't believe I almost let you talk me into moving here," I said.

Sam cut me off. "Did the arguments get heated?"

"Maybe once or twice."

"Come on, Laura. Are you holding out on me? I need you to tell me what they're going to find."

"I'm not sure," she said, but she squirmed uncomfortably.

"Did you ever threaten Rose Martin?"

"Yes," Laura whispered.

Sam swore. "Amy said she stonewalled the cops by telling them she had to talk to her supervisor before giving non-residents access to neigh-borhood documents. But she also let it slip that they keep audio record-ings of all meetings."

Laura's eyes shifted nervously back and forth, as if seeking an escape route.

"You knew that, Laura," I said.

"Of course, I knew. I'm the president. But I thought Amy erased them once she transcribed everything."

"Nope," Sam replied. "Now the cops are coming back with a search warrant, and they know exactly what to ask for. Someone tipped them off. How was your relationship with the other members of the board?"

"Pleasant, for the most part." She blinked rapidly as she thought of something. "Except for Graham. I always suspected he remained in Rose's camp, even after she resigned." A half-smile crossed her face. "I called him 'The Mole.'"

"Well, that might turn out to be an accurate assessment." Sam blew out a huffed breath. "Didn't you say Rose kept all the board meeting minutes in that big old book of hers?"

"Good idea," I said. "Let's review them."

Laura retrieved the notebook and flipped it open to the section containing minutes. "There's a lot here."

"Why don't we split them up?" I suggested.

Laura popped open the rings and removed the entire section, splitting it into three piles.

"I found something." Laura spread out a piece of printer paper with three holes punched along the side. Crinkles and folds marred the surface in the way you would expect if someone angrily crumpled the paper into a ball and threw it. Laura smoothed it out on top of the table. "This might be what the police were looking for."

Sam bent over the table, resting a large hand on the polished surface as he examined the paper without touching it. He read silently. I wanted to know what the paper said, but when I took a step closer, the scent of his aftershave reached me, and I backed away. "What does it say?"

Instead of responding to me, he surveyed Laura with reproach and directed his words to her. "This doesn't look good. This sounds like you openly threatened Rose in front of a room of board members in a meeting that was recorded and later transcribed."

"You threatened her?"

"Threatened is a strong word. That transcript has no context, no nonverbal cues."

"'If you step foot on my property again, I will kill you,'" Sam read in a deadpan voice. "Care to fill us in on the context?"

A defensive tone crept into Laura's voice. "She had photos of my house. A side of my house that is not visible from any public area. She brought the photos to the board meeting to support her claim that my house needed pressure washing."

"Pressure washing? You were fighting over pressure washing?"

"No, I was angry because she had obviously trespassed on my property. How would you feel if you knew Rose had been creeping around in your shrubbery?"

"Violated, obviously. But I wouldn't consider stabbing her for it."

"I didn't stab her! Now *you* don't believe me?"

Sam paused before answering. "I do believe you, but what I think doesn't matter. What matters is what the state attorney thinks, and what they can prove to the district attorney." He held up the paper. "You'd better believe they will be showing him this."

AFTER THE TENSE meeting the night before, I felt more determined than ever to come up with some solution that could help Laura. I worked in tech, after all. Coming up with solutions was supposed to be part of my skill set. I sat down at the workstation in my home office and considered possibilities. I grabbed the notebook I kept handy for jotting ideas and drawing diagrams and flowcharts for potential software concepts.

Laura's murder board floated to the front of my mind, so I began sketching it out from memory. Boxes represented Ed's clients. I drew a line connecting them to Ed's name in all caps at the bottom. Why had Rose created the list? Was the common factor really just contractor work?

I laid the drawing aside and wiggled the mouse to awaken the computer. The first website I pulled up was the Florida Department of

Business and Professional Regulation and selected "Verify a License." I typed the name "Ed Rivers" into the search box. The results showed he was a licensed residential contractor.

Hopper lay on the floor beside my chair, and he lifted his head at some noise outside. I reached down to pet him in an attempt to forestall a barking fit. I didn't need any more complaints from my neighbors. He laid his head back down.

It occurred to me that I could look for any complaints that might have been filed against Ed. Laura's unofficial survey of the people on the list revealed that some of them were unhappy with his work. I searched, but nothing came up under his name or license number. It had seemed like a good idea, but it was another dead end. I rested my chin on my hands and considered other avenues.

Depending on the extent of the work, a permit from the county might be required. I pulled up the website for county building services and searched using the name and contractor number I'd lifted from the Florida Department of Business Regulation, but the search revealed only two permits had been pulled by Ed Rivers in the last twelve months. When I looked up another contractor on the website, he had requested around twenty permits during the previous year. Permits cost money, and if Ed had charged his clients but never actually pulled the permits, he would be padding his profits.

I spoke aloud, "What was Ed doing? And the bigger question—why did Rose care?" Hopper looked up at me with big brown eyes, but he didn't offer any suggestions.

Maybe I was going about it the wrong way. I needed to start with Rose. Though I had denied any hacking ability to Sam when he asked, it wasn't entirely true. As a programmer who'd spent time creating cyber security solutions, I knew a few ways to get around them. I also knew that most people lacked creativity when it came to passwords. Because of all the snooping Laura and I had been doing, I knew quite a bit about Rose Martin's family members and the dates that were significant to her. Rose had snooped on all her neighbors. I decided it was only fair that someone else should snoop on her for a change.

I called Laura and asked, "What was Rose Martin's email address?"

"Why?" she asked.

"Just some research I'm doing."

The sound of Laura clicking keys on her computer reached my ear. "Looks like it was just her name with no spaces at Gmail. Creative. What's the next step?"

"I'll let you know after I see if it works. Hey, one more thing: can you snap a picture of your murder board and text it to me? And I need the names on the list."

"Will do," she agreed. "You'd better call me later and fill me in on the details."

Remembering one of our most successful forays into investigating, when Laura offered to take Rose's boxes to Goodwill but rifled through them instead, I suddenly realized I didn't need to hack her account—I still had her computer in my car.

Feeling guilty that I'd forgotten to recycle the old computer for Gwen, who seemed like a very nice person, I retrieved the CPU and carried it to my desk. After digging through my box of old cords, I plugged it in, connected it to my monitor, and booted it up. The internal cooling fan groaned in complaint, sounding like I'd awakened the hamster inside who was responsible for turning the wheel that powered the outdated unit.

Rose's home screen displayed a picture of the beach at Harbor Shores. When I opened a browser window, it took me directly to Gmail and displayed her inbox on my screen. It looked like there'd be no need for hacking today.

Reading Rose's email confirmed much of what Laura had said about her. The woman spent a lot of time sending letters of complaint. Rather than reading them all, I tried searching her emails for the names on the list. When I narrowed the search, the same topic appeared beside each name. Each subject line read, "Re: contractor complaints." After reading a few, I learned that Rose had identified neighbors who used Ed's handyman services and questioned them about their experience.

Rose had uncovered a pattern of contractor fraud targeting the elderly in her neighborhood and linked it to Ed Rivers. Could it be possible that, while Laura and Rose's relationship had certainly been antagonistic, to other neighbors, Rose was an advocate—perhaps even a hero?

Seeing the icon for Google apps to the right of the email heading, I decided to take a look at anything else Rose might have saved on the cloud. Much to my disappointment, she hadn't uploaded any documents. However, when I clicked on an icon in the shape of a colorful pinwheel, I was rewarded with a screen full of her photos. Rose's phone must have been set to back up photos automatically.

At first, the images were difficult to make out. I tilted my head and realized I was looking at a vent on the outside of a house followed by the interior portion of a vent. Then, I noticed the timestamp and date on the photos.

They were taken the night Rose was murdered.

fifteen

I DIDN'T HAVE much time to celebrate my success or even discuss it with Laura, because I'd been called in for an appointment with my boss at the downtown office that afternoon. As I inched forward with the traffic exiting onto Gate Parkway, I wondered why my boss had requested my presence. It was out of the ordinary, and dire possibilities filled my mind.

Normally, I worked from home most of the time, only coming in for department meetings. The traffic that evening nearly made me late, reminding me again why I preferred telecommuting. Upon entering the building, stressed and frazzled, I caught a whiff of coffee from the nearby break room but realized I didn't have time. My drug of choice would have to wait.

When I walked through the glass doors into the IT department, I noticed many empty desks. The desks were not empty in the way employees normally left them for the weekend. Rather, they were empty in the way one would expect after all of someone's belongings had been toted away in a brown banker's box.

Beth, the receptionist, glanced up as I entered. "Oh, hi, Emma. Patrick is expecting you. Let me just let him know you're here."

My heart sank. Something was definitely going on, and I doubted I would like it.

Beth motioned to me. "Go right in."

I threw back my shoulders and marched in to face my fate.

"Emma, nice to see you. Have a seat." My boss, Patrick, got up from his executive chair and indicated the much smaller one across from his desk. I sat, clasping my hands tightly in my lap. I squirmed as my memory flashed back to a time when the principal called my younger self into his office. "You're probably wondering about why I called you here on a Friday afternoon. I have some news to share, and I thought it might be useful to have the weekend to mull it over. Our company has been acquired by another company called TechCognize."

The name was unfamiliar to me. "Are they in Jacksonville?"

"No, they're based in Orlando."

"Oh." I was beginning to see where he was going.

"We had some overlap in our IT departments. The employees who won't be making the transition with us have been notified. We'd like you to stay on, Emma. Your familiarity with our Webvoy software would be quite useful during the transition."

With a whoosh, I released a relieved breath.

"There's one issue, however."

Uh-oh. I held my breath again.

"TechCognize doesn't allow telecommuting. You would need to be in the office collaborating with a team of developers."

"In Orlando?"

"Yes. They are offering relocation assistance. Our financial liaison can fill you in on the details. I realize you have a lot to consider."

I glanced out the window behind him in time to witness another employee yanking open the door to his car. As I watched, he pulled the lanyard from his neck and threw it down on the asphalt before driving away. "When is this taking place?"

Patrick tapped his pen on the desk calendar in front of him. "They've asked us to close this department by September 30, before the next fiscal year begins."

"So fast?" I slumped in my chair. "I own a house here."

"They are willing to secure corporate housing for you in the interim. You'll get information about all of that from HR."

I ran my hand through my hair, feeling completely at a loss. "Wow."

"I know it's a lot to absorb, but we'll need an answer soon. Take the weekend to consider it. Stop by human resources and pick up that relocation packet."

Down the hall in the HR suite, I was greeted by a jowly guy wearing glasses and an out-dated, wide, brown tie. I accepted his moist handshake before slumping down into the nubby chair.

"Ms. Stewart, I'm Anthony Miller, head of HR. Patrick asked me to go over the relocation package with you." Even from across the desk, his coffee breath was discernable. He slid a sheet of paper across the surface of his laminated desk toward me. "As part of our transition team, Tech-Cognize will reimburse you for moving expenses up to this amount, upon your submission of all receipts." He stabbed a figure on the paper with his stubby finger. "You are expected to begin work by October sixth. We understand that this timeframe is rather swift, so if you require lodging while you sell any property in North Florida and locate a residence in Orlando, we have an agreement with a corporate apartment facility. You may remain in executive housing for up to sixty days."

He continued, "As far as remuneration, TechCognize offers a cost-of-living adjustment. Based on your skills and seniority, they are prepared to raise your current salary to this amount." He shoved another piece of paper at me.

The number startled me. "What would be my title?"

"Senior Software Engineer Level Three." He continued in his monotonous tone. "TechCognize will provide guidance on rollover of your 401k. Your healthcare plan will not change, but you should receive a packet with updated providers for the Central Florida area. Any questions?"

"How about Disney passes?"

He didn't crack a smile. "Sorry, that's not included." He handed me a shiny blue folder. "You will find all the information I covered today in this packet so you may review it at your leisure. My card is in there should you have any further questions."

I shook his hand again and left, wiping my palm on my pants leg the moment I was out of line of sight. Stepping outside the overly air-conditioned office building, I stood on the sidewalk, dazed and blinking in the glare of the sun.

Behind me, one of my coworkers backed out through the glass double doors carrying a box of his belongings. I grabbed the door handle to assist. "Thanks, Emma. What do you make of all this?"

"Oh—hey, Adam. Pretty crazy. Took me by surprise, for sure." I tipped my head toward his box. "What will you do next?"

"I'm not going to Disney World." He shifted the box to one hip and dug in the pocket of his khakis, extracting his keys. "I'll try to find something here in Jacksonville. I heard NBT is hiring." He pushed a button on the key fob, causing the hatchback of a nearby car to beep and slowly lift. He stepped off the curb into the parking lot.

I walked alongside him. "Hmm. Banking? I don't know. They're probably still using some outdated computer language I don't remember from college."

He shrugged. "Better than moving away. I've got family here." He slid the box into the back of his car and slammed the hatch shut.

I pulled my own keys from my purse. "Well, good luck, Adam."

"Thanks." He slid a pair of sunglasses from the pocket of his plaid, short-sleeved shirt and put them on. "Maybe you should check out the Southside Developers networking event coming up this week. Check out the alternatives."

"Good idea. Maybe I'll see you there."

He nodded and waved as he got into his car and drove away.

I walked to my own car and sat numbly for a long moment before starting the ignition. I had a big decision to make. Did I want to return to the nine to five, the daily commute, morning meetings, and cubicles? There would be no more pajama days, and Hopper would be home alone all day. And what about Laura? She seemed so vulnerable lately, pushing even harder for me to move closer. How could I tell her I was moving three hours away? I briefly considered Sam but brushed the thought aside. That was over—a non-issue.

I inwardly groaned at the thought of Orlando. After our divorce, Ryan moved there. At the time, I'd thought it appropriate since he'd never grown up and preferred to live in a fantasy world. Like everyone else, I'd stalked my ex on Facebook. I monitored his profile in order to be certain his life without me wasn't too much better than mine, and that he hadn't married a supermodel or acquired an enviable fortune. Hopes that he'd developed a gut or lost his hair might also have played a part in my surveillance. I dreaded the thought of living in the same city as my ex-husband. I feared the accidental encounter at Publix while buying my weekly supply of Chocolate Trinity ice cream. Despite the millions of other people who lived or vacationed there, it could happen.

As I crawled along in Friday-afternoon traffic headed back to the beach, I compared it to the traffic in Orlando, with I-4 as the congested corridor. It was so much worse there. But could I find another job so quickly? People didn't leave their jobs in the fall, when the kids were all in school and Christmas loomed on the horizon.

The tech community in Jacksonville was a tight group. I saw the same people at all the networking events. Maybe it was time to do some networking of my own. But did I even want to? My current job wasn't all that exciting. To be honest, I'd been feeling restless for a while. But what else could I do?

Laura called me as I was driving home. "Hey, Em. I'm going to take some soup over to Bina. She's under the weather. You want to come?"

"Is she contagious?" I asked.

Laura's sigh was audible through the phone. "I don't think so. You're such a hypochondriac."

"Sorry. Just a reflex."

"That's all right. I love you anyway. Hugh just told me she was light-headed and a little short of breath. He said she just needs rest. I offered to help by bringing them soup."

"Okay, I'll be right there."

"Great. Can you pick up some soup on your way here?"

It was my turn to sigh. "I'll stop by Fresh Market."

"Perfect."

In the Friday traffic, it took me a little longer than usual to get to the market, but the soup was still hot when I arrived at Laura's place. After she poured the soup into a serving dish to make it appear homemade, we walked over to Bina's house.

"Look who's here!" Hugh answered the door and gave us each a hug. I detected the scent of Brut cologne, the same scent my grandfather wore, clinging to his loud Hawaiian shirt. "Come in, come in. Bina's in the sunroom."

We followed him to room overlooking the backyard. Bina sat in an overstuffed chair in a sunny corner. A colorful afghan covered her legs resting on the footstool in front of her.

"Laura! Emma! I'm so glad to see you. I would get up and hug you, but I think it would take both of you to pull me up first." She extended a gnarled hand.

Laura took the hand and squeezed it. "Don't you dare get up. You are supposed to be resting."

"How are you doing?" I sat down next to Bina and patted her other hand.

"I'm fine, just fine. The doctor says I'll be back on my feet soon."

Hugh came into the room, carrying a small tray. "The girls brought you some soup." He placed it on a raised table beside her.

Her wrinkled face creased in a smile. "That was so sweet of you. Soup sounds perfect." She picked up a spoon and began to eat, but her hand shook slightly. "Talk to me while I eat," she said. "Tell me the latest neighborhood gossip."

Laura's face fell. "I'm afraid most of it's about me."

"Don't you worry about that." Bina patted Laura's hand fondly, and Laura responded with a smile filled with all the affection she held for the tiny, gray-haired woman. "I'm sure the police will figure out who really killed Rose soon enough, and they'll all have to apologize for suspecting you."

"I doubt I'll be getting that apology any time soon. My lawyer told me they got a search warrant and seized a bunch of documents and recordings from our board meetings."

"Isn't Sam Turner your lawyer?" Bina asked. Laura nodded as Bina continued, "He's such a pleasant young man. He came over and cut the grass yesterday so Hugh wouldn't have to. I told Hugh to invite him in for a cold beer when he was finished." She turned to me. "He mentioned you, dear. Said you'd been working together to help Laura, but he hadn't heard from you lately. I spotted a twinkle in his eye when he mentioned you, girlie." Bina wagged a finger.

I squirmed in the stiff rattan chair, receiving a sharp poke in the backside from a loose piece of wicker trim. "I've been doing what I can to help Laura, but Sam has his own investigative team."

"If that's true, then why do you think he asked for your help in the first place? Sounds like a sneaky way of getting to be in your company."

Bina had a point. Why did Sam team up with me in the first place? "I think it was my idea that we team up," I recalled.

"Oh, please," Laura said, "I was there, remember? You might have made the suggestion, but Sam was all over that." She turned to Bina. "I've told her a hundred times, Bina. Sam had his eye on her from the first time they met at that neighborhood party." Bina and Laura looked at me in unison.

I raised my hands. "Don't gang up on me. Things are complicated."

Bina made a calming gesture. "I'm sorry. I don't mean to push." She glanced out the window into the backyard where Hugh was filling a bird feeder with sunflower seeds. "He's such a good man. He knows how much I love watching the birds. He built that bird feeder for me so I could sit here and watch them. Every year, a pair of cardinals build a nest in that rhododendron beside it. I think it must be the same family, but Hugh says I'm being sentimental. Then, he goes and puts out seed for them. He's sentimental in his own way." She watched him silently for a moment. "Hard to believe this Saturday we will have been married for fifty years."

"Congratulations," I said. "That's a real accomplishment."

"Have you ever been married, dear?" Bina asked me.

"Yes, but we were too young. It lasted less than two years."

"No need to give up on the whole institution," she said. "You fall off a horse, you get right back on."

"I'm happy to just walk," I said, trying to make a joke out of it like always.

But Bina leaned forward and addressed me seriously. "It's not good to be alone. Everybody should be somebody's somebody."

I wasn't sure exactly what she meant, but I smiled, and she nodded. Bina leaned back again, and I noticed her eyelids flutter. "I think we should let you rest now, Bina."

"I'm fine," she protested, but laid her head back against the chair.

"Emma's right," Laura said. "You want to be all better in time for your anniversary." She stood and gave Bina one last hug. "You call me if you need anything. Any time, day or night, okay?"

Bina nodded and smiled at her affectionately. "I'm lucky to have such valuable friends." She reached out and took my hand. "Think about giving Sam another chance, Emma. He's a good man." She looked out the window. Hugh was cutting a bright pink rose off one of the bushes in the backyard. He saw her looking, and held it up in her direction, smiling. "When you find a good one, you ought to hang on to him."

After we left Bina's, I suggested we take a short walk on the beach. I had a lot to discuss with Laura, and besides, it was a beautiful evening. The weather had started to cool, but the temperature would probably jump back up to ninety by the weekend. Florida weather couldn't be trusted. I decided to enjoy the cooler air while it lasted.

We walked past Ed and Mindy's house. Mindy was outside picking up fallen palm fronds and stacking them on the curb for yard waste pick up. When she laid the last palm frond on the pile, she said, "You two going for a walk?"

"Yes, we are," Laura said. "Why don't you join us?"

"I wouldn't want to impose," she said.

"It's not an imposition." Actually, it was, but there was no opportunity to tell Laura otherwise.

"Okay," Mindy said. "Let me just lock the door."

Moments later, the three of us were striding up the causeway toward the beach.

Bordered on either side by a nature preserve, the causeway connected the neighborhood to the shore. Midway, a tributary of the Iyola River bisected the road, passing underneath via a culvert. Occasionally, alligators lazed along the far banks of the slow-moving brown water. Other wildlife also made appearances there, like marsh rabbits, turtles, wetland birds, and even the occasional otter. Visitors entered the neighborhood by means of the scenic road. I often slowed down to peer at the water, hoping to glimpse some native critter.

Mindy sighed audibly as we passed the slowly moving water. "I'm so glad we did this. I could really use the distraction to clear my head."

"What's on your mind?"

In response to my question, her shoulders hunched up again as her short-lived relaxed state evaporated. "Ed is down at the police station right now. They asked him to come in and give them a statement."

"Really?" Laura asked. "Why do they want to talk to Ed?"

"They found his fingerprints at the Mayhew house. It was because he had been doing repair work for Alice, of course, but they still insisted on questioning him. It's just a formality, but it upset me all the same."

"Of course, it did," Laura consoled her. "If it makes you feel any better, I had to do the same thing. It wasn't that bad. I had a lawyer with me, though. Does he have a lawyer?"

"No, we didn't think he needed one. They didn't arrest him or anything like that. They just want to wrap up the loose ends, or so they said."

"Hmm," Laura said. "I don't know about that. I still wouldn't talk to them without a lawyer."

Mindy's forehead scrunched up, and she put her hand to her cheek. "Maybe you're right. I should have thought of that."

"Laura, you're upsetting her. Nothing can be done at the moment. Let's just focus on something positive." I gestured at our surroundings. "Isn't it a beautiful day?"

It was, in fact. We'd reached the beach, and Laura used her key to unlock the access gate. We shuffled down the sandy, narrow path between patches of sea oats and wildflowers growing on the dunes. All three of us kicked off our sandals and left them at the foot of the pathway, knowing they'd be there waiting for us when we returned. In a small beach town like Costa Verde, flip-flop theft was not a concern.

As we approached the water, the sand dropped off abruptly where the last high tide had eroded it. As Laura hopped down the short distance, she said, "I hope we don't get another hurricane this year. The last one damaged the beaches so much; the dunes are just now starting to recover."

I followed her down the slope. "Great job on that positive thinking, Laura."

"It doesn't matter," Mindy said. "I can't stop thinking about it, anyway. I won't stop worrying until I hear from Ed." She pulled her phone out of her pocket and frowned at the empty screen. "I thought he would have called by now. I wish he'd let me go with him."

"Alice could confirm that Ed was working for her," Laura said. "Have they even questioned her? After all, the house belongs to her."

"I spoke to Alice recently, and she mentioned that the police had been in contact with her. She told me she'd found something in her father's house with Rose's name on it, and she'd given Rose permission to stop by and pick it up." Mindy raised her eyebrows. "Apparently, Rose had a key."

"Where was Ed on the night of the murder?" I asked. Laura gave me a sharp look, but I ignored her. "Was he home with you?"

"No, he was working on another job."

"Oh, that's a shame," Laura said sympathetically. "I hope they find whoever really did it very soon."

"I'm sure you do," Mindy said. "I can tell that this whole thing has been a hassle for you, too."

"It sure has," Laura said.

Mindy's phone suddenly began playing Toby Keith's "Who's Your Daddy?" I exchanged a wide-eyed look with Laura as Mindy stepped away from us to take the call.

"Eddie?" She stopped walking as she listened. "Okay. I'll be right there. I'm sorry. Okay. I'll be right there." She tucked the phone back into her pocket and said, "That was Ed. I've got to run. See you later." She turned back the way we had come and dashed off.

When she was gone, Laura and I burst out laughing. "*Who's your daddy?*"

Laura snorted. "Ed sure has her on a short leash."

"I had a lot to tell you about my online investigation of Ed, but maybe it won't matter now that the police are interrogating him." We resumed walking. "I wonder how the interview went."

"Who knows? I'm just glad the police are talking to anyone other than me."

"I wonder how much Mindy knows." Walking on the beach brought to mind the last time I'd been there, when I caught a glimpse of Miranda's husband. "I wonder if the police have talked to Miranda."

Laura grimaced. "I still can't picture Ed with Miranda."

"I can't picture her with that old, rumpled man she's married to, but there's no accounting for taste."

"They do have proximity going for them. She's right next door."

"Poor Mindy. Why does she put up with him?" I wondered.

Laura grinned. "Because he's her Big Daddy."

I snorted. "Maybe that's it. Miranda needs his big tool next door."

She slapped my arm and said, "You're so bad! I can't take you anywhere."

"That's fine with me," I replied. "I like it at home."

"My little introvert," she said fondly. "That reminds me, you'd better show up at Bina and Hugh's anniversary party."

My nose wrinkled at the idea. "I don't want to run into Sam."

"I don't think he's invited. It's only close friends and family."

"Well, I'm not a close friend," I protested.

"You are now," Laura said. "Bina sent Hugh over with an invitation and gave me strict instructions to bring you. You don't want to let her down, do you?"

"All right, all right." I raised my hands in surrender. "They are a sweet couple. Should I bring a present?"

"The invitation says, 'No presents but your presence.'"

Tapping my lower lip, I said, "Maybe I should bring her a bottle of wine."

Laura chuckled. "I'm sure she wouldn't turn that down."

Glancing at my watch, I said, "We'd better turn around. I've got to get home and walk Hopper. The neighborhood kid sometimes rushes him on the afternoon walk. Too bad I don't pay her by the hour—or the mile." Walking back the way we'd come, I decided it was as good a time as any to talk to her about my job transfer. "I have some bad news to tell you."

She glanced at me with worry in her eyes. "What is it?"

"I just found out today that I'm being transferred to Orlando."

Turning to face me, she said, "What? Tell me you're kidding."

"Unfortunately, no. The company is merging with a big corporation in Orlando, and they're closing the Jacksonville office."

Laura stomped her foot, but the effect was extremely ineffectual, as it was done in the sand. "Emma, no! I forbid you to move to Orlando!"

"I don't have much of a choice. I can try finding another job here in Jacksonville, but that's such an uncertainty."

"You have to try."

"I will. But in the meantime, I'm going to get my house ready to sell."

"Oh, Emma. What am I going to do without you?"

"I'll come back all the time to visit."

"You say that, but you won't. We've just got to figure out a way to keep you here. Why don't you post that you're looking for a new job on Linked Up?"

"I think you mean LinkedIn. I am planning to reach out to some folks in my network, but I can't promise anything."

Back in the neighborhood, we turned the corner and found a group of onlookers standing around near Mindy's house, Sam among them. His rumpled dress shirt and tie told me he'd come straight from work. Loosening the tie, he ambled toward us.

"What's going on, Sam?" Laura asked.

"They arrested Ed. Mindy called me over to ask if I could help. I told her I can't defend him, because I'm already representing you. A buddy of mine's gonna help her out, but I came over anyway to makes sure that things were done right."

"Did they find new evidence?" I asked, thinking about all that research I had done. It looked like it was now irrelevant.

"Ed's fingerprints were found at the scene of the crime, and I guess they weren't happy with the way he answered their questions down at the station." He turned his gaze to the property line between the houses, not far from the water's edge. "Remember that knife that turned up at your property? Could have just as well been disposed of behind Ed's house, since he lives upstream from you on the same estuary."

"The police don't even know for certain if it's the murder weapon. It's a common kitchen knife," I pointed out. "And as far as the prints on the scene, Ed worked at that house as a handyman. It makes sense that his prints would be all over the place. So, why did they think they had enough evidence to arrest him?"

In a burst of exasperation, Laura asked, "Why are you arguing? They finally have another suspect!"

"Emma's gotten in the habit of arguing with me lately." Sam's brown eyes looked briefly sad before they turned away from me. "But they still have to formally charge him. There's a limit to how long they can hold him without filing charges."

"We know all about that," Laura said. "Is Mindy going to try to bail him out?"

"I can't figure out why she tore off down there. Gotta have a bail hearing first. I tried to tell her." He glanced at his watch. "I better get going. I pushed back another meeting to get here." He rested his hand on Laura's shoulder. "But this is positive news for you, Laura. One man's loss is another person's gain."

sixteen

Despite all the positive developments in Laura's defense case, uncertainty about my own future continued to loom over my head. I decided to follow my coworker's advice and showed up at the Southside Developers meeting later that week. The networking group met in a large conference room inside a suburban office building. Inside, I found my fellow software nerds clustered in groups, holding bottles of beer and making awkward conversation.

Per Laura's suggestion, I'd uploaded a current resume and changed my LinkedIn status to, "Looking for job opportunities." I sent a few emails to friends and former coworkers who worked at other companies around Jacksonville. I was doing all the right things, but so far, I hadn't found anything enticing. It looked like it was going to be hard to find a company willing to match the offer from TechCognize.

After a quick stop at the hospitality table, I gripped a chilled bottle of beer, still damp from the cooler. I turned down a slice of pizza and headed for a group containing a few familiar faces. I spotted someone whom I'd met at the previous event named Priya. She flipped her shiny black braid behind her shoulder and waved, gesturing for me to stand beside her. The conversation already in progress sounded intense. Zack, a bald guy with hipster glasses, was speaking.

"—A hundred fifty jobs."

"That many? The place doesn't look that big from the outside," said Bryan, a ginger-haired guy whose shirt buttons were straining against the expanse of his belly.

Chris, a tall guy with a comb-over, added, "They've been in business forever."

Priya leaned toward me and quietly caught me up. "Defense Synergy announced a huge layoff today."

"Yep," said Zack. "Over one hundred software engineers in Jacksonville just found out they were without a job."

"I heard they had a security breach," Priya explained. "It was serious enough to bring the whole company down."

The comb-over ruffled in the breeze as Chris shook his head. "Hope you didn't have stock in DefenseSyn."

"Heaven help anyone looking for a job right now. That's a lot of unemployed programmers hitting the market at once." Bryan swigged his beer.

I drained my bottle in one long gulp.

The host of the meeting tapped a microphone to get the attention of the room. "If everyone could sit down now, our program is about to start. Our topic tonight is 'Domain-Driven Design: Why it Matters.'"

Giving Priya a subtle wave, I gestured at my head, faking a headache. Then, feeling utterly hopeless, I quietly slipped out the side door.

I FELT uncertain about the move to Orlando, but after seeing how much competition I'd have when attempting to find another job in Jacksonville, I realized I didn't have much choice. If I needed to move in a less than a month, there was no time for waffling. I asked Sophie to put my townhouse on the market, and she told me to stop by and sign a listing agreement. Even as I drove toward her office, I questioned if I was doing the right thing. Although it was small, my townhouse was the first place I'd bought on my own as an independent woman. When I'd been married to Ryan, the mortgage was in his name only. He had always been such a controlling jerk.

I was so lost in my thoughts, I almost missed the brightly colored sign designating the squat, brown building on the corner as Apex Realty. I pulled into a space beside Sophie's enormous SUV. The huge vehicle provided more shade than the palm trees that surrounded the parking lot.

When I stepped into the building, the frigid air conditioning enveloped me. Sophie's bright hair was easy to spot in her glass-enclosed office off the lobby. She waved me over. "Hi, Emma," she said in her chipper voice. "Have a seat. I take it you're ready to list your house for sale?"

"That's right. I'd like to sell it as quickly as possible."

"I'd be glad to assist you with that. But what's the rush? Are you planning to snag a home in Harbor Shores? They don't become available very often, you know."

Unless someone dies. "No one has snapped those up yet?"

"No. The circumstances caused an unusual delay. But you can benefit!"

I winced. "Actually, I'm selling my house because I've been transferred to Orlando."

"Oh, no!" Sophie's penciled-on eyebrows arched further. "Laura's going to miss you so much. What did she say when you told her?"

"She took it pretty hard."

Sophie frowned. "I can imagine. When do you need to be in Orlando?"

"My new position begins on October sixth."

"That's quick, but I wouldn't worry too much. Your home is in a terrific location."

I raised my head and grinned at her. "Not as terrific as Harbor Shores, though. Right?"

She returned my smile and shook her head. "Nobody sells in Harbor Shores."

"Then I guess you don't get a lot of business from your neighbors." I handed her the completed forms.

"I have helped some purchase second homes." She flipped through the pages but stopped midway through. "Looks like you missed a line. Just need your initials right there."

I leaned forward to sign where she indicated. "Purchase a second home? Is that common?"

"No, not really. But those who do are usually extremely picky and require a lot of my attention."

"May I ask who?"

"Miranda and her husband, Steve, bought a mountain cabin recently. I represented them in the purchase."

"You and Miranda are close?"

"I suppose you could say that. We meet for brunch. Sometimes we work out at The Club around the same time." She examined her manicure.

"What's the story with Miranda's husband? They seem a little mismatched."

Sophie winked. "She told me once over mimosas that she likes older men. And their money."

"She said that?"

"Yes, but Steve made her sign a prenup. It's not like she can divorce him and take half of everything. He has his fortune pretty sewn up. Still, she enjoys the lifestyle he provides. She doesn't have to work on anything more than her tan." Sophie tapped the papers on her desk, lining them up in a neat stack. "Now that this is all done, we need to set up a time to do a walkthrough. I can make any recommendations needed to get your place ready for sale. Are you free tomorrow evening?"

"Let me check my calendar." I accessed my phone's calendar app. "That's Bina and Hugh's anniversary party."

"Oh, that's right. How about before then, in the afternoon?"

"That's fine. I'm working from home tomorrow. Are you going to the party, too?"

"Of course! The whole neighborhood will be there."

Laura was such a liar.

I decided to go to the party even if it meant risking a run-in with Sam. *After all, I was moving soon, so why should I care?* I almost convinced myself.

Bina and Hugh's house sat on a corner lot, and their patio could be seen from the cross street. Fairy lights hung from the trees in their backyard, gently illuminating the crowd of people talking and holding wine glasses. I found a parking spot nearby and walked directly to the patio.

Bina spotted me from her chair, looking like a queen on her throne, and waved me over enthusiastically. "Emma, I'm so glad you could make it. What do you have there?"

"A bottle of wine for you." I handed her the bottle, which was wrapped in cellophane and tied with a ribbon, courtesy of the fancy ABC store in Sawgrass.

"My favorite." She pulled me into a hug. "Thank you."

"You're welcome," I said. "Happy anniversary. Fifty years is a real accomplishment."

She gazed fondly at Hugh, who stood beside her, and patted his hand. "I'm lucky I got a good one."

"No, I'm the lucky one. She's generous to put up with me," he said, bending to kiss her cheek. "I'm going to go get some food. Want me to fix you a plate?"

"That would be wonderful," she said. He turned to go, and she watched him walk away. "He is a good one, but marriage is still hard work." She wagged a finger at me. "You need to forgive. Let go of the small stuff."

"What if it's not small stuff?" I asked sadly.

She gave me an understanding look. "Then you talk about it. Listen to what he has to say. Don't assume. Men and women, we speak different languages. You learn to communicate, and that takes time. But you gotta try."

I gave her a half smile. "I'll try, Bina."

"Atta girl," she said. "You need to settle down, have some babies, eh?"

"I don't think that's in the cards for me."

"Don't count yourself out yet. You're still young."

"Not that young," I objected. "I'm thirty."

"Honey, when you're as old as me, thirty is young. You don't want to look back on your life and regret the things you didn't do."

Another party guest came over to congratulate Bina, so I nodded and went to check out the food table. I passed Hugh carrying two heavy plates.

While I examined the buffet, Laura popped up at my elbow with a cheery, "Hey, girl."

"Hey, yourself. You're late."

"I was inside working on something. I've been waiting for you to get here."

"Just got here. Talked to Bina." I reached for a piece of rugelach.

"Don't eat that." She swatted my hand. "Too many carbs."

"I don't recall asking you to be my personal trainer." Defiantly, I stuffed the rich pastry in my mouth.

She brushed away the crumbs on the front of my shirt. "I came over here to tell you that you need to sign the signature frame inside Hugh's office. You know—one of those picture frames with a big white mat that surrounds the portrait where guests can write messages and best wishes. He had a portrait made for their anniversary, and he wants everybody to sign it. It's a surprise for Bina."

"Oh, okay. I'll check it out later."

"No, you need to do it now. We're going in shifts, so Bina doesn't notice."

"That's kind of weird, but, okay. Where's the office?"

"First door in the hallway on the left."

I stepped inside the house and found it packed with guests talking, eating, and mingling. I headed for the door as directed. When I opened it, I found two surprises. One was that it was not the office at all, but the laundry room.

The other surprise was Sam waiting there for me.

The smell of fabric softener filled the tiny room. The dryer hummed, and something inside thumped at evenly spaced intervals. My heart pounded as anger tumbled inside of me. "What is this? A setup?"

"Please don't be mad at Laura. I asked her to do this as a favor to me. I had to talk to you." He reached out and laid his hand on my arm.

His touch triggered an immediate response in my body despite my lingering resentment. "What is it, Sam?"

"Taylor told me she answered the phone at my house early one morning. She said a woman called. I think I finally put it together."

"How did you guess it was me?"

"I found your number on my caller ID. I can guess what you thought when she answered my phone that early in the morning, but, Emma, why didn't you talk to me instead of jumping to conclusions?"

"What other conclusion could there be?"

"Taylor came straight to my house after an all-night stakeout."

"Oh, please. She was also there the evening before."

"She got photos for evidence in another case I was working before Laura's. I can show them to you. They have the date and time linked to the digital file." His brow creased as my words sank in. "Wait—how do you know that?"

"I saw her. I walked over to your place after looking at Rose's house and heard you in the backyard. When I walked around, I saw you and Taylor drinking together. You looked so cozy, I decided not to interrupt."

"I wish you had. Then none of this would have happened. There is absolutely nothing going on between me and Taylor. Never was."

"How can I believe you?"

"Perhaps I can introduce you to Taylor's wife."

"Her... wife?"

"Yes, Emma. Will that be enough to convince you?" He held his hands out in surrender. "I don't know. Maybe you could try trusting me. Give me a chance. I realize you've been hurt in the past, but that wasn't me."

I examined his face, but his smooth lawyer expression was gone. Only sincerity filled his eyes. It could have been just another skill developed in the courtroom, but if it was, I couldn't see through it.

Seeing my hesitation, he raised his hand to stroke my cheek. He trailed his fingers through my hair and gently gripped the back of my neck as he leaned in to kiss me. He began unbuttoning my blouse. As his kisses burned a trail down my neck, I tilted my head back and groaned. In the case of head versus hormones, my defense decided to rest.

Our kisses increased in intensity. Sam's hands tangled in my hair as his tongue dipped between my lips. My hands stroked his back and pulled his body against mine. His hands moved to my waist, and he lifted me up to sit on top of the dryer. It felt warm beneath me as it rocked in a rapid cycle. I pulled my face back and our eyes met. I raised my eyebrows in surprise. "Hmm. This could be fun even without you here."

He chuckled in response, but the intensity returned to his face as he searched mine. "Would you rather be here without me?"

"No," I said, and kissed him. I wrapped my arms around his back and pulled his body tightly against mine, aided by the rhythm of the dryer.

Our movements abruptly halted when a female voice tinged with a Brooklyn accent spoke right outside the door. "Wheah's the powder room? This it?" The doorknob began to turn.

My eyes flew open, meeting Sam's startled glance. He extended his arm to block the door.

"Not that one, Rita," another voice chimed. "The one on the right."

The doorknob rotated back into place, and the sound of high heels receded. Our eyes met. Sam and I grinned at each other, and I covered my mouth with my hands to contain my laughter. We quickly righted ourselves and adjusted our clothing.

"This was crazy," I said.

"This was amazing," he replied, and kissed me.

"I guess we'd better get back to the party." I smoothed my hand over my hair. "Do I look okay?"

"You look beautiful." Sam kissed me again, and then he reached up to rub a spot beneath my lower lip with his thumb. "You might need to fix your lipstick, though."

"Oh, great. Is the bathroom actually across the hall?"

"Yep. Just ask Rita."

I smacked him on the arm. "Wait a few minutes after I leave before you come out."

"Yes, ma'am." He ran his hand over his own hair. "Do I pass inspection?"

"You'll do." I slipped out of the room, glancing around for observers.

When I came out of the bathroom, Laura was waiting. "There you are. Did you work everything out?"

"I can't believe you did that."

"But did it work?" She eyed my blouse and raised an eyebrow. "You missed a button." I ducked my head and darted back into the bathroom with Laura close on my heels. She shut the door behind us and leaned against it, grinning. "I guess that means it did."

"Can I get a little privacy?"

"Oh, please." She fluffed the back of my hair with her fingers. "Was it good?"

"Laura!"

"Sorry. I'm just glad to hear that phase one of my plan to get you to stay is working."

I dropped my hand from where it was smoothing down the hair that Laura had fluffed. "I forgot. I didn't tell him about that."

"I guess you got distracted. No matter. We'll just have to find you another job here in town. Let's get back out to the party. Who knows? Maybe we can do a little networking here."

After one more glance at my reflection, I followed Laura outside, where the crowd had grown since I left. Neighbors and friends surrounded Hugh and Bina, and a line had formed at the beverage table. Before I could join them, Sam caught my eye and held out a glass of champagne in my direction. I walked over and accepted it with a smile. "Usually, I expect a guy to buy me a drink *before* an intimate encounter takes place."

He clinked his own glass of champagne against mine. "I like to mix it up."

Bina waddled over as we both drank. "I'm happy to see you two getting along again."

"Yes, just a misunderstanding. Thank you for your advice, Bina. You're my hero." I bent down and kissed her cheek.

She tilted her head back and peered up at Sam, his six-foot frame towering over her not-quite-five-foot pear-shaped form. The twinkle in her eye warned me she was up to something. "How about you, handsome?" She pulled him down by the shirt collar and planted a kiss directly on his lips.

Sam appeared stunned but recovered quickly. "Hugh better keep his eye on you, little lady."

"Somebody call me?" Hugh ambled over with a plate full of meatballs. "Is she getting into trouble again?"

"Nothing you can't handle." The little lady in question playfully swatted his behind. "Did you save any meatballs for somebody else?"

"Gotta keep my strength up to keep up with you." He winked at Sam in a conspiratorial fashion. "Believe me, it's not easy."

Sam chuckled, but it sounded a little uneasy. "Tell me, Hugh, what's the secret to a marriage that lasts for fifty years?"

"The lady is always right." He speared one of the meatballs with a fork and offered it to Bina, who shook her head at first but then opened her mouth to accept his offering. "Why don't you come back and sit down with me for a while?"

"Okay, I'll be right there." She watched him go before turning to meet my eyes. "See? I got a good one. Glad you two are back together." She patted my arm, then turned to follow Hugh who had pulled out a chair, waiting for her.

Someone rolled over an enormous cake with fifty candles blazing on top. Hugh's and Bina's wrinkled, joyful faces beamed at the impressive display. Their daughter made a speech in her parents' honor, receiving supportive applause from the crowd. At her cue, speakers surrounding the patio played the first song Hugh and Bina danced to at their wedding, Elvis's version of "Can't Help Falling in Love." Hugh and Bina shuffled together on the patio in a slow, sweet dance.

The popping of corks preceded more toasts to the happy couple. The party continued well into the night. Neighbors with small children went home to put them to bed, while the empty nesters remained. The giant cake was reduced to crumbs. Bina whispered something in Hugh's ear, and he nodded before heading inside carrying her empty glass.

No one at the party noticed when Bina stopped talking except for me. The conversation continued to swirl around her, but Bina's gaze was inward. As I watched, the color fled from her cheeks. I opened my mouth to ask if she was all right, but before I spoke, she grabbed her upper arm and gasped.

"Bina?" I pushed someone aside and reached her at the moment she swayed in her seat. I took hold of her shoulder and called her name again. "Bina? What's wrong?"

Hugh heard me and dropped the two cups he carried as he rushed to her side. He took her frail hand in his own and urgently called out, "Someone call an ambulance!"

"Everybody back up!" Laura pleaded. "She can't breathe!"

Bina's face was ashen and beaded with sweat. She slumped in her chair, eyes unfocused, fighting some internal battle. It seemed that her life was draining away as we watched helplessly. Laura kneeled beside Bina with tears on her cheeks. As I dialed the phone, I saw one of Bina's hands reach out to touch Hugh's face and her lips moved silently.

"Nine-one-one. What is your emergency?" a tinny voice in my ear said.

"We need an ambulance. I think my friend is having a heart attack."

"What is the address?"

My brain froze. It was an incidence when having a landline would have been convenient. "The address!" I hollered at the group gathered at the scene. "What is the address?"

"Two Thousand Beach Hammock Drive," Laura answered.

I parroted her words back to the dispatcher. "Hurry, please. She's —" I struggled to describe the scene, the way Bina was fading, leaving us as we watched, but words failed me. "I think she might be having a heart attack."

"Emergency response units are on their way," the dispatcher said. "Give her an aspirin if you can. Four baby aspirin if you have them."

"Does anybody have an aspirin?" I hollered at the onlookers.

One woman began digging through a purse the size of a dumpster. I worried that she couldn't possibly find anything in there before help arrived. Distant sirens wailed as the ambulance made its way from the fire station two miles from the neighborhood. Someone handed Hugh an aspirin.

Hugh gently guided the aspirin to Bina's lips. "Stay with me, Beebee," he pleaded.

Bina's eyes focused on Hugh's face at the endearment. When he lowered the cup, her lips trembled but managed to get out the word, "Always."

The ambulance arrived, and two paramedics, a male and a female, leaped out and rushed to the cluster of onlookers. "Move aside, please," the man ordered, and the authority in his voice caused the crowd to obey immediately.

The woman spoke in soothing tones as she questioned Bina about her symptoms and checked her vital signs. She nodded to the male paramedic. He retrieved a stretcher and wheeled it right onto the patio. The pair maneuvered Bina atop it. The woman slipped an oxygen mask over Bina's face.

"Where are you taking her?" Laura asked.

"Saint Vincent's," the woman said. They wheeled Bina into the back of the ambulance with Hugh trailing behind. With everyone loaded, the rig sped away, sirens blaring.

"I want to go," Laura said. "Can you drive me, Emma? I don't think I can do it right now."

"I'll take you," Sam said.

Sam retrieved his truck, and we raced up State Road A1A toward the hospital. Our haste proved to be unnecessary, however, because we couldn't get back to see Bina. All we could do was wait.

The lobby of the emergency room smelled like disinfectant. Only one other person sat in the ugly waiting room chairs. He must have been there for a loved one rather than waiting for treatment because he held a small, pink purse in his lap, and he twisted the straps around and around in his hands. His face bore the same desperate look that Laura's did. Sam sat beside her with his arm around her shoulders. I paced the room, too wired to sit after the harrowing scene I'd just witnessed. On the wall above the registration window, a clock loudly counted off the minutes.

The window opened, and we all looked up expectantly, but the nurse said, "Mister Stone? You can come back now." The man with the purse leaped from his seat and rushed through the door.

Alone in the waiting room, none of us knew what to say. Laura rocked and fidgeted in her seat while I anxiously walked back and forth.

"Will you please sit down?" she finally snapped at me.

"Sorry," I said and took the chair beside her.

"I'm sorry," she said. "I'm just so worried."

I patted her hand. "I know. It's okay. It's going to be okay."

"You don't know that," she said.

"Let's try to be positive," Sam said.

Laura's green eyes squinted at him like those of an angry cat.

We both shut up. *Tick, tick, tick.* Why would they put a clock that loud in a hospital waiting room? *Tick, tick, tick.*

Finally, the window opened again. "Are you all here for Bina Finley?" the nurse asked. We jumped up and nodded. "Can you come around here to the family waiting room, please?" She pointed to a door beside the window, but it was not the same one the anxious man had disappeared through. We filed nervously across the room, and the door opened.

It was a small, dim room. The overhead fluorescent hospital lights were off, leaving only the soft glow from a lamp placed on a side table along with a box of tissues. A few chairs sat around the tiny room in a circle. The nurse followed us in and closed the door behind her. "Are you family members or friends?" she asked.

"Friends," Laura answered.

The nurse hesitated. "I'm sorry to have to inform you that Mrs. Finley didn't make it."

A stunned silence followed her words. Then, Laura stuttered, "Wh-what?"

"She passed away. We weren't able to save her."

My eyes met Sam's over Laura's head. We each took one of her hands as her body began to shake with sobs.

THE SEPTEMBER SKY blazed in brilliant shades of blue on the morning of Bina's funeral, incongruous to the emotions of the day.

After the service, friends and family were invited to Hugh and Bina's house for a reception.

I surveyed Bina's living room, filled with so many of her personal touches inhabiting every surface of the room. "Tchotchkes," she called them. Hugh sat on the overstuffed sofa, looking forlorn, his hand absently stroking an afghan draped over the arm of his seat. Cooper sidled up beside him and laid his head on Hugh's knee.

At least fifty people, standing around holding drinks or small plates of food, were there to pay their respects. Most of the faces were unfamiliar to me. I assumed they were family members, but Laura whispered in my ear, "There's Alice talking to Bina's daughter, Rachel."

I tried to be inconspicuous as my gaze traveled in the direction she indicated with a tilt of her head. A tall blonde stood talking to a short, round brunette. "The blonde?"

"Yes. The one that looks like money."

She did indeed. Like most of those around her, Alice wore black, but something about the cut of her dress, the gleam of her heels, indicated wealth. Her blond hair shone in a sleek bob that was longer on one side than the other. I guessed that her haircut alone cost more than my entire outfit.

Despite their differences, Alice and Rachel shared an air of familiarity and fondness for each other. Rachel's resemblance to Bina filled me with sadness. Alice hugged her childhood friend. When they parted, Alice dabbed her eyes to prevent damage to her makeup.

Standing apart, watching this exchange, I asked Laura, "Do you know her well?"

"No. She was all grown up by the time Jack and I moved here. But people talk. The Mayhews were neighborhood royalty."

"Royalty? Why?"

"They were wealthy, he was a politician, and the Costa Verde home was one of many they owned. His choice to settle here rather than the mansion in Charlotte or one of their other properties made the neighbors here feel important. It validated their belief that this neighborhood was special."

Once again, I marveled at people's need to feel better than others simply because of their address. "I just don't get it," I said.

"Why don't we give our condolences to Bina's daughter, and maybe she'll introduce you to Alice," Laura said.

"There's something wrong with that idea, but I can't quite put my finger on it," I said, tapping my lip. I held up my finger as if in revelation. "I know! It's the fact that we're at a funeral, not an investigation." Nevertheless, I followed Laura as she led me across the room toward Rachel and Alice.

Laura reached out her hand to Rachel. "I'm so sorry for your loss, Rachel. Bina's friendship meant so much to me."

Rachel nodded and grasped Laura's hand. She patted it with her other hand, as if to console Laura rather than the other way around. I imagined she'd been hearing the same words all day. "Thank you, Laura. Mama thought a lot of you."

Laura released Rachel's hand and reached out to touch my shoulder. "This is my best friend, Emma. She had gotten to know your mom recently."

"Pleased to meet you," she replied. "Best friends are important. Alice, here, was my BFF growing up."

Alice smiled at Rachel before extending her hand to me. "I'm Alice Mayhew. I live in Charlotte now, but Rachel and this neighborhood meant so much to me. Do you live here, too?"

"No," I replied. "I've been waiting for the right house to become available."

"Well, I've got one I'd be happy to sell you. But I imagine you've heard all about that."

I nodded. "I'm sorry for your loss."

"Thank you," she said curtly. "One thing I don't miss about this neighborhood is the way bad news travels so fast."

"Sorry," I repeated.

She waved away my apology with her elegantly manicured hand. "Don't worry about it. No one knows what to say at these things. You're not alone. Right, Rachel?"

Rachel nodded, but apparently, she didn't have any idea what to say either.

A glint of silver caught my eye when Alice waved her arm. "That's a lovely bracelet."

"Actually, they call it a cuff," she said, absently twisting it around her wrist. "It was a gift from my father."

The jewelry looked familiar to me, but I couldn't place it. "Is it engraved?"

She glanced down at the bracelet, or cuff, or whatever. "Tiffany." She shrugged.

"It's lovely," I repeated. My mind drifted as I tried to remember where I'd seen the cuff before.

For a moment, the four of us stood around awkwardly, saying nothing. Then, Laura broke the silence. "Well, we'll leave you two alone to catch up. It was nice seeing you both again, even under these unfortunate circumstances."

"Yes," Rachel said. "Thank you for coming."

"Pleasure meeting you, Alice," I said. When we were out of earshot, I said, "Well, that was awkward. I need a drink. Where's the bar?"

"Right this way," Laura said, leading me through the kitchen to a corner that had been set up as a drink station. A man bent over the table, intent on his task of fishing ice cubes from a silver ice bucket using tiny tongs. It was Sam.

I stopped so abruptly that someone behind me bumped into me. Laura turned her head, wondering why I'd stopped, and followed my gaze. Before I could escape, Sam spotted me. His hand hesitated in midair above a bottle of scotch.

"Emma," he said, oddly formal. "May I pour you a drink?"

I swallowed hard. I looked around for Laura, but she had vanished into thin air. "Sure. I'll take one of those."

"Scotch?" He sounded surprised.

I nodded. "Yes, please."

He filled a second glass with ice, poured scotch into both, and handed one to me, holding my eyes with his own as he did. "You haven't answered my calls. How have you been?"

"All right," I said. I took a small sip of the scotch and gave a small cough.

"Okay there?"

I nodded. The second sip went down smoother. I felt it warming my insides, tracing a path of heat down to my core. Already, I felt braver. "We need to talk."

His eyebrow quirked up. "Should we go into the laundry room?"

"No." I saw his smile drop away and my heart sank, but I forced myself to continue. "Sam, the other night was amazing, but there's something I haven't told you. I'm leaving. My company is restructuring. I'm getting transferred to Orlando."

"Oh." He sipped his scotch, then cleared his throat. "Yeah, you probably should've mentioned that sooner."

"I'm sorry. I should have." I couldn't meet his eyes.

He sighed. "So, that's it? There's no hope for us?"

I looked over to where Hugh still cradled the blanket made by Bina's hands. She wouldn't have wanted me to give up. If I never took any risks, I'd never find what she and Hugh had. "There's hope. I'm willing to try if you are."

Sam glanced away. "Long-distance relationships are tough."

Suddenly defensive, I said, "It's Orlando, not Okinawa."

He held up his hands as if in surrender, but instead grasped mine between them. "Now, don't get riled up. I'm just saying it won't be easy. I'm not saying I won't try."

Seventeen

A FEW DAYS after the funeral, Laura and I arranged to meet at Starbucks. So much had happened in such a short amount of time, I could barely process it. It felt important to talk to Laura face to face instead of over the phone.

We collected our orders and sat down. Laura eyed my cup. "Why did you order a pumpkin spice latte when it's eighty degrees outside?"

"What does that have to do with anything? It's September, officially fall, and I love pumpkin spice."

"Do you realize how many calories are in that thing?"

"No, and don't tell me."

"Four hundred."

"I just asked you not to tell me." I watched her take a tiny sip of her cappuccino. Laura was one of those people who took a long time to order a beverage. *Nonfat, half-caf, unsweet, soymilk, venti...* There was a lot of black sharpie scribbling on the side of her cup. Did that say *Laura*? The scribble almost looked like *Karen*. "Are you sure you picked up the right drink?"

"Of course. I can taste it. Exactly three pumps of sugar-free vanilla." She took another sip. "So, how did Sam take the news of your potential move?"

"You mean my *practically definite* move? He accepted it, but he told me he worried about maintaining a long-distance relationship."

"You see? He agrees with me. You should stay here."

A bell jingled as the door to the coffee shop opened. I glanced up in time to see Francesca power-walk into the room. She wore minuscule bike shorts and a snug tank top that revealed her figure: a miraculous combination of zero body fat and a D-cup bosom. She spotted us and waved. After placing her order, she came over to speak with us while she waited.

"Hello, ladies!" Her carb detector must have gone off, because her eyes dropped to my 400-calorie beverage. "Enjoying *una coppa grande*?"

I nodded, getting the gist of her question without knowing any Italian. After all, I considered Francesca an authority on big cups.

She continued, "Have you heard the latest neighborhood gossip?"

"No. What's going on?"

"The police released Ed Rivers." The barista called Francesca's name, and she returned to the counter to retrieve her drink while Laura and I exchanged startled glances. Francesca returned to our table and sat down without an invitation. She leaned in conspiratorially, pushing her impressive bosom against the table as she imparted her juicy gossip. "Someone told the police that Ed was with her on the night of the murder."

"You're kidding!" Laura edged forward, eager to hear the rest. "Who?"

"Miranda Fox." Francisca gave a satisfied grin. "And her husband kicked her out. Guess she won't be complaining about my exercise class anymore."

Laura gasped. "What did Mindy do?"

"She picked him up from jail." Francesca lifted and lowered one sculpted shoulder in a careless manner. "Who knows what comes next?"

My phone chimed with the ringtone I'd assigned to Sam. After I briefly excused myself to Laura and Francesca, I stepped outside and took the call. "What's going on? I just heard that Ed's been released."

"That's right. I just heard it myself from a buddy down at the station. Ed came up with an alibi."

"But that puts us back at square one. The police will be looking for another suspect."

"You're right. It's discouraging. Listen—I'd like to get Laura's defense team together in my office on Wednesday. Think you can make it?"

"Defense team? Who exactly does that include?"

"Me, of course, plus you and Laura." He paused. "And Taylor."

"Taylor?"

"Yes. Emma, do you think we can put our misunderstandings behind us and work together? After all, it would be in Laura's best interest. Taylor has been helping me from the beginning. Finding someone else to take her place at this point would be detrimental to the case. You wouldn't really want me to do that, would you?"

I didn't respond right away. I knew he was probably right. It was time to put on my big girl panties and get over it. "Okay. I can deal with it. When do you want to do it?"

His voice dropped to a lower register and lost the business tone. "Anytime you want to do it."

"I mean the meeting." I tried to sound stern despite the smile I couldn't quite restrain.

"Four o'clock work for you?"

"I can do that. I can share the information I've collected online."

"I look forward to seeing it..." His voice dropped to a low rumble. "And you."

I felt the tension in my chest release, while other parts—lower parts of my body—responded to his voice. "Okay if I grab your butt in front of Taylor to assert my claim?"

He chuckled. "I'll look forward to that as well."

AFTER ED'S RELEASE, I decided to review the information gathered before his arrest. Shifting papers around my desk, I uncovered the picture we found in Rose's old books. I'd forgotten all about it in the aftermath of the humiliation of the estate sale. I picked it up and examined it closely.

The picture was old—probably twenty years or more. It showed a small, red-faced newborn with a shock of red hair sleeping in the plastic type of bassinet found in hospitals. For the first time, I noticed there was a number beneath the name on the bed. Holding it close to my face, I peered at the tiny numbers and letters.

David Martin

Southeast Georgia Medical Center

11-03-2007

49246876413

The name of the baby was David, like the young man who'd introduced himself as Rose's nephew, but his last name was Martin. Rose's sister, Gwen, had a different last name. Knowing that births were public information, I decided to search for any online records. My search quickly revealed that Southeast Georgia Medical Center was in Brunswick, Georgia, a little over an hour away. I visited the Department of Vital Records website to search births recorded on November 3, 2007. I found "Baby Boy Martin, Mother Rose."

For a moment, I sat in a daze, wondering what it meant. Then, I snapped my laptop shut and grabbed my keys on my way out the door. Laura needed to see it.

Seated at her kitchen table twenty minutes later, Laura gaped at the laptop screen in disbelief. "Oh, my god, Emma. David is Rose's son, not Gwen's? Do you think he knows?"

I reviewed David's manner during our brief exchange. "He didn't seem to. He called her 'Aunt Rose.' So, you think Rose gave the baby up and let her sister raise him?"

"There's only one way to find out."

I snapped the laptop closed. "What? Ask Gwen? You can't do that."

Laura shrugged. "Why not? Rose is dead. Who would she have to cover for now?"

"Herself. Maybe she doesn't want David to learn the truth."

"We can talk to her when he's not around. Let's bring the photo back and tell her we found it in your car after we dropped off the books."

I stood and began pacing. "I don't know."

"What can she do to us?" She chewed her lip pensively. "Who is his father? Did the birth certificate say?"

"No. The line for the father's name was blank."

She thought for a moment. "Can you look up divorce records?"

"Sure. Who do you want to look up?"

"Rose's divorce. I want to see how the dates line up with her pregnancy."

My fingers flew over the keyboard. I searched for the county clerk of courts. I selected "divorce" from a drop-down menu and entered the last name Martin. After scanning a long list, I spotted it—a dissolution of marriage notice for Rose Ellen Martin and Paul Matthew Martin dated June 2007.

Laura was looking over my shoulder. "They divorced before the birth."

"That's the date it was filed. Getting a divorce takes time. My divorce from Ryan was quick because we chose to do a simple mediation. If you go to court, proceedings can take a year or more, depending on the people involved and their level of cooperation. It says here that Rose was the defendant. That means he filed for the divorce."

"Interesting."

It was, but I needed more. I thought for a moment before returning to the birth records. "Why did she go all the way to Brunswick to have the baby? That's more than an hour away."

"The birth certificate listed her as a resident of Saint Simons, Georgia."

"Maybe she stayed up there after the divorce."

"Why? She got the house."

My fingers flew across the keys. "I'll go to one of those sites that gives you all the past addresses for a person."

"Those are so creepy. We have absolutely no privacy these days."

"I agree, but in this case, it works to our advantage. Look at this.

When I entered Rose's name, it gave me three addresses. One of them is in Glynn County, Georgia. I'm going to do a deed search for the address." My fingers once again flew across the keyboard. "Okay, here it is. Sold 2007 by owner..."

"What?" Laura prompted.

"Phillip Mayhew."

"Let me see that." Laura craned her neck to view the screen. "What do you make of that? She was staying at Phillip Mayhew's house during her convalescence."

"Convalescence?" I jerked my head back to look at her. "What is this? The Victorian Era? Nobody calls it that. Anyway, he could have just been helping her out during a difficult time."

"Or, he could have been the father."

"So, let me get this straight. Rose gets pregnant with Phillip's baby. Her husband leaves her. Why wouldn't Phillip marry her?" I asked.

"Didn't want the scandal, I'd imagine." Laura unconsciously twisted her wedding ring. "He was a local politician in Charlotte, married to a socialite with money."

I leaned back in my chair and gazed out the kitchen window. "Didn't Bina say they used to sit outside laughing during the early days of the neighborhood?"

"That's right. Think about it. Let's say, hypothetically, that Rose and Phil were screwing around every year while his wife, Christine, was away. Then, she gets pregnant and divorced, but he won't marry her. So, she gives the baby to Gwen."

"What about the deposit slips? Was she blackmailing him to keep it a secret?"

"He could have been sending her money to support David."

"What does any of this have to do with Rose's murder?"

"Maybe Alice found out about Phil and Rose after her father's death. Maybe it made her mad enough to kill."

ALTHOUGH IT WAS rude to show up at Gwen's door without calling first, we had no way of contacting her. Laura and I worked out a plan of attack on our way over, and we exchanged determined glances before ringing the doorbell.

Gwen looked confused to find us on her doorstep. "Oh. Hello."

"Hi, Gwen," Laura said. "I'm sorry to drop in on you unannounced. I hope this isn't a bad time."

"Not at all. I'm just doing some final cleaning, finishing up some odds and ends. Would you like to come in?"

Laura employed my least favorite of her skills—fake charm. "I hate to interrupt."

"No problem. Housework is not my thing. I'm glad for the interruption. Come on in."

We followed her inside and looked around. The boxes and clutter were gone. Minimal furniture pieces were strategically placed to make the room appear spacious. "An open house is scheduled for this weekend," she explained. She led us to the seating area by the fireplace. "Is that why you decided to stop by? Are you still interested in the house, Emma?"

"Actually, there was another reason." I pulled the baby photo out of my purse and handed it to her. "When we took those boxes to the Goodwill, this fell out in my car. I just found it, and I thought you'd like to have it."

Gwen examined the photo with a furrowed brow. "I don't remember ever seeing this one."

"Is it David?" Laura asked.

Gwen nodded, still studying the photo.

"I hope you won't think I'm rude for asking, but why does it say Baby Martin?"

Gwen raised her eyes to meet mine, startled. She brought the photo closer to her face to study it further. "I guess it does, doesn't it?" Her eyes darted back and forth. If she was attempting to construct an acceptable response, she failed.

I decided there was nowhere to go but forward. "Was Rose his mother?"

Gwen dropped the photo. "I can't believe this."

Instantly, I regretted my pushiness. "I'm sorry. We shouldn't have come." I stood up, but Laura pulled me back down.

"Does David know?" she asked.

"I was planning to tell him once he turned eighteen." Gwen clenched her hands tightly together in her lap, but she couldn't hold the story in any longer, and it spilled out of her. "I couldn't have children. After three miscarriages, I couldn't take it anymore. We gave up. Not long after that, my husband died in a car accident. I was all alone. Then, Rose got pregnant without trying." Gwen sniffed. "She didn't realize she was pregnant for a while. Thought it was menopause. By the time she realized, it was too late to do anything about it. She confided in me, and I begged her to let me adopt the baby." Her eyes sparkled with tears as she looked from me to Laura. "I can't believe I'm telling you this. You're practically strangers."

Laura patted her on the knee. "Sometimes, strangers are the easiest people to confide in."

"That was a wonderful thing for your sister to do for you," I said. "But why didn't she want to keep the baby?"

Gwen bit her lip. "It wasn't her husband's." She covered her face with her hands. "I guess it doesn't matter anymore. She's gone. They're both gone."

"The father, too?" I asked.

She nodded. "And her ex-husband, Paul. I didn't keep in touch, of course, but I heard he died a few years back."

"Is David's father Phillip Mayhew?" Laura blurted.

Gwen removed her hands from her face and stared at Laura with wide eyes. "How did you guess?"

"A mutual friend mentioned that they used to be friendly."

"Friendly?" Gwen scoffed. "I suppose you could call it that. They had an ongoing affair for many years. I didn't think anyone knew about her pregnancy, though."

"Not even Phil?" I asked.

She chuckled briefly without humor. "No, he knew. He didn't want his wife to find out. Kept Rose hidden away in his fancy Sea Island cottage."

"That doesn't seem very secretive, hiding her at their beach house."

"I think Christine probably knew about them, but she chose to look the other way. A baby on the other hand... that's a different story." Gwen grabbed Laura's hand. "Please don't mention this to anyone. If David heard it from anyone but me, it would crush him."

"Of course," Laura consoled.

"That's why Rose kept away from us. She didn't want David to figure it out."

I nodded my agreement but pressed on with the interrogation. "Did Phil Mayhew give you any monetary assistance to raise his son?"

"He gave money to Rose every month, and she sent it on to me."

"And how about his will? Did he leave anything to David?"

Gwen tilted her head. "I haven't heard a thing about his will. But, before he died, he did set up a foundation with a scholarship funded by his estate. David happened to be the first recipient of the scholarship— enough for all four years of college."

"Wow. Quite generous. Didn't that raise any eyebrows?" Laura asked.

"David is very studious. It could be passed off as an academic scholarship," she explained.

"What does he plan to study?" I asked.

"Pre-med."

Laura's eyebrows lifted. "A doctor. How nice."

Gwen nodded and her face lit up with a smile. "I'm very proud of him." She stood and walked over to her handbag on the foyer table. She dug around inside, retrieved a small photo portfolio, and flipped open the cover to display the first snapshot. "The last time I saw her was when she came to David's graduation. Very rare for her to show up. We talked about telling him then but couldn't agree on how to go about it."

I accepted the brag book from her hands, examining it more closely. Gwen and Rose stood on either side of David, beaming with pride in his cap and gown. Rose had a protective arm resting on David's sleeve. The black sleeve enhanced the contrast of her pale arm with a silver cuff on the wrist and triggered my memory. "That bracelet. Rose was wearing it in the portrait that was here when I toured the house."

"Yes, she always wore it. I suspect it came from Phillip. It must have been expensive. It was from Tiffany's."

Something clicked inside my head. "What happened to it?"

"I don't know. I didn't find it here when I went through her things."

"But you said she *always* wore it."

"Yes."

"So, she should have been wearing it on the night she died," I speculated.

"Probably, but I never got it back with her things from the police. Might still be in evidence, or maybe someone stole it. I have no idea what happened to it."

"What about her phone?" Laura asked.

"I never got that back either."

"That's very strange." I thought for a moment. "Did Rose leave David anything? Did she ever intend for him to find out that he was her son?"

"I was her sole heir. She never pressed me to tell him." Gwen looked down at the graduation photo. "This family photo was unusual. She didn't see him often. After she passed away, I decided I'd tell him the truth, but I haven't had the nerve. It's selfish of me. I never wanted to share him. He's all I have. But when Rose died, I realized how fragile life can be. David should be aware that he has other family out there."

"Other family?" Laura prompted.

"A half-sister. Alice Mayhew."

Laura and I repeatedly reassured Gwen about our discretion and then walked back to Laura's house to dissect the conversation.

Once inside, I headed for her computer and took a seat in the desk chair. "I need to look something up. Can I use this?"

"Of course. But can you believe that story Gwen told us? Sounded like something off a soap opera."

"Mm-hmm," I mumbled, too focused on typing to respond coherently.

"What's so important?" Her voice sounded petulant. She wanted to gossip, and I'd retreated to the nearest computer. It was college all over again.

"I need to review the estate sale photos."

"Why?" She sidled up to me to look over my shoulder.

"That bracelet. Cuff. Whatever. I remembered where I'd seen it before."

"In the glamour shot?"

"No, before that. I hope they haven't taken them down." I was able to use a cached web address from my previous search on Laura's computer. Fortunately, the photos were still posted. I scrolled through them and stopped when I reached the image of a black cuff.

"Oh, I remember that now," Laura said. "But it's black. Rose's was silver."

I pushed my chair away from the desk. "Exactly."

Laura's eyebrows scrunched together. "I'm not following you."

I leaned in and prompted, "Don't you remember seeing someone else wearing a silver cuff recently?"

Laura's eyes widened as the memory fell into place. "Alice."

"Exactly."

"But what can we do? We can't call Alice up and say, 'By the way, did you kill Rose Martin?'"

"Maybe we can get Gwen to report the bracelet missing," I suggested. "Then, we can tell the police that we saw Alice wearing it."

"How would they know it's the same bracelet?" Laura asked.

"Cuff."

She shrugged. "Whatever."

"It's engraved."

"With the brand name, doofus, not the owner's name. It might be a special edition released in the same year, but Tiffany made many, many silver bracelets that year," she said.

I swiveled the office chair to face her. "Doofus?"

She waved her hand. "You're missing the point. We're at a dead end. Maybe Phil bought a bracelet for his daughter at the same time."

"What about Phil's will? Could it have revealed something?"

"Why don't we ask Sam?"

I withdrew my phone from my pocket and dialed his number. "Sam, is it possible to look up a will of a dead person?"

"I had a great day. Thanks for asking. How was yours?"

"Sorry. I've been playing sleuth with Laura all afternoon. I think she's rubbing off on me."

"To answer your question, if the will has gone through probate, we can look it up. Probate files are public records. If not, it's not public record yet."

"Can you see if it's there?"

"Sure. I'll bring what I find to our meeting tomorrow. You're coming, right? Still planning to grab my—"

"I'll be there." I cut him off, noticing Laura leering at me. Just like college, indeed.

UPON MY ARRIVAL at Sam's office, I found the door locked. I started to turn around and wait in my car when a voice stopped me. "Emma?"

I turned toward the source of the voice and spotted Taylor climbing out of a car. It was the same car I'd seen in Sam's driveway when the whole mess started, which immediately brought it all back to mind. I pushed the thought aside and vowed to move on. *Be nice.* "Hi, Taylor. Are we the first ones here?"

Taylor jiggled the knob. "Must be." She fumbled in her purse for a key ring and let herself inside Sam's office.

I followed her inside. "You have keys?"

"Yes. Quite a few investigations require odd hours. I have a key so that I can get in and update client files without bothering him at all hours of the day."

"Or stopping by his house?" *So much for that vow.*

Taylor dropped her handbag on the reception desk with a *thunk*. "Look, Emma, I'm sorry we got off on the wrong foot."

I took a seat behind the desk in an attempt to assume a position of power. "I'm sorry I jumped to conclusions. You seemed a bit hostile toward me the last time we were here."

"I get a little overprotective of Sam sometimes." She shrugged. "We've been working together for a long time now, and it feels like he's my partner. I used to be on the force," she explained. "I might have over-reacted. I hope you and I can call a truce." She extended her hand to me.

I nodded and accepted the handshake. Just then, I spotted Sam through the office window, swaggering up the front walk.

"Howdy!" He breezed in and bent to give me a kiss on the cheek. "Did y'all start the meeting without me?"

Standing, I glanced at Taylor. "No. Taylor and I were just clearing the air."

"Glad to hear it. I hope we can all work together for Laura's sake. Where is she, anyway?"

"She needed to run a couple of errands, so she said she'd meet me here." I consulted my phone. "She just texted that she's on her way."

"Alrighty, then. Did you bring that information you told me about on the phone?"

I picked up my laptop bag. "Got it all right here."

Laura burst through the door. "Sorry I'm late. My manicurist wouldn't let me leave a minute before my nails were dry." She splayed out her pink lacquered fingernails.

"Very pretty," Sam said politely. "I've got a few things to show you. Why don't we go into the conference room where we can spread out? I set everything up earlier today."

We followed Sam into an adjacent room that contained a long, polished table and eight rolling chairs. Neatly stacked papers waited in front of four of them. Sam took a seat and Taylor immediately claimed the one beside him, leaving me no choice but to sit across from them beside Laura. We still had a way to go, but I reminded myself that I could keep it professional.

Sam picked up the paper on the stack in front of him. "I was able to find the will of Phillip Mayhew in the public record. I've given each of you a copy, but I will summarize. No mention of any heir other than Alice Mayhew appears in this version of the will."

"This version?" I asked.

"There's no guarantee that another version might not be floating around out there. At the courthouse, I bumped into an acquaintance of mine from my old law firm, and he claimed that his daddy did some legal work for Phillip Mayhew when Old Phil was living in Florida full time and didn't feel like messing with his big firm in Charlotte. But this daddy of his died last year, and there are no records of it on file. Nothing I was able to dig up through legal means, anyway."

"Can this one be contested?" I asked while scanning the document.

"If somebody thinks they have grounds to contest and can prove it, sure. However, there is a limited amount of time to contest a will. The amount of time varies from state to state, and since most of Phil's holdings were in Georgia, his will was filed there. It looks like he had Ladybird deeds for the house and condo in Florida."

I looked up from my reading. "What's a Ladybird deed?"

"It's when a property owner adds an heir as co-owner on the deed, so that when he dies, ownership automatically transfers to the heir without having to pay estate taxes or go through probate."

"So, the house and condo went to Alice, no questions asked?" Laura asked.

Sam nodded. "Looks that way. What have you been able to find online, Emma?"

"We found a baby photo tucked inside some books donated to charity by Rose's sister." My eyes met Laura's, but neither of us cared to elaborate on our methods of discovery. "The label on the bassinet, visible in the photo, led me to find a birth record at a small hospital in southeast Georgia that identified Rose Martin as the mother. The date corresponds to the birth date of David Garrity, a young man who believes himself to be Rose's nephew. When we confronted Rose's sister, Gwen, she confessed that David is actually the son of Rose and Phillip Mayhew."

Taylor let out a low whistle. "Nice work."

After giving her a gracious nod, I continued. "Gwen told us Mayhew sent child support through Rose, plus David received a full scholarship from a foundation in Charlotte. Phillip Mayhew was the philanthropist behind the scholarship fund, and David was the first recipient."

Sam crossed his arms and leaned back in his chair. "Convenient. So, Phillip had another heir, but unacknowledged, other than some under-the-table payments to Rose. Is David aware that Phil was his father?"

"No, Gwen never told him," Laura answered.

Sam shrugged. "He might not know, but *she* did, and that would give her a motive to seek inheritance for her son."

"Not if she didn't want David to find out," Laura said. "She planned to tell him when he turned eighteen, but that was months ago, and she still hasn't done it. She made us swear we wouldn't say anything. I honestly don't believe she'll ever tell him."

"What about Alice? Is there any evidence she knows about David?"

"No, but what about that mysterious will that could be floating around?" I asked.

Sam shook his head. "We can't count on anything turning up there, particularly if Gwen isn't interested in revealing David's parentage. Taylor did some digging on Alice up in Charlotte."

"Nothing groundbreaking there," Taylor said. "She's a successful businesswoman. I didn't find anything sketchy about her. What makes you think she might be a suspect?"

"While we were at Rose's house, we saw a couple of pictures of Rose wearing a distinctive bracelet that looks exactly like one Alice wore to Bina's funeral," I said.

"How distinctive?" Taylor asked.

"It was definitely made by the same manufacturer of the same material during the same year," Laura said.

"Which manufacturer?" Sam asked.

"Tiffany," Laura replied.

Taylor huffed. "Not exactly a small outfit."

"I don't think you can completely discount it," I objected. "I'd like to look into it some more."

"*I'll* look into it," Sam said. "Now, I'd like to see what you found out on your public records search."

We went over the information I'd compiled and speculated about possible connections. Sam said, "I'm going to see what I can find out about the property on Sea Island. Taylor, I want you to do some subtle surveillance of Gwen and David Garrity."

"Anything we can do?" I asked.

"You can try to find out more about that bracelet—*online.*"

I packed up my laptop and gathered up papers. As I hooked my laptop case over my shoulder, the bag swung backward into a shelf of heavy legal books. A memory in my head jostled loose along with the books. "I have an idea of someone who might be able to help us track the bracelet."

AFTER THE CONCLUSION of the meeting, Taylor and Sam remained inside to discuss the surveillance. As we walked to our cars, Laura tugged on my arm. "So, tell me. Who's going to help us find out about the cuff?"

I retrieved my phone from my handbag. "I'm going to call Barbara."

"Who's Barbara?"

"You've met her. 'Estate Sales by Barbara.' The woman who kicked you out."

Laura wrinkled her nose. "Oh. Why on earth would you call *her*?"

"To ask about the black titanium cuff."

"Why would she tell you anything?"

"Because I'm going to tell her that I'm an interested buyer."

"But the sale is long over."

"You never know. They rarely unload the entire inventory. I'll ask her if it sold, and if not, I'll ask her to get in touch with the seller."

"You mean Alice? The woman we're accusing of murder?"

"I'll leave that part out."

Laura waved her hand. "By all means, then. Sounds like a well-thought-out plan. Give it a shot."

After Googling the number for Estate Sales by Barbara, I dialed and switched the call to speakerphone so Laura could hear. No one answered, but we listened to a recording. "Thank you for calling Estate Sales by Barbara. Due to health issues, we are no longer scheduling future estate sales, but please stop by our warehouse on Beach Boulevard. The liquidation sale will be open Monday through Saturday from nine to four thirty until October fifteenth or until all inventory has been sold."

I ended the call and looked excitedly at Laura. "Ooh—liquidation sale!"

"You're supposed to be moving soon, remember? No time for shopping." Laura glanced at her gold watch. "Besides, it's already closed."

"Why don't we swing by tomorrow around lunch?" I suggested.

She grimaced. "I guess so."

"Would you mind driving? My SUV is full of packing boxes."

She ran a hand through her hair, appearing frustrated. "Sure. Why not? It's not like I'm busy."

Eying her tousled blond curls, I said, "Let's hope she doesn't recognize you as the woman she ejected from the closet at that estate sale."

She huffed, offended. "Maybe I should just stay in the car. It's probably a dirty old place full of stinky furniture she couldn't unload."

Unable to restrain my smile, I said, "Doubtless, it will be, but you should come anyway. I need my wingman."

LAURA PARKED her car in front of the warehouse, but before she got out, she withdrew a patterned silk scarf and a pair of over-sized black sunglasses from her handbag. After putting on the items, she extended her hands, appearing to seek feedback.

Eyes narrowed, I evaluated the effect. "Who are you supposed to be? Audrey Hepburn on a Goodwill Ambassador tour?"

Laura took off the sunglasses and whipped off the scarf. "I thought I was supposed to be undercover."

"Not undercover. Unobtrusive. There's a difference." I held the door open for her. "After you, Ms. Golightly."

The warehouse overflowed with mismatched furniture and miscellany. I surveyed the room, taking in the inventory that included dinette sets from the eighties with wicker-backed chairs, overstuffed sofas with garish prints, and wingback chairs with curved wooden arms shaped like lion claws. Nothing that would be considered antiques. All the good stuff was gone. "I can't imagine why all this is being liquidated."

"I can't imagine why it exists." Laura slipped her sunglasses back on as if to block out the sight of tacky furniture.

I spotted Barbara sitting at a desk in the far corner. She stood to greet us. "Everything is thirty percent off the lowest marked price. Are you looking for anything in particular?"

"Actually, there is something I wonder if you could help me with—a piece of jewelry. I found it on your website."

"I don't keep any jewelry here, but I'll try to look it up for you." She booted up a computer that looked as though it should be liquidated along with the other inventory. "Do you remember at which sale you saw the item?"

"Yes, it was 2120 Beach Hammock Road."

Barbara raised her eyes from the computer to glance at me and then over at Laura but made no comment. Donning a pair of cat-eye readers that dangled from a chain around her neck, she turned back to the monitor and keyed in the address. "What was the item?"

"A Tiffany cuff with the dates 1867 to 1997 engraved on it."

Her penciled-on eyebrows lifted in appreciation. "Nice. Now, let me see." She scanned the screen. "Looks like that item was not sold. It was withdrawn from the sale by the owner."

"How can that be?"

Leaning back in her chair, she shrugged. "Sometimes an owner decides not to sell something after we've listed it on the website. That's what happened here. She was also planning to include a car in the sale but changed her mind on that one."

"People sell cars at estate sales?" Laura's voice held a note of surprise.

"Sometimes. Not frequently. Usually older models. Looks like there was originally a 2006 Black Raven Cadillac CTS included in the Beach Hammock sale." Barbara looked up from the screen. "I remember now. The customer was the daughter of the former owner. She decided to keep the car and drove it home."

"Wait—she drove it home?" I asked, startled. "She told you that?"

"Yes, she left in advance of the sale, told us to handle it and liquidate anything left over, because she was going to drive her father's car back to Charlotte. We did as she asked. We're a full-service operation. A lot of the time, families either can't or don't want to deal with the belongings of a deceased relative, and that's why they hire us."

I looked around at the overflowing inventory. "I understand from your outgoing message that you are no longer doing estate sales?"

Barbara gazed sadly at the remainders of years of work. "For the time being, at least. I need to take a break because of some health issues."

"Well, I'll miss shopping at your sales," I replied. "They are always so well organized."

"Thank you." She broke away from examining the warehouse and gave me a grateful smile. "I'll miss it. It's an interesting business, even if it is hard work. Every sale is different."

I nodded. "I imagine this particular one will live in your memory for a long time. Are you allowed to give us the seller's contact information?"

"No, I'm not authorized to do that, but I can act as a go-between if you want to negotiate on something. Was there anything else from the estate that you were interested in besides the cuff?"

"Not from that sale." An item caught my eye. "How much do you want for that?"

Ignoring Laura's dramatic sigh, Barbara replied, "Name your price."

WALKING BACK to the car with my arms wrapped around a three-foot-tall leaping dolphin statue, I said, "At least it wasn't a complete loss."

Laura's shoulders slumped. "I disagree. It sounded like Alice kept the cuff. Not only that, but she drove back to Charlotte instead of flying. The airport card was a false lead."

"That's an impressive amount of information gained from one shopping trip." I grunted. "Can you open the trunk? This is heavy."

"Why did you buy that thing?" Laura asked, eyeing my latest acquisition with distaste.

"I wanted to take a piece of the beach to Orlando with me." I readjusted my grip on the heavy base. "Just open the trunk, please."

"Why don't you just stay at the beach and leave that thing here," she groused, but opened the trunk with a sigh. "I guess that clears Alice, but, unfortunately, that means we're back to square one with our investigation. Again."

With excessive care, I tucked the bronze statue inside Laura's pristine trunk and closed it. Bracing myself, I said, "I know you're not going to want to hear this, but maybe it's time we hung up our Sherlock hats."

Laura actually stamped her foot. "We can't give up."

My mouth popped open, startled by her intensity. I groped for the right words to express unpleasant truths. For once, Laura wasn't going to get her way. "It's time to be realistic. I'm leaving town. My job in Orlando starts next week."

"You don't have to keep reminding me." Laura stuck her lower lip out.

I tried to distract her. "I'm going out with Sam again tonight."

She gave me an arch look. "I'm counting on him to talk you out of this move."

So much for distraction. "We'll see," I said, and got in the car.

eighteen

LAURA TOLD me she wanted to take me out to lunch at The Club before I headed off to Orlando. I attempted to dress respectably and picked her up around noon. Once seated with menus in hand, I looked around the room and spotted Miranda and Sophie dining at a table by the window.

"Miranda's here," I commented. "And Sophie."

"Mm-hmm." Laura ducked behind her menu.

"You don't sound surprised."

The menu bobbed up and down as she shrugged. "I might have tipped someone to tell me when she made a reservation."

"So, this is a spy mission?"

She peered around the menu and squinted at me. "Please keep your voice down."

Before I could respond, an elderly waiter appeared at my elbow. "Good afternoon, ladies." He filled our water goblets as he described the soup of the day.

After we ordered and the waiter hobbled away, Laura said, "We're just having lunch at the same time. No agenda."

"If you say so."

Laura leaned forward, gazing at me avidly. "Tell me all about your reunion with Sam."

I gave her a sly look. "What do you mean?"

"You know what I mean."

"It was good."

"That's all I get?"

I gestured at our surroundings, indicating the well-appointed dining room with its dramatic ocean view, soaring ceilings, and polished silver precisely positioned atop linen tablecloths. "You want me to go into details here?"

"I guess you're right." Without appearing to do so, Laura continued to monitor the pair on the other side of the dining room.

"He went for a moonlight walk on the beach with Hopper." I smiled at the memory. "Hopper loves him."

"That's one reason why you're a good match," Laura pointed out as our salads arrived. "Perhaps you complement each other."

"Like you and Jack?" I asked.

"Yes, actually. He keeps me grounded." She drizzled oil and vinegar from crystal cruets. "He takes care of me and makes me feel loved. He's very stable. That's appealing when you grew up in a military family like I did."

"I never thought of it like that," I said, taking in her crisp appearance. "I mean, I knew that was why you were so neat and organized, but..."

She waved her hand dismissively. "We moved around so much; I never want to move again. I guess it made me good at making friends, though. Or acquaintances, anyway. We never stayed anywhere long enough for anything else. Until I went to college and met you." She smiled at me fondly.

Returning the smile, I reached out to squeeze her hand. "Lucky for both of us."

While we consumed our overpriced salads, I continued recounting the highlights of my date at Laura's urging.

Throughout our meal, Laura had kept one eye on Miranda and Sophie. When she observed them preparing to leave, she gestured to our waiter. "You can clear our plates and bring the check, please."

"But I wasn't finished." I clutched my fork even after my plate had been whisked away.

"Close enough." Laura scribbled her name on the slip of paper and secured her handbag in the crook of her elbow. "Let's go."

I followed in her wake, grumbling, "I guess I can't complain, because you paid."

Laura climbed in the passenger seat of my SUV and pointed out the window. "Follow that car!"

I wondered if she'd lost her mind. "Which car? What are you suggesting?"

"I want to follow Miranda and catch her meeting up with Ed Rivers. Go! You're going to lose her."

"Which car? Where? We already lost her."

"No, she'll have to wait for the gate to open. There's still time. Go!"

Her urgency was contagious. I took off. What else was I going to do? Laura was correct in her estimation of the timing. The gate was almost completely open by the time we pulled up to the closest intersection.

Laura pointed at the black Mercedes. "That's her."

"A black Mercedes SUV? In Costa Verde? It will be like trying to follow a yellow cab in New York City."

"Skip the commentary and step on it."

I crept through the gate before it closed. We weren't far behind Miranda. "This isn't very subtle."

"She doesn't know your car."

"What about Sophie?"

"Miranda's alone. Can't you see her big, bouffant hair floating up there all by itself in the driver seat? Sophie probably drove separately."

"Why do you assume she's meeting Ed?"

"Because I called Mindy and asked if he was free to do a quick repair for me, and she said he was booked up this afternoon."

"So?"

"Then, I called Miranda on her cell phone and asked if she wanted to get together to talk, but she said she already had an appointment this afternoon."

"Maybe she just didn't want to talk to you," I grumbled. "We're probably following her to her hair stylist."

"Could be. But I've got a hunch. And, I might have been following her on and off ever since I found her name in Rose's binder."

"You are going to get in trouble, Laura."

She waved me off. "Costa Verde's a small town. I run into the same people all the time. It's not unusual."

We followed Miranda to State Road A1A and proceeded south. We passed businesses with understated beige signs, the required size and shade for all businesses in Costa Verde.

"Where is she going?" I asked. We were getting close to the end of town, where A1A turned into a two-lane road through a nature preserve. Nothing was there until you reached Vilano Beach, where Sam had taken me boating.

Miranda signaled and turned her car into the driveway of an enormous home just north of the preserve on the ocean side. We passed the drive and continued south in order to preserve our cover.

Laura snapped a picture with her phone as we drove past. "Did you see that?"

"See what? I'm driving here."

Laura craned her neck to look behind us. "The house had some scaffolding on the front like it's being remodeled. I'm pretty sure that was Ed River's pickup truck in the driveway." She reviewed the photo on her phone. "Yep. He's got that bright yellow toolbox bolted in the back."

I cringed. "You think he takes remodeling jobs and has his mistress meet him there when the house is empty? That's disturbing." I chuckled. "So where are we going now?"

"Park at the beach public access lot. It's just up ahead."

"Then what? Where are we really going?"

"We could take a walk up the beach."

I glanced sideways, suspicious of her innocent tone. "Why?"

"It's a beautiful day. We've wasted time on this pointless mission, and I'd like to redeem the afternoon by walking on the beach." She grabbed the dashboard. "It's right there! Turn in!"

"You must be desperate for some beach time," I said, but I complied. The serenity of the ocean was just what I needed after this crazy experience. Luckily, there was a parking space available at the public beach access point.

"We're a little dressed up for this activity," I pointed out.

"Easily remedied," Laura replied, slipping off her shoes.

I slipped mine off, too, and left them on the floorboard. Once out of the car, I could smell the ocean. I closed my eyes and inhaled deeply. When I opened them again, Laura was already shuffling up the sandy pathway toward the beach.

"Are we on a schedule?" I asked, hurrying to catch up.

"No, of course not," Laura replied, tossing the comment over her shoulder. "I'd just rather be on the beach than standing around in the parking lot."

At the end of the path, I looked left and right, weighing whether to head north or south. Normally, I based this decision on which option had the fewest people, but Laura headed north without pausing. *Okay. Decision made.* I followed, because the decision to back Laura up had been the default since the early days of our friendship. Of course, I knew she was up to something, but maybe my presence would temper her impulses.

Of course, it didn't. Right away, it was apparent that Laura wasn't looking at the ocean, absorbing the serenity of the waves, or searching for shark teeth. She was making a beeline back to that house where she thought she'd seen Ed's truck.

Struggling to keep up with her, I said, "Laura, I don't know what you think is going to happen here, but if you're planning to peek inside windows, I'm out."

Once we'd reached the oceanfront portion of the house in question, she indicated it expansively, as if giving a tour. "We won't have to peek. Look at those windows."

Naturally, a house built on the ocean would have sizable windows. After all, they'd paid millions for that view. What I never could figure out is why they didn't also pay for curtains. From our spot about twenty feet away, we could see clearly inside the house, where two figures faced each other. The glare on the glass obscured the details of their features other than height. One was taller than the other, but neither was broad or bulky.

"I don't think that's Ed," I observed.

"No, it's not," Laura agreed. She took a few steps closer, edging into the dunes.

I grabbed her arm. "Laura, they'll see you."

"They seem rather preoccupied." She crept closer.

Any restraint I might have imagined my presence would provide was negligible. I glanced over my shoulder to see if anyone on the beach seemed suspicious, but the few umbrellas lining the shore were angled to block out the sun. Conveniently, they also blocked us from view. When I turned back to Laura, panic jolted me forward. She was practically in their backyard. I tried to grab her, but she shook me off.

The glare faded with proximity. The two figures inside were now clearly visible. One was Miranda. I recognized the smaller of the two as well, and it definitely wasn't Ed. It was Mindy.

We'd gotten close enough to overhear voices inside, all the clearer because those voices were raised in anger.

"—ridiculous! You lured me here—"

"I was able to *lure* you here because you *thought* you were meeting my husband! I know you're sleeping with him!" Mindy was pointing at Miranda accusingly.

Wait. Not just pointing. There was something in her hand.

"Laura! Get back here! We've got to call the police!" I took hold of her arm, and this time I pulled with enough force that she couldn't ignore me, though she still strained to see what was going on inside.

She spotted what I'd already seen. "Is that a *gun?*"

I fumbled in my pocket for my phone but found only my keys. Panic tightened inside my chest. "I must have left my phone in the car. You have to call 911."

Laura waved her arms helplessly. "I left my purse in your car."

A shot rang out.

Startled faces emerged from behind the umbrellas on the beach.

"Was that a firecracker?" one sunburned man asked.

"Call 911!" I shrieked. "Someone's been shot!"

The man's equally sunburned wife was already digging through her beach bag.

I ran toward the couple, then looked back for Laura. She stood frozen in the dunes, like a startled rabbit.

"They want to know where we are," the woman said, her voice shrill with panic. "What do I tell them?"

I grabbed the phone from her hand. "We're about a quarter mile north of the public beach access lot on A1A in Costa Verde. The shots came from inside a house. I don't know the address, but there's scaffolding on the front."

"Okay, help is on the way. Stay on the line," the dispatcher's calm voice instructed. "Did you hear the shots?"

"Yes." I struggled with what else to say. *I was peering through the window at the time?* "I think I can get past the house to the driveway. I'll direct the police when they arrive."

The dispatcher's voice grew stern. "Ma'am, this could be an active shooter situation. You need to stay out of sight."

"No, I—" I realized I had to tell them what I knew. "I recognized the woman with the gun. She's not a threat." I considered that for a moment, then added, "To me." Mindy had seemed like one of the least threatening people I'd ever met. Everyone has their limits, however. It appeared that Ed's cheating had caused her to snap.

Ignoring the dispatcher's warning, as well as the woman whose phone I'd commandeered, I retraced my steps back towards the house. Snagging Laura, still frozen, I pulled her with me around the side of the house and into the driveway. Ed's truck was gone.

The dispatcher squawked in my ear. Based on their tone, it was not the first time the dispatcher had prompted me.

"I'm still here." My senses seemed to be fading in and out as adrenaline took over. "I'm here, and I think the woman with the gun left." Sirens wailed in the distance. "I can hear a police car. I'm going to wave them down."

The dispatcher squawked again, but my brain didn't process it. With the street in sight, Laura picked up the pace and hurried ahead of me. She waved her arms at the approaching vehicles: a police car, an ambulance, and a firetruck pulled up to the house, lights flashing.

THE SHERIFF's department issued a BOLO for Mindy, along with the license plate and description of Ed's truck. An ambulance rushed Miranda to the hospital, badly injured but not dead. What felt like hours later, when we wrapped up our police reports, they allowed us to leave.

As Laura and I were both barefoot, they offered us a ride back to our car. Laura and I agreed that we'd rather walk back along the beach. It gave us a moment to process what had happened and wind down before attempting to drive.

During the ordeal, the tide had gone out a bit. Eyes downcast, we followed a pathway of tiny shells that lay exposed by the receding water.

"I would never have guessed that Mindy was capable of anything close to this," Laura said, breaking the silence.

"I barely knew her," I said, "but I guess everyone has their breaking point." Spotting a small shark tooth gleaming black against the sand, I bent to pick it up. The tip was tiny but sharp. Like Mindy.

"If we hadn't overheard them, what do you think would have happened?" Laura gazed out at the horizon. "Do you think she'd go back to Ed like nothing happened?"

"Who knows," I replied. "I can't imagine she'd planned to make a getaway in Ed's extended cab with the yellow toolbox bolted on the back."

"It won't take them long to find her in that," Laura agreed. She turned to me. "I'm sorry I dragged you into all this. When I first tried to persuade you to move into my neighborhood, I thought I knew my neighbors."

"Too bad I'm moving away." I gave her a playful punch on her upper arm. "After all this drama, I might actually be able to afford it."

nineteen

THE POLICE CAUGHT up with Mindy in her getaway pickup within hours. Because she'd tried to flee, the judge ruled out bail. She would remain incarcerated until the trial. The gossip chain around Harbor Shores had no shortage of fodder. Miranda had been released from the hospital, and her husband took her back. Maybe he thought getting shot was punishment enough—or the prenup wasn't as favorable as everyone had assumed. Ed retreated to the home he'd shared with Mindy. Some things even a handyman couldn't fix.

No matter how much Laura and I both dreaded it, the day finally came for me to start my new position. The parting with Sam was hard, but he assured me he'd visit often. Thinking of him gave me a painful feeling of longing inside my chest. I was heading back to see both of them at the earliest opportunity.

ONLY ONE WEEK into the new job, and I was already miserable. My corporate apartment was a depressing place—even more so, because they didn't allow dogs. Hopper was staying with my parents until I could find permanent housing. Walking through the door at the end of a long, taxing day and knowing he would not be there to greet me was one of the hardest moments of the day. The only thing that got me through was looking forward to the weekend when I could return to Harbor Shores and visit Sam and Laura. But first, I had to escape the traffic hell of Central Florida. During rush hour, Orlando was emphatically *not* the happiest place on earth.

I drove past a colorful billboard bearing an image of the world's most famous rodent and said aloud, "This entire town is a people-trap built by a mouse."

Inching forward in Friday traffic, I grimaced at the electronic information sign estimating thirty minutes to reach Ivanhoe Boulevard. That was bad news because, based on the mileposts, Ivanhoe was only five miles away. Still, at least I'd be out of the snarl in thirty minutes.

Forty minutes later, I read another warning on yet another variable-message sign estimating thirty minutes to Maitland Boulevard exit a few miles away. Commuting on Interstate 4 constituted cruel and unusual punishment. The signs tricked drivers into thinking there was an end to the traffic, but it was as endless as an Escher staircase. Hope always remained out of reach, just over the horizon. It reminded me of the failed investigation that Laura and I had attempted. Just when we thought we'd made progress, another obstacle always appeared in front of us.

So far, the transition to my new hometown had proven equally frustrating. The commute was hell, the office was a maze, and I spent the bulk of my time in pointless meetings. Thankfully, it was Friday, but at the rate I was going, I'd be lucky to make it to North Florida before the weekend ended. I couldn't wait to get back and have dinner with Sam. I intended to finish packing over the weekend. Everything would go into a storage pod because I didn't have a permanent address yet.

I stopped at Sunshine Corporate Suites, my temporary home-away-from-home, long enough to pick up my suitcase. Each door of the complex opened onto an outer walkway. In front of one door, the guy who lived above me had rolled his desk chair outside, so he'd have a comfortable place to sit while he smoked. As I watched, he crushed the cigarette against the railing and tossed it over, heedless of where it landed, which was directly in front of my door. I had to find a better place to live. Temporary housing made Harbor Shores look like Park Avenue.

THREE HOURS LATER, when I finally made it back to my townhouse in North Florida, I had piercing pain in my forehead, a crick in my back, and an exceptionally bad attitude. I parked in front of the sign in the yard bearing the words "SALE PENDING."

I grabbed my overnight bag and dashed inside to freshen up before Sam arrived. Because I was running behind, however, I only had time to use the bathroom and wash my hands before I heard the doorbell. I examined my reflection in the mirror, hurriedly smoothed my hair with my damp fingers, and went to answer the door.

Sam swept me into a hug that left only my tiptoes in contact with the ground. "Have you been gone for only a week? Feels like longer."

"The drive alone felt like it took a week." I self-consciously smoothed my hair again. "I wanted to fix myself up before you got here."

"You look beautiful. Let's go grab some dinner. I'll buy you a drink, and you'll forget all about the drive."

I climbed into his truck, and he drove us to Beaches Fish Camp where we snagged a table with a view of the sunset over the water. As predicted, once I had a cool glass in my hand, my perspective shifted. I reached across the table to clasp Sam's hand. "I've missed you."

His brown eyes met mine. "I've missed you. I gotta tell you, I don't like this long-distance thing."

"Me, either," I admitted.

"Tell me how things are going with your new job," he prompted.

I sighed. "It's been an adjustment, getting used to office life again. They assigned me a cubicle that's in the manager's line of sight. I feel like I'm under a magnifying glass. Then, there's the meetings. So many meetings, and most of them feel so pointless. But my coworkers are friendly, for the most part, and everyone's been very kind to me."

"They'd better be, or I'll come down there and show 'em what's what." His wide grin took away any threat from his words.

"I'd like to see that. My personal bodyguard."

He leaned forward and murmured in a low voice, "I'm happy to guard your body anytime."

After dinner, we went back to my place. Most of my belongings were in boxes and I'd sold most of my furniture, but I still had a mattress on the floor. As we lay side by side, I leaned my head on his chest and listened to the sound of his heartbeat as it resumed a normal pace. "Yes, I missed you a lot."

His voice rumbled beneath my ear. "Is it too late to change your mind about that new job?"

I sighed. "I don't know. In the tech field, people are always moving around when they get a better offer, but I don't like to burn bridges."

His fingers traced circles across my bare back. "I don't like the idea of us driving back and forth to see each other."

"I don't like that." His fingers abruptly ceased their motion. I lifted my head and pouted. "No, I meant I don't like the commute. I *did* like what you were doing on my back. You have talented fingers."

He raised his eyebrows. "Do I?" His fingers began to swirl on my back again, then traced a line down the length of my spine. I shivered as his light touch caressed the curve of my waist and then traveled down my hip with exquisite slowness. "I wonder what else my talented fingers can do?"

AFTER SAM LEFT the next morning, I focused on packing. September was nearly over, and so was my life in North Florida. I was wrapping my dishes in bubble wrap and sealing boxes shut with packing tape when I heard a tap on the door.

Laura came in without waiting for an answer. She held a bottle of orange juice and some plastic cups. When she saw what I was doing, her face fell. "This is really happening, isn't it?"

I nodded. "Appears so. Is that orange juice?"

"Pre-mixed mimosa." She found an empty spot on the counter and lined up the cups. "You left that stupid dolphin statue in my car. I'm holding it hostage, so you can't go."

"You can keep it safe for me."

She filled the cups and handed me one. Taking a sip, she gazed around at the messy surroundings. "Where's Hopper?"

"At my parents' house."

Propping one hip against the counter, she pouted and said, "The news said there's a storm on the way."

Raising my cup to my lips, I froze. With some astonishment, I asked, "Are you actually hoping a hurricane comes to prevent me from moving?"

Laura lifted her chin. "If that's what it takes."

I glanced at the window, framing sunny skies. "I don't think it's predicted to hit here."

"The spaghetti models are all over the place," she said dismissively, refilling her glass. "When is your closing?"

"It hasn't been set. The buyers have a few days to get an inspection before the offer is final."

"So, there's still hope." She tapped a finger on her pursed lips. "Possibly, I could sabotage the inspection somehow."

"Wouldn't put it past you," I said, hiding my grin. "After all, we are jail sisters."

AS THE PREDICTIVE models of the hurricane's path began to converge, things started looking grim for our area. When I went to Home Depot to buy more packing tape, large boxes containing portable generators lined the aisles. Having grown up in Clearwater, I had weathered hurricanes in the past. I knew the drill, but I'd never had a house on the market before. I decided to put up the hurricane shutters when I got home, just in case. I was struggling to put them up when my phone rang, and I ran to get it.

"Hello?" I asked breathlessly.

"It's me," said Laura. "What were you doing? Exercising?"

"No, I'm trying to get these stinking hurricane shutters in place."

"What's going to happen with the house sale if a hurricane hits?" she asked.

"I swear, you are hoping for this. You want something to go wrong."

"No, but I don't want you to leave. I just lost Bina. Now with you gone, I don't know what I'll do." She sniffed audibly. "And now Jack's stuck out of town on a stupid business trip. The flights are all booked."

She sounded so pitiful, I wanted to cheer her up. "I got an email from my office. They've decided to close Monday and Tuesday because of the storm."

"That's good news. Why don't you come over here and we'll have a hurricane party?"

"That sounds like almost as bad an idea as breaking into the Mayhews' house turned out to be."

"The storm's not that bad. And anyway, it's just going to skirt the coast. Come on. It'll be fun."

"Famous last words."

"I really need you, Emma," Laura pleaded. "I can't get my hurricane shutters up without Jack's help. Can you come over here and stay with me?"

"But, Laura, you're closer to the ocean than I am."

"And you're right next to the Intracoastal Waterway. A flood's a flood."

"Guess you have a point. I'll pack up my supplies. Have you done any preparations?"

"I filled up the bathtub with water, and I got a case of wine from Trader Joe's."

"Ohh-kay. I will gather up some things and be over as soon as I can."

Less than a week ago, the storm was a seemingly insignificant disturbance in the Bahamas. It was nothing out of the ordinary for September in Florida, but the storm strengthened and picked up speed in a way that no one expected. We thought we were ready. We weren't. By Monday night, parking lots in front of the big box stores sat empty, their windows covered with storm shutters. Gas stations displayed hand-lettered signs that read "NO GAS."

I grabbed the large bin I always kept stocked with water, batteries, flashlights, canned soup, protein bars, and instant coffee—all the necessities. After loading it into my car, I headed toward Laura's house. The bridge that led off the island was backed up with cars, and I was traveling in the opposite direction. What the hell was I doing?

I hit the Bluetooth button and called Sam. "I just wanted to let you know I'm going to be in your neighborhood. Laura begged me to come stay with her during the storm."

"Are you sure about that? Your house is farther from the ocean," he said.

"I mentioned that fact, but Laura-logic prevailed. Besides, I don't have any furniture."

"Why don't the two of you come over to my place?"

"That would be kind of awkward, don't you think? The three of us having a slumber party together?"

"Um…"

"Don't go there. Anyway, she has hurricane shutters, and I have supplies."

"Okay, but I'm going to come check on you as soon as the storm lets up. And I can venture over there even earlier, if you need me."

"Thanks."

He paused. "*Do* you need me, Emma? It would be nice if you did."

I sighed. "I appreciate you, Sam. Is it that bad if I feel capable of doing things on my own?"

"I know you're capable. I'm just saying that people who care about each other rely on each other. After all, you're on your way to help Laura because she's important to you. You're important to me."

I chose my words carefully before speaking. "You're important to me, Sam. I'm just not used to relying on other people so much. I appreciate your offer."

I heard his gusty exhale above the car noise. "Okay, Emma. I'm still gonna check on you, okay?"

"Okay. Thanks. Gotta go. I'm almost there."

As I made the last turn into Harbor Shores, I considered my conversation with Sam. We had been skirting around using words that defined our feelings for each other. "You're important to me" was as close as we'd gotten, and, yet, even those words made me a little antsy.

I pulled up to Laura's house and found her outside, struggling with the hurricane shutters. I rushed to help her. The shutters were the kind that had to be attached to a bracket already on the wall. Laura, with her five-foot-two stature, was not well equipped for the task. I fitted the shutters in place and held them while she attempted to fasten the wing nuts to the bolts on the bottom ledge.

While we were struggling with the unwieldy task, Ed Rivers drove slowly past and then came to a stop. He lowered the truck's window. "Need a hand?" he called out.

"An extra hand or two would be useful," Laura replied. "Thanks."

I still wasn't sure how I felt about Ed Rivers, but I stepped aside and let him do the heavy lifting while I assisted Laura with the wing nuts. The task went much faster once Ed retrieved a cordless drill fitted with a wingnut driver from his truck. The effort left all of us out of breath. Ed removed his hat to cool off. His shiny, bald dome gleamed with sweat.

"Thank you so much," Laura said. "How about an iced tea?"

I looked at her with one eyebrow raised, but she was in her Southern hostess mode and either didn't notice or chose to ignore me.

"Iced tea sounds good to me," Ed said, and followed her inside the house. I saw no alternative but to follow them.

"Anything else I can do for you, to help you get ready for the storm?" Ed asked. "I helped Jack build a garage door brace last time a storm blew in. I can put that up for you if you don't know how to do it."

"I forgot about that. Would you mind, Ed?"

"No problem," he said, and walked through the dining room and the mudroom to enter the garage. Shortly thereafter, we heard the whirring of his power drill.

"Laura," I said, "I don't like being alone in the house with that man."

"He's my neighbor."

"Who we've been investigating," I whispered.

"But the police released him."

Suddenly, I noticed the sound of drilling had stopped.

Ed stood outside the laundry room door, which was directly across from the door to the garage. When he noticed we'd stopped talking, he turned to us and said, "Got you all set. The garage door is one of the most vulnerable spots in a hurricane."

Laura handed him a glass. "Anything else you'd recommend?"

He took a long gulp of tea before placing the glass on the counter. "I'll check the rest of your doors and windows." He walked down the corridor leading to the bedrooms without waiting for a response.

I looked at Laura, forehead tensed with concern, and pointed insistently at the laundry room door, where the light shone out on the place where Ed had been standing. "Did you ever take down your murder board?"

I saw her eyes widen, confirming my fear. The board must still be up, and Ed probably got a good look at it. She looked over her shoulder to where Ed had disappeared and hurried to turn off the light and shut the door.

I heard Ed clomping down the hallway, shutting doors one by one. When he reappeared, he said, "You ought to shut all your interior doors during a storm. It helps disperse the pressure in the house. Helps your roof stay put." He secured the patio door by sliding the bolt into place. Then, he walked to the mudroom door and locked it. With the sound of every bolt sliding into the latch, my heart raced. My muscles tensed as I fought a sudden urge to flee.

"Storm's not too far away," Ed said, approaching us. "Everybody's getting ready to hunker down. You ladies plan to ride it out here alone?"

"We'll be fine," I said. "How about you?"

"I've got our house nailed down." He took another drink of iced tea before placing his glass next to the sink. "Guess I'd better be heading back."

Laura escorted him to the door. "Thanks for your help, Ed."

"No problem. Call me if you need anything else."

Laura closed the door behind him and leaned against it. "Do you think he saw the murder board?"

"Maybe." I shivered. "That whole encounter gave me the creeps. I didn't like being alone in here with him."

I reopened the laundry room and flipped on the light. The Roman shade was up, and photos of all of Ed's customers circled the board, with bright pink notes below each boldly labeled with the job he did for them. It appeared Laura had continued adding to the board since I last saw it, because she'd managed to secure copies of the estimates from some of the neighbors she'd consulted. Beneath Phil Mayhew's obituary portrait were Rose's photos of the venting system taken on the night of her murder.

I hoped Ed hadn't seen it.

OMINOUS WEATHER REPORTS DISTRACTED my thoughts away from the handyman. Predictive modeling showed the storm skirting the coast, too close for comfort. That night, Laura and I stayed up late watching TV and drinking wine. We ate a dinner composed of miscellaneous stuff from the freezer: a chicken pot pie, mini pizzas, and a pumpkin pie left over from a BOGO sale last November. Around midnight, we parted ways and headed off to bed.

The wind woke me four hours later. It sounded like a wild creature howling. I tried to get back to sleep, but my mind wouldn't stop spinning. I checked a storm tracker app on my phone and was startled to find that the storm, predicted to stay mostly offshore, had taken a sudden turn toward the coast. The outer rain bands had been passing over us all night, and the eye of the storm was heading our way at a speed of fifteen miles per hour.

I got up because there was no way I could go back to sleep, and I put on my clothes and shoes. An emergency notification blared from my cell phone on the nightstand, and I grabbed it before knocking on Laura's door. She answered quickly; the alert had awakened her as well. The howling wind outside seemed to be intensifying, but inside, a sudden quiet settled over the house as the power went out and the air-conditioning unit fell silent.

We went into the living room and lit some candles. Laura's face glowed in the light of her mobile phone as she scanned the weather report. She looked up from the phone, and her eyes were wide with fear and confusion.

"It's not supposed to come here," she insisted.

"It's coming. It changed course." I scanned the room we were in, noting the boarded-up patio door. It felt scarier not being able to see what was going on. I heard the sound of glass breaking outside. Something heavy slammed against the hurricane shutters, and Laura and I both jumped.

Laura had her hand over her racing heart. I felt my own thumping in my chest. I said a very bad word that no well-bred Southern lady should use, and Laura didn't reprimand me. That's when I knew how scared she was.

I moved to sit beside her on the couch, and we wordlessly put our arms around each other. I felt her body shaking. A loud crack detonated outside as a hardwood tree snapped. Flying debris pelted the shutters with a sound like gunfire. The metal around the sliding glass door began to creak.

"Let's move to another room," I said urgently.

"There aren't any windows in the study," Laura suggested. We grabbed our phones and a candle and headed in that direction. The house sounded like it was groaning. The front door was rattling. We ran down the hallway into the study and slammed the double doors behind us. I moved the love seat to block the inward-facing doors. Even though the air conditioning was off, I felt chilled and shaky. We sat on the floor, huddling together.

Laura looked up and made a whimpering sound. I followed her gaze.

Along the ceiling, a wet stain was beginning to spread. We watched it bleeding across the whiteness of the ceiling. The paint and drywall began to split, and water began to drip. The wind made an eerie, high-pitched whine as it whistled through the cracks.

"I heard the bathroom is the strongest room in the house because of the plumbing," I said. "Let's go."

We pushed aside the loveseat. The noise outside was deafening, like a train approaching. We ran to the hall bathroom and slammed the door. Laura and I squatted beside the tub and held each other. The pipes creaked. We heard a crash from somewhere in the house. The door rattled but remained shut, though the wind howled.

I'd dropped my cell phone during our flight from the study, but Laura still had hers. The Florida Storm app showed the eyewall of the storm directly above us. It felt like hours went by as we crouched in that bathroom, but my watch said it was minutes. We had hours left until sunrise.

After a while, the wind fell oddly silent. "What's happening?" I asked.

Laura checked the app. "Could be the eye. It's not over yet." She looked at the tub. It was half full because storm preparation experts told us to fill our tubs in case we didn't have running water after the storm. "We could drain that and sit in it. It's strong and surrounded by pipes."

"I don't think that's necessary," I said, lulled by the hypnotic quiet outside. I leaned against Laura's shoulder and closed my eyes.

"Maybe we should get out and go to another house," Laura said.

"Where would we go?"

"A two-story? I'm scared. There could be a storm surge," she said.

"I don't think we have time before the other eyewall hits. Better stay put," I asserted, but inwardly I felt uncertain. My brain felt foggy from lack of sleep combined with a flood of adrenaline.

After a few minutes, the sounds coming from outside confirmed that if we'd wanted to leave, we had missed our window. The wind picked up its howling refrain once more. The sound slowly intensified, like the growl of an engine revved by an impatient driver, until it peaked to a relentless roar. The toilet gurgled, and the showerhead rattled. My ears popped with the plummeting barometric pressure. I felt dampness soak my pants leg and looked down, stunned to see water seeping under the bathroom door. I grabbed a towel and shoved it against the doorjamb.

"It's the storm surge!" Laura shrieked, but as we watched, the seemingly insufficient barrier of the towel held back any additional water.

"Maybe just a leak," I said. My eyes scanned the ceiling above us for signs of wet spots or cracks. It appeared to be holding despite the vibrating rumble of the structure.

When it was nearly daybreak, the howling abated. A banging on the front door shattered the stillness. Eyes wide, I looked at Laura. "Was that someone knocking?"

"Who would be out in this?"

The pounding repeated, a rapid *boom-boom-boom.* My muscles were cramped, and pain shot up my legs as I slowly rose from my spot on the bathroom floor. I helped Laura up, and we went together to answer it.

Ed stood outside in a black rain slicker, water droplets glistening on his bald head. "I came to check on you." He shouldered past us into the house. "The creek behind our houses is rising."

I looked outside and saw the street in front of the house littered with branches and other debris. Absently, I noted a boogie board caught in one of the remaining trees. Daylight was coming. Then, a lingering burst of wind blew the door shut with an ominous bang.

"What are you doing walking around the neighborhood, Ed?" Laura took a step back, away from him.

"I told you. Checking on you. How's the garage brace holding up?" He moved toward the hallway.

"I don't know," Laura said.

He glanced toward the laundry room. "Where have you two been holed up?"

"In the bathroom," she said, eyeing the water creeping across the floor.

Ed advanced, backing us into the hallway and blocking us with his considerable frame. Laura backed up until she bumped into me.

"You stick your nose where it doesn't belong, and you might get blown away in this mess," he said, still advancing.

"What?" Laura's voice cracked, and she cleared her throat. "What are you saying?" She stepped backward, and I had to move with her, as we were practically pinned together.

"I saw that board on your wall. Why are you keeping track of my work? What are you doing with that information?"

I took another step backward and heard a splash as my foot met the tile.

"Nothing. It's just names we got from an old HOA notebook."

"You got it from Rose," he said.

"We don't understand what it means," I insisted.

"I think you do," he growled with a quiet yet menacing tone of voice. He shoved us back into the bathroom where we'd previously found safety. I huddled in the corner between the toilet and the wall. "Rose started nosing around in my business. Threatened me. Then, Mindy saw Rose nosing around outside the Mayhew house, taking pictures. That woman never knew when to quit. Couldn't even leave the dead alone. She had to be stopped."

Laura was gripping the sink with white knuckles. She whispered, "What are you going to do?"

"I saw that board, and I figured you knew too much. If that information Rose dug up ever got out, I'd be out of business. Mindy did what she had to do to silence Rose, but now I've lost her, too. I have nothing left but my job."

A realization hit me, followed by a wave of nausea. If he was confessing, he wasn't planning on letting us go. "You can still get out of this, Ed."

He gave a humorless laugh. "I don't think so. Not unless a tree falls on you two or something. This storm arrived just in time." He edged forward. "I thought I'd help it along." In the mirror, I saw his gaze drop to the water-filled bathtub. "Like I said, the creek is rising." With a burst of motion, Ed's arm bolted out and grabbed Laura by the back of her neck. He shoved her face-first into the tub. She struggled wildly, but he didn't let go.

Water sloshed everywhere as Laura's legs flailed. I screamed and threw myself on Ed's back. Wrapping my arms around his muscle-roped neck was like trying to choke a tree trunk. I tried to kick him in the kidneys, but he swept one leg under me, and I fell to the floor. Laura's movements were becoming weaker.

I looked around for something I could use as a weapon, but there was nothing in the bathroom more substantial than a plunger. I hurried to the hallway, where my gaze landed on the dolphin statue. Laura must have brought it in from her trunk. I grabbed it by its bottlenose, took a couple of steps for momentum and swung it, base first. Ed dropped like a stone.

I stepped over him and pulled Laura out of the tub. She lay draped over the edge, coughing and sputtering. Ed didn't move. I spotted

Laura's phone under the edge of the vanity. Instead of calling emergency services, I dialed Sam's number.

"Laura? Are you two okay?"

At the sound of his voice, my adrenaline-fueled strength left me, and a sob caught in my throat. "Sam. Can you come over to Laura's? I think I might have killed Ed."

"What? I'll be right there."

I sat there unmoving until I heard the door burst open behind me and turned to find Sam standing in the doorway. "Are you all right?"

I nodded and pointed wordlessly to the legs protruding from the bathroom. Sam stepped over them and bent over Ed's crumpled form. He felt for a pulse. "He's alive." He looked up at Laura, still huddled in the corner, and me, frozen in place, on my hands and knees in the hallway. "Get out of there, Laura. Emma, go call nine-one-one. I'm going to keep an eye on him in case he wakes up. I don't know how they're gonna get here with all this mess from the storm."

WHEN I WALKED OUTSIDE to wait for the cops, I was shocked by the devastation surrounding me. An enormous oak tree rested in the roof of the house next door. The houses backing up to the pond lay within its watery boundaries. They must have at least six inches of water inside. One of the flooded homes was the former residence of Phillip Mayhew. The "For Sale" sign canted sideways in the waterlogged front yard.

Harbor Shores lay in shambles. I wondered what amount of time and money it would take to return the neighborhood to its pre-storm condition.

Many of the residents had opted to evacuate, but a few that remained stood outside their homes, dazed by what they saw. Pine trees snapped in two pointed upward with shards of bright yellow wood. Broken glass sparkled on the doorstep of a home with nothing but gaping holes for windows. Shingles sprinkled the ground like confetti. It was the morning after an out-of-control party that no one had enjoyed.

The sound of a siren wailed with increasing intensity as it

approached. Miraculously, the road to enter the neighborhood was passable, though the patrol car had to swerve around fallen branches and puddles of indeterminate depth. When I thought he was close enough to see, I waved my arms wildly to direct him toward Laura's house.

From the front, Laura's house looked undamaged, largely thanks to the hurricane shutters. Behind it, however, lay the swollen creek that overflowed its boundaries and crept inside beneath the patio door.

The patrol car pulled to a stop at Laura's curb, and two deputies emerged. This time, it was a welcome sight.

I ran to meet them. "There's a man inside—a large, bald man—who attacked us."

"Is he armed?" the older of the two asked.

"Not that I'm aware of," I said.

The two cops approached the door in a tactical formation, but Laura flung it open. Her sudden movement made them jerk into a defensive crouch, hands on their weapons.

"Help!" she said. "He's waking up!"

They followed her inside, weapons now in hand. I heard Sam's voice say, "Over here, officer."

Laura came running outside and flung herself at me. We held on to each other wordlessly. In that moment, I realized I could have lost her, this sister of mine not of birth, but of friendship. She stepped back from the embrace and held me at arm's length, examining my face for damage. Her hair was wet, and there were red marks in the shape of fingers on her neck. "Are you all right?" she asked.

"Me? I'm fine. You're the one I'm worried about." I tentatively reached out to touch the marks on her neck. "I thought he was going to kill you."

"You're not the only one," she said. She began to shake violently, and she wrapped her arms around herself in an effort to hold herself together.

I draped my arm around her shoulder, and we turned to face the house in time to see the police leading Ed Rivers out of the house with his hands cuffed behind his back. He caught sight of us, and his face twisted in hatred. One officer opened the rear door of the patrol car while the other one put his hand on Ed's bald head and directed him down into the vehicle.

Sam walked out of the house and strode toward me. I didn't protest when he wrapped me in his arms. "I'm so glad you're okay." His arms rubbed up and down my back. Without releasing me, he turned his head to address Laura. "Are you all right, Laura?"

"Just a little bruised," she said.

"You sure?" he said, eyeing her neck with concern. "Those marks look bad."

She shook her head but winced. Waving her hand in a small, hopeless gesture, indicating the destruction around us, she said, "I imagine the ER will be a little too busy today."

One of the deputies approached our little scene. "Somebody want to tell me what happened here?"

twenty

THE HURRICANE DELAYED the sale of my house, but, after an additional inspection, the buyers agreed to close. Packing everything up overwhelmed me. Laura offered to help, but when she arrived at my door wearing a white blouse and slim-fitting cigarette pants, it was clear she had other plans.

"When you said you wanted to help, were you thinking moral support?"

"I have to talk to you." Laura surveyed the landscape of boxes in my living room. "I realize you've got almost everything packed up, but I have an idea I want you to consider."

"I do not have 'almost everything' packed up," I said, gesturing at the disarray. "I thought I was further along. All the small stuff takes forever to pack, like the rest of my salt and pepper shaker collection."

She pursed her lips. "You wouldn't want any of those to break. You put so much time and effort into building a collection that tacky."

"I've told you, it's *kitschy*." I set down the roll of tape in my hand. Obviously, I wouldn't be getting any work done, anyway.

She spread her arms in dismay. "What happened to the sofa?"

"I sold it. Barbara offered to consign all the big pieces of furniture.

It's easier than moving everything, and I still don't have a permanent residence in Orlando. The corporate housing is furnished."

"Well, I need to talk to you about something. Is there anywhere left to sit?"

I gestured for her to follow me to the kitchen. "I still have the table and chairs. I'm planning to donate them."

"After you put so much effort into painting them different colors?" She sat on a lime green chair, while I took the yellow one.

I stroked the brightly painted surface. "I think they're cheerful. Did you just come over to talk about my poor taste in furnishings?"

"On the contrary. Ironically, I have a proposition for you that could utilize your keen eye."

I raised an eyebrow. "Let's hear it."

She clasped her hands together, leaned forward, and beamed at me. "What if you and I go into business together?"

I leaned back in my chair, causing it to creak alarmingly. "Are we going to start a detective agency?"

"Very funny. No, I was thinking of something you already enjoy— estate sales. What if we started our own estate sale business?"

Her words struck a chord somewhere inside me. My hobby and my work, combined? "But we don't have any experience in the estate sale business, Laura. How would we do that?"

"You've been to so many of them. You see how they work." She swatted away my concerns with a wave of her hand. "Plus, this is Florida. It's full of old people. They're dropping like flies all the time around here."

"Your sensitivity never fails to amaze me."

"Just another reason to partner up. We complement each other. You can handle the marketing. You get what I mean." She flapped her hands. "Build the website, manage the social media—stuff like that."

"And what will your role be in this?"

"I can arrange all the things in the houses to make them look nicer. And I can network with people in my social circles to identify potential clients."

"You would work for a living?"

Laura chewed her bottom lip. "Lately I've been feeling at loose ends. I need a new project. Besides, Emma, you hated that cubicle. If we did this, you could set your own hours and work from home again."

An image of my cubicle came to mind. I realized how much I didn't want to return. "I don't know, Laura. Starting a business from scratch is never easy, and there's a lot of work involved in setting up estate sales. I'm not sure you realize what you would be getting into."

"I've been doing research. I even went back to that dirty warehouse and talked to Barbara. We can pick up where she's leaving off. She's willing to mentor us. I think it could work. Will you please at least think about it?"

I sighed. "I'll think about it."

She clapped her hands. "Excellent. Now, why don't you get cleaned up and we can go get a drink to celebrate?"

"I have to finish packing. My house sold. Whatever I decide to do, I can't stay here. Besides, drinks cost money, and you're trying to talk me into quitting my job."

"If we talk about our new enterprise, it will be a business expense, and we can deduct it."

"I must be crazy to even consider this."

She grinned. "It might be crazy, but I can guarantee it won't be boring!"

LATER THAT EVENING, I stood in the middle of the room, mentally cataloging all that remained. If only the Grinch would break in and steal it all.

The sound of Sam's V8 engine roaring up to the curb in front of my house brought me to my senses. He was better than a Grinch, and his heart wasn't two sizes too small.

"I thought I'd to stop by and see if you could use some help." He bent to give me a lengthy kiss.

After an enjoyable public display of affection, I pulled him inside, shut the door, and gestured at the piles of belongings I had yet to pack.

"You have perfect timing. Let's load it all in your truck and take it to the dump."

He let out a low whistle. "I was hoping I could take you out to dinner, but it looks like we'll need to order in." He looked around. "Where's your guard dog?"

"Still at my parents. They offered to keep him until I get settled."

"Did they get any damage from the storm?"

"Not at all. Their place was well out of the path of the storm." I pointed at the rolled-up newspaper he held tucked under one arm. "Is that more paper for wrapping my breakables?"

"Sure." He unrolled the thick stack and held up the front page. "After you read this."

Scanning the front page, I noticed the obituary photo of Phil Mayhew above the fold. The headline read, "Police Suspect Foul Play in Death of Charlotte Politician."

Sam spoke up before I could continue reading. "Turns out Rose was taking photos of a vent installed by Ed Rivers in the home of Phil Mayhew. It was supposed to ventilate a gas water heater, but it had been improperly installed. They tested the house and found dangerous levels of carbon monoxide—levels that could kill someone elderly, with health problems, like Phil. Now they're thinking it wasn't his COPD that killed him. Rose must have suspected, and she was trying to get the proof on the night she was spotted taking pictures outside Phil's house."

My mouth dropped open. "You mean, not only was he committing contractor fraud and targeting the elderly, he actually might have indirectly killed Phil Mayhew?"

"That's right. Ol' Ed Rivers isn't getting out of jail again this time. Didn't you say Laura was here earlier? I'm surprised she didn't tell you already."

"Guess she hadn't heard the news. She spent most of her time trying to talk me out of the move."

"Did it work?" He raised his eyebrows hopefully.

"I'm pretty sure that the people who bought my house expect me to vacate the premises." I bent to retrieve a piece of newspaper from the stack on the floor and began wrapping glassware again. "Other than that teensy complication, I think I actually liked her proposition, which must mean something is inherently wrong with it. Laura always gets me into trouble."

He took a piece of paper and began wrapping a vintage saltshaker. "What was her proposition?"

"She suggested we could start an estate sale business."

He glanced up to examine my expression. "You think that would be something you might enjoy?" He turned over the little Dutch boy figurine in his hand. "You do seem to enjoy shopping at them."

I nodded. "I do. I must admit, the idea sounds intriguing. And I *really* hate Orlando."

He searched my face. "Owning your own business is a lot of work, I won't lie. But at the end of the day, knowing that you're working for yourself instead of lining the pockets of some boss or a big law firm like I was makes it worth the effort. At least, it did for me."

I picked up another piece of newspaper that happened to be the classified ads. How appropriate. "But walking away from a real job seems foolish."

"A job you don't enjoy, in a city you don't like, far away from a man who loves you."

I jerked my head up in surprise, but he just smiled that slow, sexy smile of his. He took the figurine from my hand and set it down on the table. Then, he took both of my hands in his. "I do love you, Emma."

Instead of the fear I expected to fill me at such a pivotal moment, I felt only excitement and a deep sense of peace, if those two feelings could co-exist. Evidently, they could. I took a deep breath and said the words I never thought I'd say again. "I love you, too."

He pulled me to him and held me tightly against his body before releasing me enough to press his lips against mine. When he finally pulled away, he let out a deep laugh that I felt rumbling through him where our bodies still pressed against each other. "You're amazing. How am I going to keep you here with me?"

"I don't know." I gestured at the moving boxes that surrounded us. "I'll be homeless soon."

He cocked his head. "I can think of one solution to the problem."

"What's that?"

"You could move in with me."

"You're kidding, right?" I searched his face, but his dark eyes were serious. "This feels a little premature."

He held out his hands. "My backyard is fenced. Hopper would love it. This feels right to me. But if you want to say it's temporary, until you get your business started or while you look for another place..." He grinned. "I can make sure Sophie never finds you one."

I swatted his arm. "There's more than one Realtor in Costa Verde."

He arched an eyebrow. "Ever since we met, you said you wanted to move into Harbor Shores."

I smiled. "That would be one way to get into the neighborhood, and it's easier than committing murder."

acknowledgments

Thanks to my Dad, who let me stay up late to watch *SNL* and *In Search Of...* and then slept on my floor to keep away bad dreams.

Thank you to my sons, who tolerated me reading all the books with funny voices. I love you both so much, my little sausage links.

Thanks to the BFC, the women who make Thursdays my favorite day of the week.

To the Wildcats—thanks for all the prayers and chicken salad.

Thanks to my critique partners, Jennifer and Avery, who have been reading this and providing input and encouragement since the first draft.

And the biggest thanks of all to my patient, loving partner on the road trip of life. I love you more.

If you enjoyed this book, please do one or more of the following:

- Leave a review on your favorite book review site
- Tell a friend about The Estate Sales Mysteries
- Ask your local library to put Shelley Marsh's work on the shelf
- Recommend Fawkes Press books to your local bookstore

VISIT US ONLINE
WWW.FAWKESPRESS.COM
WWW.SHELLEYMARSH.COM

DYING
to Live Here
The Estate Sales Mysteries
SHELLEY MARSH

MORE
Than She
BARGAINED
For
The Estate Sales Mysteries
SHELLEY MARSH

EVERYTHING
Must Go
The Estate Sales Mysteries
SHELLEY MARSH